JASON SHOHARA

KAMI JIN

PAPER PEOPLE

LitPrime
"Your story is our priority"

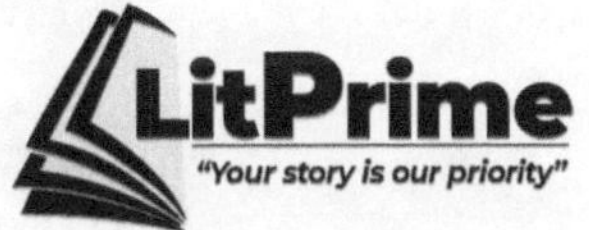

LitPrime Solutions
21250 Hawthorne Blvd
Suite 500, Torrance, CA 90503
www.litprime.com
Phone: 1-800-981-9893

Published by LitPrime Solutions   03/28/2023

ISBN: 979-8-88703-211-5(sc)
ISBN: 979-8-88703-212-2(e)

Library of Congress Control Number: 2023905617

CONTENTS

INTRODUCTION

The news today announced that there are now more millionaires and billionaires in the United States than ever before. What they don't tell the world is that there are even more that enter the realms of poverty. More people are displaced on the streets of major metropolitan cities and suburbs because they lose their houses and have nowhere to else to go. Homeless shelters are often overcrowded, especially in the winter months. People are forced to live in cardboard boxes – if they are lucky. Some camp under freeway overpasses and bridges just to shelter themselves from the cold. Some huddle near church doorways just to get a slight breeze of warm air that flows through the cracks of the bottom of the doors. Yet, people often say, "Do nothing for them."

Corporations often say that their employees are their "best and most valuable assets." Yet when it comes time to reducing staff, their employees are the first ones to be laid off, often given very little or no severance pay, and a severe loss of benefits. Yet, while their employees lose much, big executives of these companies often are rewarded with millions of dollars in bonuses while displaced workers are often forced to find a way to make ends meet on their own – often without assistance. And it is big corporations – once they have turned their backs on their employees – will not even provide one ounce of care to assist one in time of need to get a person back on his or her feet in order to survive.

Take a tour through your local neighborhood or metropolitan city and just take a look at the litter, all the trash on the streets and the highways that pollute the environment and the scenery. It's as if people eat in their cars from paper plates and plastic containers are just literally thrown their waste onto the streets and highways.

Now, take this illustration and apply it to a higher level – with people. Corporations and society have treated people very much in the same way. Take a tour through the slums and the skid rows of your metropolitan cities and see all the littering of people on the streets. Only, this time, the pollution really does affect the environment – especially when facilities are not provided in these areas to deal with personal waste. Some of that is disposed of against walls of buildings that create such a foul odor that one can smell it for miles. Yet, society has really not figured out a way of eliminating poverty and homelessness.

What has happened to the notion that "All men are created equal?" Why do we still find ways to destroy people's lives by throwing them out onto the streets, tarnish their livelihoods and personal records yet still find ways to reward bad behavior?

Why do we continue to find ways to kill each other through wars, but we can't find ways to eliminate poverty, hunger, and homelessness in our own backyard? Why do we continue to add a few more people to the roles of the millionaire and billionaire list while the rest of the world continues to starve?

The prophet Micah said:

"Nation shall not lift up a sword against nation, neither shall they learn war any more...And none shall make them afraid" (Micah IV)

It is my hope and prayer that nations will cease all wars and come together in peace – and then work in harmony so that mankind in every corner of this world can live in peace, tranquility, and equal prosperity.

— Lloyd Kaneko

PART I

PREFACE

WHITTIER, Ca, April 11, 2008/WorldNewsWire – Scientists have just discovered a phenomenal wristwatch that appears to have been developed well into the future. The mechanics of the watch are highly unusual and appear to be fabricated of materials not commonly known to scientists today.

According to a witness, a strange, unidentified person, wearing a bright orange jumpsuit, apparently left the watch on the doorsteps of a Jason Shohara of Whittier, California. Apparently, the watch has a computer port compatible with current computer technology. The watch was reported to contain a diary of a person who lived in the future – around 2208 A.D.

Presently, world scientists and law enforcement officials are puzzled as to how this unusual piece of jewelry has traveled back in time and currently do not have a solid explanation as to how it was delivered from the future into the current time.

CHAPTER 1

Thank You for Having Me Over

] Login, A Gordon Sakata
"Welcome A. Gordon Sakata. Please enter today's date."
] Date: 01/15/96
"Today is January 15, 2196. Please enter the time."
] Time: 18:00
"The time is 6 O'clock. Welcome to the Cyberspace living room."

To begin with, let me thank you for inviting me into your living room to shoot the breeze. I know that your time is precious and very valuable. For that matter, so is my notecase! So it confounds me to wonder why you bought my story from the bookstore or downloaded it from your favorite internet source. I know, computers need input – or, so the theory goes.

Getting off the informalities, let me introduce myself to you and your kin. Or, should I say, your "memory banks?" My name is A. Gordon Sakata II. Yes, as the name implies, it sounds like my heritage is Japanese or from some distant, foreign nation at that. No, my ancestry is Napajanese – from the country island of Napajan in the Southern Pacific Ocean.

"Where's that?" you ask. Well, it's about 2500 miles south, southeast of Japan. It's a little known Pacific island that isn't densely populated with human beans – I mean, beings! My American ancestors moved to Los Angeles, California early in the 1930s and I understand that my relatives looked so much like Japanese that they were even mistaken for their kind and were forced into concentration camps in California. I remember my great grandfather talking a lot about a camp called "Manzanita" – or, was it "Manzanar?" I can't exactly remember the place because it isn't exactly on the revised state maps of California. He also used to talk a lot about his great, great, grandparents' temporary accommodations at a place called "Santa Anita" and said that they stayed in horse stalls before they were relocated to that other place. In fact, one of my relatives never made it there. I understand that the government went to his house late one night and he was whisked away to another concentration camp in Arkansas. I know, you said that you've never heard of Napajan. That's because the island country itself was taken over by the Japanese during World War II and since then, it became an extinct nation. They never had a chance! The Japanese took over the country in a matter of 1.7654 hours! It was like saying "You want this country? It's all yours!" You would say that, too, if you had nine guns pointed towards your tree-house!

Well it was extinct until about the early to mid-22nd Century when a very large pocket of oil was discovered under the tiny island. The oil companies quickly moved in and turned the once tropical island into a steel jungle. Napajan managed to maintain its control over the oil until just recently in this century when the Republic of North America attempted to annex the country by declaring it a "colony." A war almost started a few years ago with China. It was no secret to the world that Napajan was very rich in fishing resources and was a very close trading partner with the Chinese.

There are no airports in Napajan. The island is too small to accommodate those intergalactic liners. Even the smallest 500-passenger ones would cause a major earthquake when they attempted to land on the island's leeward side. The only way of getting to Napajan is by sea liner via Saipan.

Say, while you're reading this story, it would be a good time to get that pot of coffee going. I take it with cream and chocolate ice cream, thank you. Just kidding! Coffee is awfully bad for people with bionic peripheral limbs! It clogs up the electrical systems. Especially the memory banks! You see, I broke my right wrist in a sonic-skating accident when I was 10 years old and I severely severed my wrist as the mini-rockets on my skates exploded. I went into a forward tumble down a steep hill. They said that my wrist was so damaged that it was beyond repair so they replaced it with a bionic arm. Yes, I know, they always told you to wear protective headgear as well and – well, you guessed it – I wasn't wearing that either – so, part of my brains had to be replaced with memory chips as well. It all worked out for the best I guess. It increased my memory capacity tremendously. And my ability to process information was far beyond that of a normal human being. Anyway, along with this bionic arm, I got a watch which is actually a computer that runs this bionic arm. It controls the movement in my arm just as I think about it with my brain and the computer processes it. The computer also processes all my thoughts and records my observations and stores it for future reference. When the memory senses inactivity for an extended period, such as, if I fall asleep or take a nap, the computer will automatically logs itself off. The only thing is that the battery, although somewhat solar powered, needs an occasional boost once in a while. So it needs a little recharging with regular hydro-electricity – which, in the 23rd Century, is a little scarce. They said that one of these days, I can eventually get the battery changed to an atomic driven one. But extreme cold weather would affect the performance of the battery also.

If I accidentally separate this watch from the port on my arm, my arm does not function – so I have permanent medical clearance to wear this watch no matter where I'm at – even on an intercontinental air vehicle in the process of clearing passenger security.

As for the physical part of myself, I am about 6 feet tall, 184 pounds and I don't wear glasses or contacts because my bionic brain controls my eyesight very well. I do not align myself with any political party. I'm more of a progressive independent if you will although some might say I have traits like that of a reformist. I do believe in the basic fundamentals of democracy in the way that it was originally intended, but the way that it is practiced now, you would hardly call it a "democratic process." Before I broke my wrist, I was right-handed. Now, I am ambidextrous. When I write with my right hand, it is very sloppy, and unintelligible. Then, my left hand is the exact opposite. It is very neat, readable, and immaculate.

This probably explains the appearance of my apartment. My living room and dining room was very neat and immaculate. My bedroom was very sloppy, cluttered and messy, the bed was never made, clothes laid all over the room and piled high on the floor. Sometimes, I even have a hard time walking in my own bedroom.

I used to have a collection of trains – mainly monorails running through my apartment. But I sold the vintage collection because I needed the money and the collector offered me a very handsome price for my trains. I used to enjoy riding public transportation until it became too costly to ride them. Many of the good routes where discontinued due to budgetary reasons and those were the routes that got me to where I needed to go. The only way I get around the city now is with my car. The color of my car is purple. That's my favorite color and it just so happens to be my family colors – purple and white.

As for my family, lost my parents when I was in my 20s due to unexplained illnesses and have been living on my own since then. I don't have any brothers or sisters. I have a few relatives that I visit primarily during the holidays and I have a few friends around the city. Most of them are work associates. I also enjoy early classical music from the Baroque and Renaissance Eras. There are some contemporary songs I like also, but the classical ones appeal to me the most.

At one point in my life, I wanted to become a great philanthropist and give a lot of money to charity. But with the job on the line, and money tight, it has really been hard to fulfill this dream. I like going to church on Sunday. Besides singing in a masterworks chorale, I also sing in the church choir as a baritone. So, I would guess these are my "hobbies" so to speak.

However, I have a real compassion for people. I really care for how people are treated in and by society even though, my weakness often interferes from me doing greater works in this area. The weakness is that I'm rather shy, and a non-assertive person. I've taken workshops to be a little more assertive and I guess that takes practice. But my shyness often serves as a barrier for such progress. One would find this difficult to believe because I love speaking and performing in public.

That's about enough about me. As for the city itself, in the 21st Century, there were so much debate over a phenomenon called "Global Warming" that some scientist theorized that man's behavior was causing the destruction of the environment through air and water pollution. The ozone was being destroyed by harmful particulate matters that were being emitted into the air that it was causing a destructive "hole" in the very layer that protected the Earth against the harmful radiation of the Sun. And, man was also known for discarding wasteful products into the oceans which polluted the waters and made the waters unsafe to drink. There were data that supported this theory. Yet, companies developed their own conclusions and statistics to disprove the conclusions of other scientists. This led to the great debate of the environment of the 21st Century. Eventually the environmentalist won out in all corners of the Earth. Their conservation efforts were so successful that by the 22nd Century, the Great Ice Age began. Of course, in today's world, it would have to get awfully cold because we are currently living in that ice age. We're all waiting for the "Great Melt-down!"

Getting back to business, you said that you wanted my story and you're going to get it. I don't know when you're going to print this story or where, but you said that it would get printed somewhere. Let me tell you about my profession as a computer anthropologist – someone who studies the history of computers and its impact on the human society. It was a great profession until the early 2100s when artificial, non-human-like droids took over our business. There were massive layoffs in the computer industry. Everyone that banged on keyboards at home and at work had been replaced by these dumb machines that had minds and logic of their own and were capable of carrying on discussions. There were models just like you, but with much less intelligence. I personally started working at an aerial photography firm in the South

Beach area during the mid-2170s as a computer operator. Yes, I had no other choice. I remember in my early adulthood that I set out to become a famous screenplay writer. I even took courses at South Beach University and received a Bachelor of Arts degree in creative writing. You can very well see how far that got me in entertainment! Not very, indeed! Luckily, the undergraduate courses that I took at Eastern City College in engineering were good enough to land my first full-time job. Well, it paid money and it was better than being unemployed for thirteen months after my graduation.

What kind of computer? It was nothing like yours. At the time, it was considered a microcomputer the size of a file cabinet! The whole computer system itself took up two rooms and was able to transform aerial photography into mappable images by removing camera lens distortion. During that time in produced negatives called "orthophotographs." The photos were taken from a twin-engine jet plane. Now, I know that's out of your dictionary, so I'll explain that type of aircraft later on.

Anyway, getting back to my first paying job, this computer was a prototype and there were only five of them in the whole world. And like typical prototype computers, nothing was written about them. No, not even something to tell you how it worked! So being the aspiring writer that I wanted to be, I sat myself down one day and began to write step-by-step instructions on how to operate this machine. People thought pressing the reset key on a modern computer was difficult when you wanted to reboot a machine. This machine required that you use a series of toggle switches or a bootstrap to restart the computer. And, the computer was well known for being down more than it was being up and running!

Well, that's how I broke into computer training. Management got wind of this book I wrote and wanted me to train other operators. I was probably so successful at it that I got a free trip to Algiers, Algeria to train operators over there for three months in 2179. I really can't tell you how homesick I was. Especially, when my residence there was during the holiday season starting from Thanksgiving through New Year's. But, I really can't say enough for the great hospitality I received there. Training Algerians was particularly special and the food there was great! I got hooked on the greatest wines and dates over there that you can't find anywhere else in the world! I know you, as a computer, wouldn't be able to appreciate it very much so I won't elaborate on the subject.

The Super Nova Personal Computer started to creep into business around the early 2180s when I was working for a company called Huge Airlines and Manufacturing Company that was near the old Los Angeles International Airport. I believe in your data banks, it's now called the Los Angeles Air and Space Port Facility. I remember reading about the original personal computers that were manufactured in the 1970s. They were quite large and had two disk drives. You started the machine with a diskette. Then it took you a half dozen or more diskettes to start the program that you wanted to use. A few years later, it became better. They started to market a computer that had a floppy disk drive and a whopping 20 megabyte hard disk drive. Don't choke! I know you have a 7.65 terabyte disk that's no bigger than my pinkie. But you know darn well what dinosaurs are — and, those were dinosaurs. Well, when these new Super Nova Personal Computers came out, I started to informally help other people use these programs. I didn't have any formal training to start — that came later. That is to say, people used to train and help support other people using that kind of technology. It was the beginning of an industry that was known back then as Nova Personal Computer Training and Support. And I tell you, corporations in America definitely did not know how to manage that sort of new technological advance at the time.

At Huge Aircraft Manufacturing Company, which later became known as the "Huge Air Crash" of the century, only people who had their hands on those machines were managers who found time to play a game called "football", of course, behind closed doors! Everyone else had to do the work by pencil and paper — which, probably was not a bad idea at the time. Those computers were very unreliable and the computer programs themselves were very "buggy." Oh, excuse me. I really didn't mean to scare you off. I know computers like you are very susceptible to viruses.

Getting back to the thought of training and support, I continued to do that for a while until I became very concerned with the economical situation at HAMC (pronounced "hammock"). I don't think that acronym is part of your dictionary. Part of the company was sold off to a big auto company in Detroit. I remember being there for the big party at Pleasureland. It brought back memories of the times I used to spend there during my days as a toy soldier during the Christmas season while I was working my way through college. After the party, massive people were laid off at will and I wasn't about ready to sit there and get my head cut so I immediately began to send out resumes by bulk although I had been looking casually for another job or a transfer for other reasons.

I was successful in getting a very good job in PC Training and Support at General Wilkerson's Federal Savings Bank in the San Fernando Valley, a little northwest of Los Angeles. But boy, did it double my commuting distance! I estimated that I was commuting through Los Angeles traffic for over 62 miles each way, or 124 miles round trip. Keep in mind, I wasn't the only crazy commuter in Southern California at the time. The town of Whittier, where I lived, was about half way between Riverside and the General's bank. I knew people who used to commute from Riverside to the San Fernando Valley. The job was very rewarding for a while. That is, I loved teaching people the art and science of using personal computers at work – that was before drones like you took over our business. And, being able to help people over the telephone was very enjoyable. But, it was time for a move upward in my professional estimation and the situation a Great Wilkerson's in my sixth year there turned for the worse. I'll talk about this in more detail later on also.

When you invited me into your living room, you were interested on the matter that I talked about in front of the Congressional Committee to Save Corporate Republic of North America. I should say that during my time as a systems analyst at General Wilkerson's, the economy across the country was very bad –especially for the state of California. Companies were moving out of the state by the droves. Companies like Huge Airlines and Manufacturing were losing jobs because of the lack of governmental defense contracts. It pretty much cut their work force from over 45,000 employees in half. Real estate in California was astronomically high in the 2180s and 2190s so it wasn't profitable for companies to operate in California anymore. Companies were sending blue-collar jobs south of the border and being a Napajanese in California, or resemblance thereof, was almost like reliving times of World War II. Yes, the Japanese were blamed for most of the economical problems in the United States. But the world's economy eventually caught up to Japan as well. Japan started to blame their woes on the Napajanese, who were worse off than the Japanese. There was a major drought in Napajan. Coconut and Bird of Paradise sales were down. Besides, they didn't buy much anyway. The Napajanese couldn't afford anything. Around the world, no one was buying anything, not even wrist televisions made by Chronoplex! Yes, sir, that was the break of the famous middle class in America. During these economic trials, the rich seemed to have gotten richer while they were lining their pocketbooks with money collected from the middle class. And you know, in the state of California, legislature still finds ways to vote themselves automatic pay raises in excess of $1,500,000 over and above what they were making the year before. Ironically, it now takes the legislature 1.74 years to pass an "annual state budget." I tell you, times were still bad even after the second Civil War! It was a war that was relatively peaceful my comparison to World War III, for the feud between Northern California and Southern California was over water rights. But how they were getting money from the lower class is beyond me! And I tell you, I consider myself an ordinary Napajanese-American – more "American" than "Napajanese."

The economy improved slightly after the merger between the three North American countries once known as the United States, Canada, and Mexico. But corruption in all three governments and private sectors were still wide-spread, particularly in unchecked private sectors. The Japanese were still considered the bad guys, but like the Japanese-Americans, we Napajanese-Americans were all caught up in the middle of the hysteria. It still is difficult to tell the difference between the two races because we were so similar to each other – even in name!

You know, by and large, the problems that we have today can be traced back to some of the stupidity in American management that we discovered in the 1980s and 1990s. Yes, we haven't changed very much, and the only way we're going to change is to understand what made the United States of America great in the first place. Then, and only then, will Republic of North America rise again to greatness.

] Logout
"Good Evening, A. Gordon Sakata. Please come back very soon."

CHAPTER 2

On the Matter of Late Great American Society

] Login, A. Gordon Sakata
"Welcome A. Gordon Sakata. Please enter today's date."
] Date: 01/15/07
"Today is January 15, 2207. Please enter the time."
] Time: 18:00
"The time is 6 O'clock. Welcome to the Cyberspace living room."

When the forefathers of the United States of America created the Constitution, they ensured that every citizen would be guaranteed the freedom of speech and expression through the First Amendment. The growth and spirit of these freedoms sparked the birth of a growing nation that was once admired everywhere on this earth. People, including my ancestors, sacrificed much to immigrate here to have a slice of that freedom. After all, in many nations, an individual was forbidden to speak his piece and ideas or, he or she was severely punished for "talking against the establishment."

With these freedoms, which have blessed the Republic of North

America, new ideas and directions were generated. Corporations in the RNA are starting to thrive because ideas and innovations are not suppressed by businesses that have long gone out of operation. It was perhaps during the 1970s, 80s and 90s, the last few years of the 20th Century and before the merging of the three nations, that a double standard existed in Corporate America. Society said that it was okay to express yourself freely. Corporate RNA said that it wasn't okay to express yourself – a total contradiction of the First Amendment. Companies practically discouraged creativity by greedy management. Yes, it was okay to create new innovations as long as the company got the credit and patent rights to an individual's achievements. After all, can you name famous inventors after Thomas Edison, the Wright Brothers, Henry Ford, and the like? No! Why? Because it was more important, at that time, the company, and not the inventor him or herself had all the glory and the credit. It was, after all, for the good of the company! Yet, who were the ones that pocketed the bulk of the money? They're all in the upper class and took a ride on the work and dedication of others. Oh yes, there were many innovative ideas generated by companies in this period, but just name a few good individuals who should have received the recognition for their ideas.

For instance, I can remember working at the aerial mapping firm in the South Beach when a very talented engineer developed a system that would have had a great impact on criminal science. When it came down to who was going to get the credit for the invention, the company won out but eventually lost its chief engineer because of it. I remember it well. They spent a lot of money to relocate him from Province and probably paid him a nice respectable salary. Obviously, that investment was wasted just because someone else wanted credit for an idea.

Corporations in States, at that time, encouraged a win-win resolution to problems. Most problems often resulted in a "lose-lose" resolution. Now I know that this is not the only isolated problem of its kind. After all, one has to look seriously at the migration of employees who, on the average, could not stay with a single company for more than three years. They were always jumping from job to job and never gained any kind of continuity! They were always starting from ground zero.

Unlike the Napajanese in those days, workers there were dedicated to one company. Yes, there was rivalry between corporations there. But companies there encouraged the participation of employees and valued their ideas. And, a lot of these characteristics of corporate Japan and Napajan can be attributed to what was taught and practiced in America before World War II when American companies were more open to new innovations. Such incentives like "Quality Circles," or small problem solving groups, were an American idea practiced by participative management in American industry but it was never fully appreciated. The Napajanese, on the other hand, found the beauty of freedom of speech and expression, encouraged creativity rather than stifled it.

During the closing years of the 20th Century, one can clearly see that organizations were operating under the umbrella of paranoia. There was a great distrust between blue collar-workers and management. We have also seen the destruction of labor unions, for they were faulted for America's inflationary problems. They only wanted a fair piece of that pie. No, it was certainly the greed of capitalistic individuals that caused the great downfall of Corporate America. That was so much to say about the famous "trickle-down economics" theory. Oh yes, the rich did get richer during those recessionary times. But it was because the government, before the Economic Revolution of 2105, granted them enormous tax incentives when a matter of fact, nothing trickled down! Yes, there was money to be equally distributed amongst all of the citizens at that time, but a few found ways of keeping it all to themselves and sharing it with nobody. There was truly no reason for the problems of homelessness. The problems were that American Society had just lost its values that once made the country the greatest nation on Earth. The values of many were not shared by the values of a few.

Similar problems exist in today's world. I can remember, one time when working at HAMC when I experienced typical problems of greed and paranoia from management. I recall seeing instances where ideas were generated and proposed by individuals only to have the names later changed on the paper to give true liars the fame and glory of someone else's diligence. A paper I wrote once to propose a new training program for quality groups was literally torn apart, and I was chastised for my ideas only to find out that the same ideas, retyped and changed with another manager's name appear in another program. Knowing management behavior in that organization at the time, I never did like to include all the details that would have made a program highly successful. Oh yes, it was certainly a means of working under paranoia. For these practices were typical. The turnover of that company was incredible. Their airplanes were always taxiing.

I was finishing up my graduate work at the University of the Westwoods where my studies and research had included subjects in Adult Education, Management, Organizational Development, and Training and Human Resources Development. I designed a training course for HAMC which gone through unbelievable scrutiny by my supervisor and her manager. They were highly critical all over the document through their criticisms that were contained on my draft of the proposal. Ironically, it was highly praised by the resident expert on the subject in the corporation itself. I met with my supervisor and the manager to discuss about the proposed plan.

"Gordon, we just cannot accept your proposed training plan," said Karen, the manager.

"But I'm sure it will benefit not only the department, but the company as well. My research and interviews with other experts in the field indicate that this is a viable training plan that will succeed. Even Abe, the head of the project, agrees that this will be a good training program for the company," I said.

"I'm sorry, your concepts and training approaches are really incompatible with our training methods here," said Karen.

Katrina, my supervisor only sat in silence during the entire discussion and did not say a word. Two months after the meeting, we had group meeting with Katrina. She passed around her new training plan for the department. Besides myself, there were Shawn and Debra whom I've had very good working relations. Debra was already aware of my training proposal that I was working on previously.

"We are going to implement a new training program that I have designed," said Katrina as she passed around the proposed plan. Debra leaned over and whispered to me.

"Gordon, isn't this your training plan?"

"Yes. This is plagiarism at its best."

"Do we want to share something?" said Katrina?

"Oh, no. We were just commenting how well your training program is." I said.

Her plan included only parts of my original proposal since the draft never included everything that was contained in the research paper. The white paper was presented to the International Society of Small Group Problem Solvers. They had an international conference that was scheduled later on in the year. A few months later, I received a letter from the ISSPS.

"Congratulations, you have been selected by the committee to present your paper during our International Conference ..."

I knew that I couldn't register myself as representing HAMC because this research paper was never sanctioned by them in the first place. It was my project from school. So, I registered myself as an "independent consultant" and presented the workshop under that capacity. When the conference came, our group attended the event.

"Do you see who is presenting a workshop?" Katrina said to the rest of the group.

"Yes, it's Gordon." said Debra.

"We have to do something about this. We have to stop him from speaking."

"You can't stop him from speaking. He's been invited to speak here." said Shawn.

"But the company hasn't approved his appearance here."

"He's here on his own, as an independent consultant. There's nothing you can do about it," said Debra.

"We'll see about that."

I was allowed to speak at the conference and gave a successful workshop. But when I returned to work the following week, I was severely chastised and reprimanded my management. I was suspended from work for two weeks without pay.

"Since when do I have to take out a license to speak in public?" I asked.

They didn't have a response.

Computer, you have heard of the term "back-stabbing." I've seen the term in your memory banks. It was a way of life in Corporate America at the time. When I was a supervisor of a training and documentation group there, we had the responsibility of publishing operating procedures that never previously existed. It was a wonder how people did their work over there! Well, after finding that out as an analyst, I was promoted to the position of supervisor and was given a staff of writers and a trainer. The trainer was one who replaced me in that vacant position. I remember her well. She came to her first interview in rags. That's to say, she didn't present herself very respectably as a professional. Her training experiences were only that of teaching first- and second-graders in elementary school. And she had a work history that took up two pages, none of which lasted for more than a year to a year-and-a-half. But mysteriously, she was admired by my immediate boss, and I was encouraged to hire her for the position against my own will.

I can remember one instance when she collaborated with a secretary to get access into the personnel files of my employees. She was almost sued, for it but the victim decided to drop the charges. That would have been advantageous for me because I would have no longer had to tolerate her behavior. Nevertheless, I was forced into a situation of having to live with this kind of behavior. After a change of management, it was almost like the department's leaders encouraged that kind of behavior. She would always not show up for standing staff meetings but always met with my bosses to launch accusations against me and my employees. Later, I was abruptly removed from my position with management's excuse that I was ineffective and incompetent. My employees didn't think so – nor did my record, which reflected that we published eight manuals of operating procedures with only three writers during my tenure. You know, Computer, it was ironic that I eventually had to work for her. Yes, management encouraged despicable behavior and often rewarded the tyrannical. One day I was called into Tom Franklin's office. Tom was the department manager which I worked for at HAMC.

"Gordon, you don't mind if I take the title of 'supervisor' from you, do you?" said Tom.

"It's your department. You can do whatever pleases you."

"Good. Because I am appointing Katrina as your supervisor."

"Why?" I said.

"Because I think she will be a more effective supervisor that you will."

"What will become of me?"

"You will become the department's administrator. That will not change your salary or your benefits." He said.

This was certainly office politics. Three months later, he was transferred to another department. But what was even worse, this was the beginning of Huge Air Crash. Fortunately, I wasn't in the airplane when it did crash later on in the 90s.

You know, come to think of it, American Society also began to lose favor with the rest of the world. Oh sure, we were always complaining about acts against humanity found in other nations. But, the American society failed to raise the mirror in front of itself to discover that we, too, had a great deal of crimes against humanity to deal with in the former country. Historically, it can be said that the wealthy were able to cover up their crimes much better than the less fortunate. That was also reflected in the records of the judicial system, which existed then also.

These were just minor issues compared to the major global issues on the national and political levels. On September 11, 2001, the world watched in horror as two planes crashed into the World Trade Center in New York and one plane crashed into the Pentagon in Washington D.C. Yet, another hijacked plane was taken down over the skies of Pennsylvania. It launched the United States into a war against terrorism. But just who were these terrorists? Historians say that they originated from a country called Afghanistan. Yet, the United States went to war against a tyrant called Sadam Hussein who ruled the country of Iraq, trumping up claims that the terrorists were in that country and that Iraq was in the process of manufacturing weapons of mass destruction. The "war" lasted for more than three decades, and the U.S. military became like a permanent fixture in that country. The death toll was enormous. Even by the year 2008, it claimed more lives than that of World War I, World War II, the Korean War, and The Vietnam War put together. And the war continued long after that year. The real tyrant of the World Trade Center disaster eluded capture for decades afterwards.

There were calls to impeach the President of the United States for war crimes. But the Congress, made up of a majority of the opposition party, did nothing. It couldn't. They had just enough to have a majority, but didn't have enough to be effective. By and large, it was a highly ineffective Congress. The government was costing the people money. Education, the health system and municipalities were losing valuable funding because a lot of the money once used for these more important purposes were diverted to fund the war and for military expenses. Municipalities were going under with some cities closing their borders or even merging with other cities and/or county governments having to take over bankrupted cities.

Then, on the financial front, banks were going under in droves. The government would often bail out poorly run corporations and businesses, but they would not provide any assistance to families and individuals who were crying for help because they were losing their houses due to bad loans and the loss of employment. Then, the government did something to assist families and individuals by passing emergency bills. However by then, it was too little too late.

Yet, the government continued to encourage corporations to export jobs overseas. There was this phenomenon called "globalization." This phenomenon was taking its toll on the American people. No, not the corporate executives – it was taking a huge toll on the common worker.

The government said that they were listening to the people. Actually, they turned a ignored the needs of the people and listened more to corporations. In fact, this was the starting point of "government by corporations, for corporations." The government turned its back on the people and largely didn't trust them at all. In fact, using the Iraq War as an excuse, they began taking away a lot of civil liberties that were once guaranteed and protected by the Bill of Rights.

People lost their right to privacy when Congress authorized the government to wire tap private citizens who were suspected of being a "terrorist." In those hysterical times, the mere fact that you were a Muslim classified you as a "terrorist." And I really must say, that having lived in an Arab country where the majority of the populations were Muslims. All these people are not terrorists. In fact, most Muslims are very kind, gentle, friendly and will give the shirts off their backs just for your safety and well being. But somehow, Americans had a knack of stereotyping people. And, this process of stereotyping has often gotten them into big troubles on the international platform. Such as, if you merely wore a turban on your head or dressed with a head scarf you were a woman, you were suspected of being a terrorist. If you wrote anything contrary to what the country believed, you were considered a traitor and a terrorist even though you done nothing but expressed a thought – which is guaranteed under the freedom of speech, the First Amendment.

You know, Computer, I think it would have been healthy for all Americans to live abroad in an Arab country at least for 3 months so that they would learn how to appreciate Muslims. I really believe that most people in the Republic of North America have the wrong impressions these people because they have never lived among them.

In the year 2015, the Republic rescinded this right and took it away for all citizens permanently. This was largely a corporate-driven initiative. After all, the government no longer belonged to the people. Executives never recognized freedom of speech in their organizations anyway. They often encouraged their managers to practice methods of prohibiting free speech among their employees. All they did here was elevate the matter ten steps higher – to the federal level.

During this time, the Administration bowed so low that it allowed its military to detain prisoners and impose and carry out cruel and unusual torture on "prisoners of war." Actually, they weren't referred to as "prisoners of war," but as "political detainees" and were not subject to the protection of the Geneva Convention. The Administration allowed the CIA to carry out water boarding, a form of torture that consists of immobilizing a person on his back with head inclined downward and pouring water over the face and into breathing passages, which sometimes lead to suffocation and death. Yet, there were other instances where prisoners were stripped naked and abused. Pictures were taken of these prisoners naked while a soldier was abusing them. Yet, the Administration demanded that its prisoners be treated according to the Geneva Convention.

Yes, these were interesting times, because this is the birth of what has affected life in the 23rd Century in the Republic of North America. If you thought times are bad in the 21st Century, you should see what it's now like in the 23rd Century – all just because of what you started in the 20th and 21st centuries!

Take the matter of insurance companies. In the 20th and 21st centuries, there used to be these organizations called "insurance companies." People would pay premiums (money) to these companies for policies or coverage which should have protected them or aided them financially during crisis such as health care, life, accidents, and a variety of other issues. People would pay a certain percentage of the "bill" and the insurance company would cover the rest. However, there were times when the insurance companies didn't cover anything at all, yet they collected huge premiums and denied coverage saying that a certain medical procedure would be "experimental." Therefore, they would deny the individual coverage. In some cases, the denial of medical care would result in death in favor of profits to a corporation or some big executive. Where's the value of human life? Yet, the government again did very little to aid the consumer or the individual. But instead, rewarded the insurance company for "saving money."

I do have to say one thing for the 23rd Century. All health care is much better for all. It's not free and it is also not cheap. But, the government has ensured healthcare for all individuals. People who could afford medical care were expected to pay for medical services. People who couldn't pay for such services were subsidized by the government, which was a costly venture for the government itself. Insurance companies have been extinct since the 22nd Century, and since then healthcare has become a world-wide right for all citizens paid and funded by the government. Our priorities are not on making money for corporations but keeping people of nations healthy. It cost more to care for a sick nation. As a result, people live longer than those in the 21st Century.

But in the shantytowns of the city, this did not hold true. People were dying rapidly for the lack of access to medical care and assistance. People who died in these areas of the cities were not afforded a proper funeral. There were makeshift morgues and the cadavers were often cremated in the open. Very rarely were the next of kin even notified. The ashes were just tossed among the other trash that lined the city streets – not even buried into the ground with respect.

Around the early part of the 21st Century, there was still the notion of having a two- party political system that was good for the country. That didn't settle too well for a lot of citizens who were becoming rapidly frustrated with the Democratic Conservatives and Liberal Labor parties. Both parties claimed that there were different. But in action, they were behaving very much the same. Both parties were full of corruption influenced heavily by corporate lobbyists who often influenced legislations in favor of Corporate America and wasn't in the general interest of the public – often times, their legislation ran contrary to what the people wanted. Slowly and gradually, a third party, that started around 2014, began to pick up momentum. A small group of independents demanded a change in government and formed the Democratic Reformist Party. The DRP didn't abandon all of the ideals and principles of democracy and freedom that were once relished by the American people, but it recognized that it was time for change. The current process and structure of government was getting too expensive, costly, and didn't serve the people. So, it started an initiative for a peaceful transition into a new government by the people and for the people.

At first, the DRP struggle and encountered many obstacles thrown by Labor and Conservatives. People in the DRP party really were neither on the left or the right, X or Y. In fact, most of them were on a higher plane of thinking at level Z, the apex of the pyramid. At first, people really didn't know what to think of people in this party. Most of them were formerly in the Labor and Conservative parties and became disenfranchised with the entire political system. In fact, you might say, most of them were really centrists. Conservatives often referred to them as "communists" referring to the old political structures in Europe and

China that was often a "bad" word in America. The Labor Party often accused them of being "socialists." They were neither that, too. The DRP believed in the fundamental belief that all men were created equal and should have equal rights and benefits guaranteed by the Constitution. But, they believed that this equality was not just applicable to the people of the Republic of North America, it was a God given right to every being on Earth. The DRP, however did not force their beliefs on other nations. They believed that they should serve as a model for all other to follow. They also believe in equal opportunities and free quality education for all and that health care was a right, not a privilege and should be fully funded by the world, not by private industry for the gain and profit of companies. The DRP did not advocate for military power for solving problems of the world, but using diplomatic channels as its primary means of resolving conflicts. The DRP also believed in an affordable government and took steps towards simplifying the government by eliminating a lot of waste and bureaucracy. The DRP were the first to ban lobbyist in government as well. In their opinion, this didn't give the people an equal voice and access to government – especially when lobbyists were making favors in Congress in order to have their representatives favor or "twist" certain legislation in favor of corporations rather than the in the general interest of the people. The people in the DRP really were gifted in thinking at a higher level than Labor and Conservatives combined. And this gift of higher thinking led them to successes in the House of Representatives, the Senate, and eventually in the 22nd Century, the White House.

It started out as a national movement, but in the late 21st Century it became an international phenomenon. The DRP had international chapters all over the world.

] Logout
"Good Evening, A. Gordon Sakata. Please come back
very soon."

CHAPTER 3

Life in Los Angeles in the 23rd Century

] Login, A. Gordon Sakata

"Welcome A. Gordon Sakata. Please enter today's date."

] Date: 03/01/07

"Today is March 1, 2207. Please enter the time."

] Time: 18:00

"The time is 6 O'clock. Welcome to the Cyberspace living room."

I love to go to the Los Angeles Regional Library in Downtown Los Angeles and look at the pictorial archives of what life was like in the 20th and 21st Centuries. For a man that was about 35 years of age like I am, it must have been very nice living in those days.

The archives reflect that the weather was usually at a calm 75 degrees during the spring; very warm during the summer months; and very mild during the winter months. Southern California then was known as the "Sunshine State." There were beautiful landscapes, especially with the Los Angeles Regional Observatory and the famous "Hollywood" sign that stood in back. Then, there were other pictures reflecting life at beach cities, orange groves, and various sporting events. Times must have been very exciting then.

I wish life was like that these days. We're in a severe ice age right now. Our warmest days average around 50 degrees Fahrenheit during the summer months, around 30 degrees during the winter months. About 50 years ago, it used to be much worse on the opposite end of the thermometer. During the summer months it would average around 125 degrees F. for the highs, and around 90 degrees during the winter months.

When they started efforts to reverse the trend, an exact opposite effect occurred. About 15 years ago, the Earth entered into an ice age and we have been in once ever since then.

As for the County of Los Angeles, there used to be many cities within the county borders. Now, there are only a few. Some have gone bankrupt and either merged with other neighboring communities, absorbed back under county government authority, or, if it were a beach city, chances are, it was submerged during a great flood which changed the coastline of the state.

Freeways still exist in Southern California but have greatly changed since the advent of the new semi-automated cars which pilot themselves and run on way less gasoline that the cars of the early 21st Century. Cars back then used gallons of gasoline. Because gasoline is so scarce these days, vehicles now run on mere tablespoons of gas and get better mileage also. As for the automation of the cars, all one has to do is tell the car where you want to go, and it will program itself to go to that destination. No steering involved, nor any of the fuss that drivers had to contend with in the older non-automated cars. The anti-collision avoidance systems built into cars are much more advanced. The cars now keep their own safety distance between the vehicles in front of them as well as vehicles that are to the sides of the car. It can even tell if you are intoxicated.

Life, however isn't very rosy. People are continuously being laid off from their jobs by automation – or, droids. This is very similar to the pattern that the United States experienced when the people then lost a lot of jobs due to "globalization." As a writer and a techno-academician, my job is in jeopardy because my work is gradually being transitioned into "smart-droids." Or, robots that are expected to replace humans in the classrooms – especially at the college and university levels. When I was a Director of Training and Human Resources Development, I managed a large staff of employees until I decided to become a consultant for a major utility company. Then, during another project I was working on, my father passed away. While I was working on that same job, I was laid off and could not find employment for the next four years.

My unemployment benefits expired after thirteen months or just after the first year. And it seemed my life just started to fall apart after that. My credit ratings plummeted, prospective employers would not consider you for employment because I was either too old, not qualified, over qualified, barely qualified – but not qualified enough, had a bad credit rating, or because I was already laid off from another company.

Yes, there were sympathetic people, but these people could help and were absolutely of no help.

"Oh, we're sorry you can't find a job, Mr. Sakata. Have you tried collecting unemployment?"

"Yes," was my response. "But that's already run out. I need a job right now."

Yet, the unmerciful bill collectors kept coming like condors flying over a nearly dead corpse – waiting for the kill. I was perhaps more fortunate than others. I was barely making it by living in a friend's closet. When I was down at my lowest point during my fourth year of unemployment I would still continue to get calls from agencies.

"Mr. Sakata, this is Universal Credit Corporation calling about your account."

"Yes, what about my account?" I said over the vision-phone.

"Our records show that you haven't made a payment in over 60 days. Can we set you up with an automatic payment plan?"

"No, I've sent you dozens of letters explaining that I've been unemployed for over 4 years and you continue to ignore my pleas for assistance. All you want is your money. You wouldn't even lend a helping hand finding me a job!"

"Sorry sir, that's not our problem. But if you don't make a payment to your account, we are going to have to turn your account over to a collection agency."

"How do you expect to get blood of a rock?" I said. "And yes, it is your problem. If I can't make any money or receive a steady income, you can't get paid – that's the bottom line. Do you understand that?"

"We understand that sir. But that's still not our problem."

"What part of this problem don't you understand? I would like to talk to your president about this."

"Who?"

"The president of your company. Do you know who that is?"

"Sorry sir, I do not know who that is. He is in the States. I'm calling you from India"

"Is that why I'm having such a hard time trying to understand you?"

"I demand to talk to someone here in the States!"

"Just one moment sir, I will transfer you."

He transferred me to a representative in the states.

"Hello Mr. Sakata. My name is Marianne, I am assistant manager of customer relations. How may I help you today," she said

"What is your position in the chain of command?" I asked.

"I am an assistant manager here in Kansas City."

"That's not good enough. I want to speak to your president right now!"

"We can't let you do that sir. He is in New York. I am the person that you will have to talk to."

"What's the matter, is your president too embarrassed to take customer complaints? What kind of customer service skills does he have? I'd say it's very poor. He doesn't have the courtesy of answering my letters that I've sent him four years ago explaining my problems finding a job."

"What letters were those sir?"

"You wouldn't know about them because you are in KC, he's in New York. The problem with your company is that you are too big and your lines of communications are very poor!"

After arguing with the assistant manager and got absolutely now where I received another call three months later.

"Hello Mr. Sakata. My name is Mark, I am the account manager of General Collections Services. I am managing your account and would like to arrange to set up a payment schedule on your past due account with Universal Credit Corporation," he said.

"Like I told the people at UCC, I'm broke, I'm unemployed, and I haven't been able to find a job for over 4 years. How do you expect to collect money off of me when there's no money to be had?"

"Sir, that's not my problem. I'm only trying to collect on an outstanding debt. Your credit rating will reflect poorly on your ability to pay on your accounts."

"Then why don't you rate the companies poorly for their inability to give me a job?"

"Sir, I understand your frustration. But that's something that you are going to have to work out on your own."

"What's going to happen if I can't pay?"

"We can put a lien on your property."

"I don't have any property for you to put a lien on." I said. "I'm living out of a closet."

Four months later, I was evicted out of my closet. By my own friends who were threatened of having their property seized because of me. I went to the Mega Homeless Shelter in Arcadia and had to wait for five days before getting a roll-away bed to sleep on temporarily. They gave me my own 5x8 foot space as I tried to get my life back together again.

It was like starting my life all over again. Almost as if they put a brand new hard disk in me and I had to reformat myself, reboot, and reprogram my life from scratch. In the shelter there was a dining hall were meals were served. Another area was designated as a living room or lounge area. And then, there was the rehabilitation zone where people tried to find jobs. Most of the available jobs were meaningless. The good jobs were being taken over by droids. I found a temporary summer job working with a traveling circus in the city as a maintenance worker caring for the elephants. Nothing difficult, just really hard work feeding and cleaning up after their mess. But I did this for about three years.

I went back to school to learn some other skills as an auto mechanic. Fortunately, I already had technical skills in computers, so I was able to adapt those skills in programming automobiles. That's basically how I got my life back on track before coming a professor at Whittier University in computer anthropology.

Others, however, also lost their livelihoods. They lost everything they owned – furniture, clothing, tools, automobiles, pets – everything including their homes. Many were forced into shelters like the mega malls that once serve as luxuries for shoppers in regional areas. Now, these mega malls are now centers for the homeless. Some homeless families moved into shantytowns in various cities – metropolises of tin shacks and cardboard houses. There were some districts in the city that were thriving with abundance and wealth. But, they were the people often taking advantage of the people that were being displaced into the cold streets of Los Angeles.

What could we do for these people? Government did not have an answer. Municipal governments did nothing but pass them along to other municipalities.

"Not on our city streets," they said. Instead, they passed zoning ordinances to construct mixed residential and commercial areas claiming to revitalize the city of its "blithe." But, it was a losing battle. Millions of people were being displaced by the day with droids that were taking over many jobs – including those jobs that were once thought to have been protected just for humans such as law enforcement. Police personnel were being replaced by street cameras and mobile droids. No job was safe anymore.

Government had turned its back on its people. People were no longer valued, nor considered an "asset" in companies. And, there wasn't a plan to handle the "waste" of people by discarding them out onto the streets of the cities. The government felt that nonprofit organizations such as the churches could take care of them. But the churches themselves were having and increasingly difficult time taking care of the destitute and the poor. Churches were losing members in their congregations because they were either moving away, getting older, or losing their homes and forced into other means of living elsewhere. Their monetary base of giving rapidly eroded and governments were no help in the matter. Many government agencies had difficulties paying their own employees, let alone, funding unnecessary wars just for political reasons that did not serve the nation or its people well.

Cities like Los Angeles were becoming overcrowded on the streets – especially in the racially segregated shantytowns. Over 60 million people resided in Los Angeles alone. Most of them were homeless and unemployed. It was as if they were litter tossed onto the streets. There were multitudes of people all over the city.

And, speaking about litter, trash could be seen all over the city streets and highways. There was no budget to pick them up. In some places, the litter would be piled at least 10 feet high or higher and the distinct aroma of the discarded materials could be smelled for a radius of several miles beyond the city limits. The trash would be so bad on some streets that you couldn't even drive through those areas. You often had to program your car to take an alternate route.

The buildings themselves were filthy and full of grime. Every building in the city was almost black. No one has maintained these buildings for centuries and it gave the city dark, grave-like, haunted, appearance. How can a civilization permit its people to live in such conditions?

Getting back to the cold weather, the warmest places in the city were usually in the shantytowns at night. People typically burned the trash to keep themselves warm. The fires contributed to the serious air pollution in the city. On a typical day, it would be very hazy with yellow clouds hovering over the city. You couldn't even see the sun for 98 percent of the year.

If lucky, they could find room and board in a nice facility like in one of the regional homeless complexes around the county. But those places were often overcrowded and filled rapidly.

In the 23rd Century, it has become increasingly obvious that the common man has been used as "pawns." They have been used only for the convenience of a very few. And when they no longer served them, nor were profitable for them, they were discarded – like trash.

Life in Los Angeles was very much reflective of the life in the RNA. It had an insatiable appetite for perfection. People were highly praised and treated as heroes like winning the gold medal during the

Olympics. They were happy if you won a silver or bronze. But they were elated if you won the gold instead. People who made such made such great accomplishments were rewarded richly. Yet, for the common man who didn't make grand accomplishments but contributed their skills and talents to society were treated differently. If their skills or talents were no longer useful, they were no longer treated as humans, but as inanimate objects. They were considered as societal rejects. Either you developed a skill that a robot couldn't do, or, forced to live in the world as an animal – a sub-human. And sub-humans also had emotions and feelings the same as ordinary people.

Can it get better for these people?

Will it get better for these people?

Is there an answer for these people?

Are there any viable solutions?

And for that matter, does anyone care?

There is a Japanese (not Napajanese) translation that can best describe people as being treated as "paper plates" or as "paper people" – that phrase can be said as, "kami jin." "Kami" meaning "paper," "jin" meaning" "people."

] Logout
"Good Evening, A. Gordon Sakata. Please come back very soon."

CHAPTER 4

In Search of Tabitha

] Login, A. Gordon Sakata
"Welcome A. Gordon Sakata. Please enter today's date."
] Date: 03/30/07
"Today is March 30, 2207. Please enter the time."
] Time: 08:00
"The time is 8 O'clock. Welcome to the Cyberspace living room."

I received a telephone call early this morning from cousin Larry who said that Tabitha was laid off from her job a while ago as a payroll clerk for a shipping company in Los Angeles. He was rather concerned because he hadn't heard from her for quite a while. Tabitha was my closest cousin. We were practically like sisters and brothers. Where I was the only child in my family, she was also the same in hers as well. Every time we got together during the holidays, we were inseparable. We did a lot together on the side. But now that I come to think about it, I also haven't heard from her in quite a while also.

Last Thanksgiving, we took family pictures, and one of the shots had just the two of us. I was lucky enough to have found that picture since I needed it to go looking for Tabitha in places unknown. One of them was the Asian shantytown on the north side of Los Angeles. From Whittier it was easy to get to and I wasn't about to take my car. If I took my car, it would have been stripped or stolen very easily regardless of all the security devices features installed on it.

Several decades ago, the Regional Transportation District built a nice light-rail system from the Los Angeles Central to Whittier. The end of the line ended only two blocks away from my apartment. I personally do not like riding public transportation because of the cost, but it's better than losing the car, for one, and secondly, it's better than navigating through all the litter on the streets.

I really didn't know where to begin looking. I hoped that she wouldn't be in one of the shantytowns. But I know after speaking to her at Christmas time last year that she was going through some very tough times. I decided to take the train into Union Station and then transfer to the subway into the center of the city.

I tried searching in the homeless shelters of the city first. I began with the Thomas Johnson Mission, but had no luck there. They haven't seen here there. Neither was she seen at the Los Angeles Shelter for the Homeless. I talked to people on streets with only suggestions that I'd try the Asian shantytown which was located in the old Chinatown district of Los Angeles.

After a futile search in the center of the city, I got on a bus and headed for the Asian shantytown. The Asian shantytown is one of the largest in the city and I knew that my search for Tabitha there would take forever.

The best I could ever do is start from one corner of the district and work my way through the other side. As I got there, I was immediately approached by beggars wanting money and donations. I was short on money myself and just barely had enough to get me back to Whittier on the train. But I began my frugal search showing pictures of Tabitha to people in tin shacks and cardboard houses.

"Have you seen this person?" I asked.

"No." was the common response.

Then, as I worked my way towards the northeast corner, I got lucky.

"Yes." replied an old woman cooking a meal on an open flame. "She's in one of the shacks on the outer edges in the northeast quadrant near the Metro Station."

I continued my search, this time looking for the Metro Station. Finally, I found the Metro Station and began looking for her in that area. In a small section, sandwiched between several small tin shacks I saw the faint resemblance of Tabitha. She did not look well. She was frail to begin with even when she was in her prime. But this time, she looked very skinny as if she hadn't eaten for a long time. I approached the woman who was trying to warm herself near an open flame.

"Tabitha? Is that you?"

"Gordon? Hello! What are you doing here? Why did you come here?"

"I heard that you were in distress. We haven't heard from you in a long time. How are you feeling?"

"It's been cold and I'm not doing well, brother." she said.

"Sis, you can't stay here in these conditions."

"I didn't want to impose on anyone."

"You'll be of no imposition to anyone. Come live with me in my apartment. It's better there and we can get you proper medical care."

"No, that's going to be too much trouble for you."

"It's no trouble at all. Come with me. Let's get out of here."

I wrapped her in a blanket and held her tight as I escorted her to the train stop. She was coughing severely, her face was red, she was hot as if she was running a fever and needed medical attention soon. We arrived at the train stop and got hopped on the train back to Whittier.

"How did you ever end up here?"

"I was laid off from Carlyon Shipping Enterprises and replaced by droids."

"But why didn't you get help?"

"I tried. I collected unemployment for a while, but eventually, that stopped and I couldn't make house payments anymore. I lost the house, my pets, the car, everything." She said.

"But couldn't any of your relatives help?"

"When the checks stopped, so did my lines of communications. I couldn't afford paying the bills that continued still continued to come long after I spent my last check. I couldn't get a job after that even though I kept trying without any success."

"Why couldn't you get a job? I thought you had a lot of skills?"

"They often said I didn't have the skills they were looking for. The skills I did have, droids could do it for much less money. In fact, they said droids were better at working 24/7 with very little cost involved. Humans were only capable of working 48 hours a week."

"Did they offer you another job or form of employment, retraining or anything of like that?"

"No, they said I become too costly for them. You know, with all the benefits that they had to pay on my behalf. With droids, they didn't need to pay any benefits. If one broke, they just replaced it with another. I guess that's the way they figured they could treat people. If a person cost too much, they would just simply replace him or her with a droid."

"And they did this without any regard for your life?"

"That's pretty much it. They gave me a paltry 3-month severance. But that didn't last long. Other than that, I was on my own."

"And how long did you serve that company?"

"Over 37 years."

We got back to the Whittier train stop and got off the train. Her condition deteriorated even more. She could barely walk off the train.

"Tabitha, could you walk just two more blocks?"

"No, Gordon. I feel very weak. I don't think I'm going to make it."

"I'm going to call for an ambulance."

I called for emergency services and we were taken to the nearest emergency room which was about four blocks away. In the emergency room, she deteriorated very quickly. The doctors and medical staff did all they could to revive her, but it was too late. She departed this Earth in peace.

Three days later, we had a small, simple memorial service for her at First Friends Church after her internment service at Rose Hills earlier in the day. There were a few friends and relatives gathered as we each contributed our fond memories during the service.

"When she was alive," I said, "I had seen the pain, agony and suffering that passed through her. It was as if she was imprisoned in a cage waiting to be released from the bondage of hell. The trials of man were lifted from her. When she passed away, it was like white doves encircled her body and lifted her towards Heaven. She was released from her misery and departed with a smile happily into a new world. I will miss her very much."

] Logout
"Good Evening, A. Gordon Sakata. Please come back very soon."

CHAPTER 5

The Decline of Spiritual Values

] Login, A Gordon Sakata
"Welcome A. Gordon Sakata. Please enter today's date."
] Date: 04/11/07
"Today is April 11, 2207. Please enter the time."
] Time: 20:00
"The time is 8 O'clock. Welcome to the Cyberspace living room."

The founding fathers of the great United States dedicated one nation under God. Their trust in God was inscribed everywhere, including the currency that's even seen on our money today, "In God We Trust." I have no doubt that those people knew who God was and the value of His almighty power. Back in the revolutionary days, families worshiped together, and there was a true sense of community among neighbors. In the beginning of the 20th Century, this still held true to some extent even though we've seen a gradual decline in the moral values of the United States. These values were reinstated as a nation when the three North American nations merged as one. But in the closing part of the last century, we saw a spiritual decay that not only influenced society, but also Corporate America.

In the 1960s, there was the rise of cults in America which in essence tarnished the biblical truths set forth by God in the beginning. There was the rise of the "New Age" movement that resembled Christianity's values but was far removed from Christian belief and doctrine. Yet, there were others proclaiming to be prophets who led many astray – many of whom were led to their untimely deaths either by drinking tainted "Kool Aid" or being burned into oblivion. Yes, everyone started to have different beliefs and "knew" that their thoughts were always the "right" ones. Which one was truly right? There were too many to tell! But if one boils everything down to the basic truth, it was God's truth that ultimately triumphed in the 21st Century.

Yes, there were those who even claimed that God was a "she" – where they got that idea is beyond me. For where can they extract God as being a female when people say, "Our Father in Heaven"? However, I am not one to argue. Even now in the 23rd century, maybe the phrase should finally be rewritten to say, "Our God in Heaven." God is neither a he or a she, male or female. So to some, God could also be Mother. So why not make it a non-gender specific statement? After all, God Is who He/She Is – "The Great I Am."

Oh yes, it was certainly easy for people to twist the truth and the facts without really knowing what the facts are. Ultimately, that had quite an impact in Heaven. Yes, Heaven did leave their "calling card" if you will. The Great Earthquake of Los Angeles was miniscule compared to what happened later. Why, they used to think that the Great Mississippi Flood of 1993 was so terrible. The Great Los Angeles Flood of 2103 made the Mississippi River disaster look like Walden's pond. Even to this day, one can fly over the area and see the old Los Angeles International Airport under 50 feet of water. Much of the flooding subsided back into the Pacific Ocean. But it did dramatically change the coastal outline of the Pacific Coast.

The great Quaker belief that the "Light of God" resides in every being is very true. This light is placed in every child at conception. It is this light that has driven nations to greatness and its abuse of the light led to downfall and disaster. Abortions were many during the closing of the last century. Why, it's really beyond me. So much potential talent was destroyed that the United States itself really didn't have a development plan for continuing greatness. After all, their arguments over abortion killed off many children who probably could have contributed very much to society but weren't even given an inkling of a chance to survive. Oh yes, many could have been adopted into wanting families. But many ultimately were not given the chance. In certain history books, there was a story that describes a mother who was contemplating abortion. She nevertheless changed her mind. Her child grew up to be one of the greatest men of the 20th Century – Albert Einstein. Abortion is not in God's master plan! However, who's to say that God doesn't have contingency provisions for emergencies?

As for Corporate America, there was certainly evidence of a lack of respect for humanity. In the early part of the 2008s began the Great Third Depression of the United States. No one was spending money, the government was printing more money but it certainly was not trickling down to the common man, and people were losing jobs by the multitudes. Although we cannot exactly pinpoint the problem in the closing of the 20th Century, it probably started when immigrants from Europe first stepped foot on this continent. People were certainly not treated like people. If people respected the fact that the Light was in each and every individual, then people would have treated each other more kindly and with more respect as fellow human beings. There was a definite split in society – those who were economically affluent versus those who were certainly not. The less fortunate people, normally working in jobs such as mills, mines, and factories were treated with far less dignity than those who were much more affluent. I remember sitting in break the room at HAMC when suddenly, the workers from the manufacturing lines were severely chastised for their work. It was almost like they were being treated like animals rather than humans. Factory workers historically were always treated with much disrespect, which had probably caused the birth of labor unions in those times. Yet, I recall that at General Wilkerson's, employees often felt like they were being treated like "dogs." Yes, some people got treated like dogs. Management provided jobs but did not ensure security and therefore had the freedom of putting a lot of people out of work – at will even!

Yet, some dogs were treated like people. I read an instance in history where this one person housed his pet dog in an air conditioned dog house. Yet, I've seen pictures in history books where people lived out of cardboard boxes, if they were lucky. Computer, I think there's something wrong with this picture! Where did some people get the "license" to treat other people with less dignity than animals? Was the root cause of this really money and the thirst for power? It certainly was not for the good of mankind!

Jesus commanded us to love one another as he loved us. He loved us even unto his death – even his enemies. So should we do the same? In fact, some of the superiors that I had worked for had that trait of love. They treated their employees with humility. It wasn't learned in college or any other school; they just were people who possessed high moral values. Unfortunately, many of them really didn't get very far up the corporate ladder. Oh sure, there were great schools of the time that taught excellent courses in managing a business and graduated many folks into the management ranks. What they didn't teach them was managing their people with a degree of humility. No, I don't think it really mattered to them or the schools of business and management. They were apparently always taught to be more concerned about the "bottom line" which I guess had something to do with money again. Unfortunately, it was often done at the expense of other humans.

I think that if God were truly given a chance in Corporate America, then that driving light would have driven the old United States to an even higher degree of greatness. There would have been a sense of direction for the country. Unfortunately for the nation, everyone had different values, concerns and priorities which disrupted the country's directions. I think this ultimately led to the demise of the United States and the creation of the Republic of North America.

A nation must truly give God a chance to lead His will and direction for a nation. Unlike what others may have thought at that time, there is only one God in this entire universe. I know it now because I've been there in my visions on many occasions. I can genuinely say, this is the truth, the whole truth, and nothing but the truth.

Now we really cannot blame corporations, back then, of inferior values. Society as a whole was just as corrupt. In fact, I have learned of stories where Christians have turned against Christians, Hindus against Hindus, Muslims against Muslims, and so on! What went on in some Christian churches was anything but Christian.

There was an instance in one church where one associate minister just ripe for the position of a senior pastor. The transition was ugly indeed! Some members of the congregation rose against this young fellow and launched accusations against him. The accusations were all unsubstantiated, but it caused a horrible split in the congregation. The departing pastor submitted a letter to the church board recommending that he not be promoted. The church was basically going broke – that's to say that there wasn't very much money in the funds to hire a minister from out of state. The personnel committee decided that what the church needed was a woman minister to lead the congregation. This led to an even greater divide amongst the membership. The members that led the uprising also went to the regional minister. Without a formal investigation of the entire matter, the regional minister threatened the promising young pastor that if he were to be called to the senior position, he would never preach in another church again.

I have remained firm in my belief all these years that Christians should act as sisters and brothers both in will and in practice. If we should call ourselves "sisters" and "brothers" then so should we behave like that and nothing less.

It came about in the mid-1990s when America first began to see definite evidence of societal decay. Hatred among races was at an all time high. There was a rise and increase of militias and a peculiar burning of African-American churches in the South. This sparked a progressive phenomenon that was eventually put to rest in the mid-2090s when people of goodwill rose up to fight against those full of hatred.

I guess you might say it started happening around the year 2001. As I mentioned before, a very tragic series of events happened in the eastern United States where terrorists hijacked planes and flew them into the New York Trade Centers, the "Twin Towers." There were two planes that crashed into the buildings that ultimately brought the grand skyscrapers down and killed thousands of people. Another plane on the same day, crashed into the Pentagon in Washington D.C. These acts shut down the country. No planes were allowed to take off or land for days. You might also say that America became so paranoid that it couldn't even trust an ant off an ant hill in its own backyard! They created a department of "Homeland Security" which did anything but keep the nation secure. Extremists managed to infiltrate the country once again and destroyed the Hoover Dam in 2015, cutting electrical power off to the western United States for several years.

In 2008, gasoline prices rose over $4 a gallon, but that was only the start. It continued to rise above $15 a gallon. It was, perhaps the ugliest period in American history. People were rioting in the streets. Gasoline stations were being burned at will, and there was no mercy on oil executives. There were public hangings almost every day, and the American justice system turned against the people who were making trillions of dollars a day at the expense of average Americans who could no longer even afford to ride a bus, the cheapest of public mass transportation in the country. For those who could afford gasoline, cars were being destroyed every hour – often with the drivers in them. And, these were making big news on local television news at 5 o'clock.

The churches pleaded for peace and sanity. But people were no longer listening. Often, the churches themselves were associated with a corrupt, ineffective government both on the federal, state and local levels. Someone let Corporate America into the legislative houses. It was time to take the government back, even if it meant tearing the current government apart and making an entirely new government that was going to be responsive and accountable to the people.

As I mentioned in the previous chapter, Computer, the DRP was started sometime during the 21st Century. It had its rough climb to success – not only by the two major political parties at the time, but also by Corporate America, that had a iron grip on the government. The DRP was one of the peaceful third-party political alternatives. There were several others that often supported violence and often took that violence to the streets of the cities. The People's Political Party was one of the more notable examples. If the United States had its hands full with international terrorism and al-Qaeda, this domestic terrorist group was not only dangerous, but much worse than al-Qaeda – this was America's nightmare. Not only did the PPP destroy government buildings and facilities (municipal, state, federal and foreign), but its members also destroyed a lot of corporate offices and headquarters also. And, the offenders of these crimes were often hard to apprehend or never apprehended at all. Many people say that their tactics and training were like the old classical Japanese Ninjas. They would come in the night and do their damage, then disappear and blend into the natural surroundings without a trace or glimmer of evidence. Their crimes were so advanced that the FBI couldn't solve a lot of cases. Exactly who were these people? Were they aliens from another society or world? No one knew – no one had a description of them. They often eluded the most advanced security systems and camera monitoring networks. They were never detected by the street cameras that replaced the walking street patrols in many cities. No, they didn't even leave a footprint or something that a heat detection device could even pick-up or sense at a moment's notice. But the ironic thing about this whole matter is that these people had the support of the people. Law enforcement officials just could not get the cooperation from the public because police were seen as representatives of an ineffective government that didn't represent the will of the people.

Oh yes, the government was occasionally successful in capturing the criminal. That was because they had a network of, oh, how would you describe these people? Spies? Snitches? These people thought that they were being sheltered by the great "Witness Protection Program." But when you take a drive around the city once in a while, you'll smell the stench of death in the air – cooked meat. Someone had a barbeque or a block party and got roasted for turning someone in.

] Logout
"Good Evening, A. Gordon Sakata. Please come back
very soon."

CHAPTER 6

The Raping of the Common Worker

] Login, A. Gordon Sakata

"Welcome A. Gordon Sakata. Please enter today's date."

] Date: 09/04/07

"Today is September 4, 2207. Please enter the time."

] Time: 18:00

"The time is 6 o'clock. Welcome to the Cyberspace living room."

General Wilkerson's Bank took a turn for the worse in the late 1990s. GWB wasn't the only company in Southern California that was laying off common workers and middle managers at the time. It just was especially interesting at General Wilkerson's. You see while GW was laying of its employees, the executives there managed to still retain most of their privileges. While the common worker was being displaced into other job positions, if there were any to be had, or out into the world of the homeless, the executives managed to retain their corporate jets (although they claimed that they sold one of the two jets to a private company. The private company turned out to be a subsidiary of GW, and while the common worker was losing property, including their homes, GW executives were riding around in longer stretch limousines. They continued to hold fundraising drives for their annual "Good Government" campaign, and continued to raise the premiums of employee life and medical insurance to the point that each employee was paying for over 90 percent of the cost of their insurance premiums. They continued to call these as "employee benefit" packages. Also, contributions to the employee's retirement funds were being secretly "reallocated" to other accounts. Two percent of the employee's contributions would go to the individual's retirement fund while the other 98-percent went into another account. Yet, the employees were often told how great the retirement fund was working and encouraged employees to continue their contributions into the retirement programs.

The federal government was not any better. In 1995, bickering between the presidential administration and Congressional leaders led to the worst government shutdown in ages. "Non-essential" government employees were laid-off twice in a matter of a couple of months because the President and his staff (Labor) and Congressional leaders (Conservatives) couldn't come to a budgetary agreement. Oh sure, the President, senators, and representatives were paid – with absolutely no cut in pay, thank you! But other government employees were laid off for the holidays. Some could barely make ends meet while others were having severe difficulties making mortgage payments and caring for their children. Yet, the battle between the two parties continued, as if they didn't have anything else to worry about!

As people were being laid off, it was reported in the news that oftentimes these people would lose their retirement benefits. What was interesting is that the profits and savings of these retirement benefits would end up in the pockets of the executives who just laid off the employees. Was this a classical case of the "rich getting richer and the poor getting poorer?"

Computer, a while back I talked about the phenomenon called "globalization." More than anything else, that caused the raping of the American worker during the 20th and 21st centuries. The mere fact of people losing their jobs to other people in other countries was just a stepping-stone. Government was not out to protect American jobs and corporations were out to look for "cheap" labor. They say it was an effort to keep cost down. But it was more of an exercise to maximize profits for rich executives rather than benefit the masses. Because the only thing that the "masses" benefited from this entire "trickle-down theory" was, was a kick in the teeth by a phenomenon called "inflation" and higher prices. People had to pay more for what they purchased largely influenced by rapid spikes in energy.

Bad loans from financial institutions compounded by people losing their jobs caused defaults on loans and a serious housing crisis in the 21st century. People were losing their homes without any government intervention or assistance, but the Administration then, insisted on funding an unpopular war that was started on false premises.

This was perhaps the beginning of the raping of the common man in the Republic of North America. Where globalization caused the loss of American jobs to other countries in the 20th and 21st centuries — automation caused the loss of even more jobs to robotics during the 22nd and 23rd centuries. For humanity, this was not good. It displaced millions of people –families and individuals – forced them out of their homes and disrupted their livelihoods. It separated fathers, mothers, sons, and daughters, aunts, uncles, cousins and close friends. And the most unfortunate thing about all of this is that the government did not have a master plan to transition the people into a better way of living.

It was a good thing I left General Wilkerson's when I did. I find computer anthropology to be much more challenging and rewarding, although I do find time to relax and participate in a master chorale in Whittier.

Well, it's time I retire to the guest room, so I'll log off for now.

    ] Logout
"Good Evening, A. Gordon Sakata. Please come back
very soon."

CHAPTER 7

An Incredible Vision of the Past

] Login, A. Gordon Sakata
"Welcome A. Gordon Sakata. Please enter today's date."
] Date: 09/8/07
"Today is September 8, 2207. Please enter the time."
] Time: 18:00
"The time is 6 o'clock. Welcome to the Cyberspace living room."

I just had an incredible experience last night! You know it's as if I were experiencing déjà vu! I had this unbelievable feeling that I've been through this before 200 years ago! You know, I once performed at the Hollywood Bowl and Carnegie Hall. As I drove past a place called the Whittier Civic Auditorium, I felt like I'd performed there before also. No, not in this lifetime – but in another! I kept hearing the various parts of Aaron Copland's *Lincoln Portrait*. I don't know why, because the Civic Auditorium has never been noted for big, grand concerts. Not like the major concert halls in downtown Los Angeles. There must have been some special occasion. You know, the group that I sing with, the Whittier Choral Society, performs in the Whittier Civic Auditorium frequently and has a long history dating back to 1982. I'll have to look at their history books to see if such an event ever took place over there once upon a time.

This special ring that I wear on my right ring finger is 14-carat gold with the family crest, a crescent eagle. The story goes that this ring is a replica of the original that was once worn by one of my American ancestors of the third generation. According to the story, the original was lost sometime during the early 21st Century in World War III. In fact, now that I come to think about it, I have been having some very peculiar dreams and nightmares about having done all of this once before.

For example, I had a dream of being alone in a beautiful forest somewhere in the Sierra Nevada Mountains in California. Although I've never been to a place like that, it appeared very scenic and has compelled me to do some research about that area to see if a place like that exists.

Yet, on other occasions, I would pass by this little famous hamburger stand called "Tomás" on the corner of Rampart and Beverly and I had visions of frequenting the place often with a person whom I've never known. Although I must say, she was quite cute! That is, the person in these dreams.

You know Computer, as I tell to you about these experiences, I am compelled more than ever to look into these mysterious visions. They must be telling me something. What, I don't know at this point. But I'll be more than happy to return once again with more data.

] Logout.
Good evening, A. Gordon Sakata. Come back soon.

CHAPTER 8

Excursion to the Greater Whittier Library

] Login, A. Gordon Sakata
"Welcome A. Gordon Sakata. Please enter today's date."
] Date: 10/12/2207
"Today is October 10, 2207. Please enter the time."
] Time: 090:00
"The time is 9 o'clock. Welcome to the Cyberspace living room."

I woke up a little late this morning, and I really wanted to get an earlier fresh start on this project. The morning was gorgeous — Mid-40's and very clear. So incredibly clear that one would forget that we still have problems with air pollution in the 23rd Century. Back in the late 2190s they launched an initiative to clean up the air. Sure, the electric cars made a significant impact on the environment. But big businesses still got away from cleaning up their act. Somehow, they always managed to find a way to stall the progress. Well, the progression of their efforts became increasingly worse. And, we're still paying for their mistakes even today.

I had a little problem making my remote connection here in the Greater Library of Whittier to my Cyberspace living room. Please forgive me, computer, but getting a link these days is getting harder. I guess it must have been due to the increase in the population of the city! Sometimes, I just can't find space to link at all. That's not fair to us long-term residents!

Now, I need to get signed onto the library's archives. I haven't done this in a while and it may be a little difficult to do. I haven't upgraded my wrist-top for a while, and it really needs a 2 terabyte memory upgrade. We'll see what happens.

> (Computer)>Login
> (Computer)>Please enter your name: A. Gordon Sakata
> (Computer)>Please wait.....
> (Computer)>Please enter your password: ********
> (Computer)>Sorry, your account has expired. Please see
> the System Librarian. Come again soon!

I hate computers!

Well, I went to see the Systems Librarian, Jennifer, for a new account. She was quite pleasant after I practically gave her my whole life's history, credit references and everything else she could have and did think of.

"Hello, Jennifer." I said.

"How may I help you today?" she asked.

"The system says my account has expired."

"Oh! I'm sorry to hear about that. No problem. Just fill out these papers and we'll get you right back on line.

She gave me a stack of papers about ten pages worth. "What's all the paperwork for?"

"Sorry," she replied." If it were only the city, you would have to fill out the top page only and show your driver's license. But now, we're mandated by the FBI, Homeland Security, and the RNA government to file papers for the Republic's security purposes. You know…anti-terrorist laws. That's why there are ten pages that need to be completed.

"It's as if the government didn't have anything better to do, but to kill whatever trees are left and create more paperwork on its citizens! This is disgusting!"

"I'm sorry for the inconvenience, sir."

"I know, you're only doing your job."

So I sat down and began to fill out all the papers. About an hour later, I completed filling out all of the information on all ten pages and returned the forms back to Jennifer.

"Here you go." I said to Jennifer.

"Thank you, sir. Here are your new temporary access codes."

"My temporary access codes?"

"Yes. When we are notified that your security clearance has been approved by the government, your new permanent access codes will be mailed to you."

"Thank you, Jennifer. I didn't realize that everything required a security clearance now days just to surf the internet."

"That's big brother for you! Have a nice day."

Let's try this again.

> (Computer) >Login
> (Computer) >Please enter your name: (Gordon) A.
> Gordon Sakata
> (Computer) >Please wait.....
> (Computer) >Please enter your password: ********
> (Computer) >Welcome, A Gordon Sakata. We haven't
> seen you for over 20 years. How are you doing?
> (Gordon) >Fine thank you. Let me go into archives
> please.
> (Computer) >Just a moment while I connect to your
> search engine...
> (Computer) >Archives is now activated. How can I
> help you.
> (Gordon) > Find "*Sakata*"
> (Computer) > One moment please...
> (Computer) > Two entries found:

A) A. Gordon Sakata (1951)
B) A. Gordon Sakata (2051)

Interesting, there are two identical names in the archives. I knew my ancestors arrived here from Napajan in the early 1930s and I've heard of family stories about a distant ancestor with an identical name. Gordon, I found you – sort of.

(Gordon) > Select B
(Computer) > A. Gordon Sakata, Born April 11, 2051
in Los Angeles, California.
(Gordon) > Select A
(Computer) > A. Gordon Sakata, born April 11, 1951
in Los Angeles, California.
Died: Estimated April 1, 2009, Manzanar, California

What a coincidence! Could it be that I was named after the infamous A. Gordon Sakata I who, according to legend, performed in the Hollywood Bowl with 1000 singers on October 8, 1994 and once in Carnegie Hall in New York? Gordon, I've heard a lot about you.

(Gordon) > Go to interactive mode.
(Computer) > One moment. Please check your voice
input device.
(Gordon) > No voice. Please continue.
(Computer) > Now ready for interactive mode without
voice.
(Gordon) > Play back A.
(Computer) > One moment...
(Computer) > Now ready, please strike the ANY key
to continue.
(Gordon) > [ANY]
(Computer) > Now playing...

This is absolutely fascinating! I'm watching video clips of my ancestor who looks almost like me. Or, should that be the other way around? The record shows that he was into computers and was a personal computer trainer at General Wilkerson's in Northridge. But his residence was right here in Whittier near the house that I'm living in right now!

It says here that he created a ring with a crescent eagle. A golden image of a raised eagle with the head looking to the right and both wings spread over the head. It says that this was a replica of the family crest handed down through the ages since the early times of his ancestors in Napajan. It also notes that the original ring was lost and he had an exact replica made which that one was also lost at the time of his untimely death in camp. But wait! If he wore the replica to his death, then the one I'm wearing right now must be the original ring that was created more than 200 years ago! My father gave me this ring when I turned twenty-one. It's a family heirloom. According to family stories, Gordon I had a fondness for turning twenty-one. It says that the original ring had great mysterious powers, but nobody could determine what those powers or secrets were. Well, I guess I'll keep in tradition – I haven't found any mystical power to this ring. It's pretty and I do get a lot of compliments about this ring. In fact this ring is so unusual, there are these two things sticking out of each wing. They're microscopic, and I've been always afraid of breaking them one of these days. It's kind of bothersome however. I got poked with one of the metal things sticking out. No one could ever tell what the meaning the two pieces or things are about. They really don't logically fit with the general design of the eagle itself. I would imagine that I could very well take a pair of side-cutters and clip them off. But I've been told not to destroy any part of the ring because of its "mystical" powers.

It also says here in the text that he too performed the narration of Aaron Copland's *Lincoln Portrait* at the old Whittier Civic Auditorium on Saturday, May 31, 2008. That must have been in the small performing arts center before the big quake of 2012 destroyed the original building and when this campus was known as "Whittier International University". This is also quite a coincidence! I've been invited to perform the exact same part in the new Whittier Civic Auditorium which now seats around 3800 people. He was also a member of a member of the Whittier Choral Society.

In his younger days, he used to participate in an activity called "drum and bugle corps" and was also decorated as an Eagle Scout in the 1960's. It says that he loved camping and he spent 10 days one summer in 1967 in New Mexico at a big place called the "Fillbrook Scout Ranch". Interesting, it also says here that he lived for three months in Algiers, Algeria while training people to use a special computer called a "Gestalt Photo Mapper".

Anyway, when World War III broke out, he was sent to a concentration camp around 2105. It says that he was first sent to the Santa Anita Race Track in Arcadia, California first which was some kind of staging center as the Napajanese on the Pacific Coast were gathered supposedly for their "safety". From there, he was sent to a place called Manzanar in central California at the exact site of his father's relocation in the 1940s.

He was an advocate of peace, and it says here that he was rather quiet and reserved. But when he spoke, he spoke with wisdom and dignity, and everyone listened intently. In camp, the article says that he often mediated disputes between camp officials and the internees. The story is unclear from this point. But it says that he was mysteriously abducted one night and taken into the mountains where eventually, he met his untimely death. Four to five months later after the war ended, he was discovered by his wife, who was pregnant in camp. The story says that he was found barely alive, and according to some family interpretations of the story, he had these visions that he shared with this wife just before he died. It says that he is buried under a pile of rocks somewhere near a lake up in those mountains – probably somewhere in the Sierra Nevadas. One of these days, I must make it a point to visit this site and pay my respects for this person whom I bear the same name.

> (Gordon)>Logoff
> (Computer)>Good afternoon, A. Gordon Sakata. Come again soon.

Rich and I had a chance to sit down and talk. I loved a good

Southern-style barbecue. Rich had the best on the ribs on the West Coast. He was a eighth generation chef and said that his ancestors were chefs during the slavery period just before the Civil War. My cooking was okay but nothing worth speaking of. People often liked my Pig-Pot Stew. It was a genuine dish of Napajan – very Pacific-Islander-ish if you will. But I can remember when my people were often treated like slaves during the Japanese occupation. The Japanese were notorious for over-fishing our shores for Kamanpura. It was like the monk fish and it had the texture of a lobster when cooked right. I think the Kamanpura was driven to extinction during those days of World War II. Yes, people historically treated other people like "Kushunbis". A Kushunbi was a festive Napajanese plate made of banana leaves. Since Napajanese lived in tree houses most of the time, banana leaves were very plentiful. The only kind of thing I can think of that comes close to a Kushunbi is "paper plate." That's because Kushunbis were often thrown away after their use.

How do you compare people to throw-away paper plates you ask? Simple, just look at the matter of slavery for example. Slavery existed in early Biblical times during the time of Moses. When a slave's use was expired, he was often "thrown away". In the days of the Roman Empire, slaves or "gladiators" were thrown into the arena to sacrifice their lives for the entertainment of others who were of a more privileged class in society. In certain places in Asia, a woman was treated as "property" instead of a human being. And if the "property" did not perform to expectations, she often was put to death or cast aside. In Germany during World War II, the Jewish people were driven from their homes only to be put to work as slaves or put to death if they were too weak or sick to perform the needs of the Master Race.

There's basically no difference in American Society. African-Americans were hustled from their native Africa and put aboard filthy sailing ships only to be brought to market and sold as slaves or, once again, "property". Those who did not survive the journey across the Atlantic were tossed over-board. Those who tried to escape slavery and were caught were often put to death by their owners or severely punished.

Modern day America had its own form of slavery. Only then, it was hidden under the name of what used to be called "Corporate America."

In Corporate America, life and times were probably tougher than slavery in early America. That's because back then if one didn't like the "system," he or she was often put to death. In Modern Day America, if one does not like the "system" one often is forced to survive through a "living hell." Before the second American Revolution, there were distinct class differences. The upper class of affluent – well-to-do people – who often ran large corporations, big businesses and influenced government, politics and policies usually in favor of the rich. These people were genuinely in the minority while the majority of the people belonged to the "middle class" who were less affluent and often burdened with paying more than their fair share of taxes and, by governmental standards and legislation, received very little in benefits in return. Nevertheless, a lot of books on the market then educating people how to manage their "wealth" also encouraged people not to pay taxes. As a someone once said, "The rich do not pay taxes."

Then, last, but not least, there were the impoverished class. These people earned hardly anything, hardly paid taxes, yet received a lot of benefits from the government in terms of assistance.

But socio-economic classes and divides exist elsewhere in other nations, you say. This is very true. But the matter goes even deeper than the divide between the rich, the middle and the poor! Nowhere but in the United States of America where it is written:

> *"We hold these truths to be self-evident, that all men are created equal, that they are endowed by their Creator with certain unalienable Rights, that among these are Life, Liberty and the pursuit of Happiness.—"*
> *The Declaration of Independence*
> *July 4, 1776*

If in fact all men are "created equal", then certainly the rights guaranteed by its Constitution would be applied equally both in government, private and Corporate America. However, in Corporate

America, people are often denied the freedom of speech and expression even when there should be allowances for constructive criticism and comments of its management. People are often displaced from employment because of so-called fabricated economic conditions and excuses that often people – mostly of the middle class – are left without jobs, yet forced to pay for bills and living expenses by meaningless and limited resources from government resources and agencies. Some people are often disqualified from benefits because, according to some agencies of the government, their "spouses make too much money." Yet, when an individual applies for a job, it is done on a singular basis – not a joint effort! Taxes are taken out from an individual, yet they do not qualify for assistance when desperately needed. Furthermore, as the middle class is laid off and dislocated, managers and executives often reward themselves with tremendous bonuses and rewards often resulting in awards in millions of dollars per individual.

Back in the days when I was working as an administrator at HAMC, I remember processing some papers for the department manager. A colleague of mine, Patrick presented me with some documents that the managers wanted to file with the division office.

"Hi Gordon, could you please process these Cost Improvement Performance Award Bonuses for the department manager?" said Patrick.

"What are the CIPs for?" I asked.

"Do you remember the 500 employees that were laid off from the department two weeks ago?"

"Yes"

"This is his cost justification. He wants to collect a bonus for their layoffs."

"That's ridiculous. He's just displaced 500 employees out of their jobs and now he wants a reward for that?"

"Yeah! A $1 million bonus no less!"

These people were not sanctioned for displacing thousands, if not millions, out of their fair share to the pursuit of an acceptable quality of life, liberty, and happiness. Their life of luxury has cost the lives of millions of others their good fortune and perhaps the biggest victim of their arrogance are the federal government, state government, and local municipalities. A government auditing agency in the year 2010 showed that the middle class virtually had shrunk to nothing while the poverty class rose dramatically. Millions were displaced out of their homes and into the streets, and the Upper Class continued to pay nothing in taxes. The federal government was going bankrupt. And so were the states and local governments. The person who invented or coined the term "trickle-down economics" probably created one of the biggest fallacies of American history. Nothing trickles down!

It's late in the afternoon, and I'm awfully hungry! I think I'll go to Rich Henderson's "Mr. BBQ" for some lunch. Computer, I'll see you later at home.

]Logout
Good Afternoon, A. Gordon Sakata. Come back soon.

CHAPTER 9

Enough is Enough

] Login, A. Gordon Sakata
"Welcome A. Gordon Sakata. Please enter today's date."
] Date: 08/25/2208
"Today is August 25, 2208. Please enter the time."
] Time: 12:00
"The time is 12 o'clock. Welcome to the Cyberspace living room."

Hello Computer. A lot has happened since I last our last conversation. I met a 30 year old woman named Wendy in a cyber café one evening, and since then, we have dated quite frequently. She's everything I've ever imagined of – like the girl of my dreams that I mentioned in one of my previous chapters. She's a cross between a Norwegian and an Arab – blonde hair with olive skin and blue eyes. There's so much that we have in common that I don't know where to begin.

We both enjoy going to the beach and especially taking hikes up the mountain. She owns a house in Altadena in the Pasadena area around Eaton Canyon where there are some nice hiking trails. She doesn't have any family here. She says that all of her family lives in foreign countries – probably from Norway and somewhere in an Arabic country like Egypt.

She's primarily a vegan although I've seen her sneak in some bits of meat off my plate once in a while. Her favorite colors are also purple, but she drives a white car. Whereas I'm the shy person, she is very outgoing and assertive. She is left-handed, does not wear glasses and stands about 5 feet 8 inches tall.

Where my handwriting is very sloppy, hers is very neat, precise, and almost being very formal. Her hobbies are gardening and she has this fabulous apple tree in her backyard along with other fruit trees. As for her house, it's very immaculate throughout the entire house. Really not like my apartment at all.

We went on a little excursion to Las Vegas recently and became engaged to be married. We haven't set a date yet. She wants a really big wedding at the First Congregational Cathedral in Los Angeles.

In fact, now that I think about weddings, I really should do something about my appearance. My hair is getting long, and I really need a haircut. Computer, remind me to go to Cost Cutters in the Whittier Mega Complex. It's one of very few places remaining that sill employ real people to cut people's hair. Most other places use droids. It's like getting two clips for a hundred dollars, and that's it! That doesn't even include a shampoo! [RECORDED INTO YOUR DATE BOOK.]

A lot is also happening in the nation and in the world as I speak. Like that of the times in 2203, the matter of war has once again reared its ugly head. This time, America is preparing to go to war against Napajan as the President claims that the Monarch of Napajan has committed his nation to weapons of mass destruction both biological and nuclear. I find this incredibly hard to believe. What would a small island in the Pacific be doing with nuclear and biological weapons of mass destruction even though it already has conquered bigger nations like China, Japan, and Taiwan? And so what if the little country has aims on economically taking over bankrupt Australia as its next "merger and acquisition?" That's none of America's business. No, there must be another ulterior reason for this massive build up of military power in the Pacific. One of the last great oil fields of the world has been discovered and controlled by the Napajanese just west of the island and America is starving for more oil to feed its frenzy of sports utility vehicles (SUV) that remained strong in the market after the Iraqi War of 2007 and the great oil shortage that soon followed the war that crippled America. Conditions then became so bad that nothing moved – not even trains or trucks or airplanes. The transportation system in America came to a complete standstill, yet the people that were able to move about were those in government and the upper class.

Speaking about the upper class, they have been in the news recently also. 95-percent of the RNA was unemployed and more are being laid off in favor of automated processes and artificial intelligent robots. This is not only an American phenomenon, but a world-wide problem. Corporate executives are laying off people by the millions especially in countries once thought to have been rich in "low-cost labor" employees. People were getting displaced by the millions every day, yet the governments of their countries are doing absolutely nothing about it. It only goes to reason, particularly in America. People in the rich class of America controlled both Corporate America as well as the government (federal and state). This pattern is nothing new, it goes back to the time the United States was founded long ago. Only the rich are entitled to gain any access to public office by means of their affluence. The term, "buying an election" isn't really far from the truth. Those who hardly made any money, such as those from the middle class could not afford to run for any office, no matter how much they received in contributions. But it was easy for the rich to buy their way into office with their own funds and through political contributions, usually by large corporations. Since you had the rich and affluent in power in government, laws and policies were written in favor of those who were rich and affluent in American Society. Hence, the burden of the middle class to pay for everything while the rich got away with paying for nothing. After all, the middle class had very little to say in government, even though most representatives said that they represented their "constituency". This was a fallacy. The more money you gave to your representative, the more attention you received from him or her. The less money that you gave, if you gave anything at all, the less attention you received from your representative for the voice of money spoke louder than words from the general public. If there isn't any monetary value that could have been made from a situation or a problem, the problem was often ignored. If it did have a monetary value, the more attention the matter received. Therefore, since there isn't any money to be made from the homeless, these people often were ignored as well as those who were unemployed and soon joined the ranks of the homeless. In other words, if corporations couldn't make money out of an individual, he or she was laid off in favor of something or being that was more profitable not matter what the talent and professional skill levels were. They were often discarded like paper plates. Now the world, had one big problem, these "paper plates" were piling up and could not be recycled like aluminum.

The displaced people began to rise up in arms. Small pockets all over the world began to administer "street justice" throughout cities all over the world. Here in the RNA, the PPP was one example of those "small pockets" only on a larger scale. Local police and law enforcement agencies, made up primarily of droids, were of little use in stopping these activities since they too had little funding from governments (local, state, and federal). In the RNA, these outbursts were more prevalent. The Republic's people demanded a better way of life that was equitable to all and not for only an elite minority of the population. People were tired of being displaced by machinery. Yet the government insisted on paying unemployment benefits for only thirteen weeks. This was not enough. Capitalism in America had run its course. After all, it was well known that capitalism bred corruption, greed, and crime. Furthermore, it only favored an elite few. Those of the elite class still had their fingers in governments all over the RNA. The big "middle class", which now became the "poverty class" said, "Enough is enough. A new revolution is in order."

Still, the federal government had its hands tied on other matters like that of Napajan. Military troops and equipment were being sent to the neighboring Pacific islands in a massive build up of war while the poverty class was waging its own war against the RNA. The government was more concerned about the matter of surviving a nuclear or biological holocaust while the Republic's people were more concerned about just being able to survive at home.

In the meanwhile, Napajanese and Napajanese-Americans were having a difficult time being caught up in this madness. Napajanese-Americans had the highest rate of unemployment amongst all races at 98 percent – largely due to discrimination and being associated with a country with which the country was nearly going to war. Even if you looked like a Napajanese (Japanese-American, Chinese-American, Korean-American – or, any Asian for that matter), people discriminated against you. If you went to restaurants, only non-Asian people were allowed to use the restrooms. If I were lucky, there would be a portable outhouse in the back of the restroom for us to use. Otherwise, it was only a bucket with drawn curtains. The buckets were never emptied so there were always overflows. Many people just dug holes in the ground and lined it with two logs. In the restaurants themselves, there were sections for non-Asians and a back room for Asians. Usually, the Asians had to sit on floors since there were no chairs or tables. That's why most Asians dined at fast-food facilities or ate at home.

Interracial relationships were also not tolerated – particularly, if it had to do with an Asian and any other race. I remember there were a lot of instances where Wendy and I received a lot of stares when we went out on dates. At some restaurants, we didn't even get any service at all, not even a glass of water. We continued making our wedding plans despite the fact that it was becoming increasingly hard to find clergy to marry us. They often said that interracial marriages would be detrimental to the institution of marriage. Bishops and high priests often warned the local clergy in the region to refrain from performing marriages to interracial couples. Those who did were often removed from their parishes or churches and replaced with someone else who subscribed to their doctrine or "book of discipline."

On the revolutionary front, there was an incidence in Northridge at the old General Wilkerson's Headquarters, now the corporate office of the Oregon National Bank and Loan. A group of unemployed workers who were just laid off from the Oregon bank stormed the corporate office and carried the chief executive officer to the corner of Prairie and Oakdale and hung him on the nearest microwave tower. As he died, the massive crowd chanted, "Down, down upper class." This was not the only incidence. Across the country, corporate executives were targets of assassination plots, many plots were successful – some were not. But the rise of these incidences were quite evident. People wanted their jobs back and Corporate Republic of North America was not about offer a helping hand. The riots continued. Executives continued to make purchases of big ticket items like limousines made in Japan for they were the only ones that were able to afford such luxury items.

On the spiritual front, many of the elitist were of such faith that they often considered the Bible as The Law above and beyond the laws of the RNA. Whatever the Bible said, they took it literally. Therefore, causing such primitive behavior for treating people they way they did. If you didn't agree with these strong-willed Protestants, then you "were against them." They automatically placed you on the "undesirable list" or the "black list." Being on that list was very cruel. It inhibited any person from gaining any kind of employment, of what employment there ever is. Even if you have talents and skills that were much needed in society, you were often one of those "paper plates."

] Logout.
Good-bye A. Gordon Sakata. Come back soon.

CHAPTER 10

Making Wedding Plans

] Login, A. Gordon Sakata

"Welcome A. Gordon Sakata. Please enter today's date."

] Date: 08/27/2208

"Today is August 27, 2208. Please enter the time."

] Time: 06:00

"The time is 6 o'clock. Welcome to the Cyberspace living room."

There was much talk about preparing for war and going to war against Napajan that I thought right now would be the best time to ask for Wendy's hand in marriage.

"But where? And how?" I asked myself.

No one in Los Angeles would marry us – not even the local judges. We can't even get a marriage license here in California because of the ban on interracial marriages.

I'll try calling Wendy and see if I can drop in on her today. I tried calling her on my cell phone but had problems connecting. Then on my fourth attempt, I finally got a good connection.

"Hi, Wendy! What's up?"

"Absolutely nothing!" she replied. "I'm getting quite bored with all this talk about war."

"How about some company?" I asked.

"Get your Heineken down here right away!" she said.

So, I immediately showered, dressed, and hopped in my speeder on my way from my condo to Wendy's house in Pasadena. My car was running awfully low on gasoline. It only takes 2 tablespoons. But I can go 500 miles on 2 tablespoons. In the 20th Century, cars were lucky if they could drive 200 miles on 12 gallons of gasoline. In the 23rd Century, you can get gasoline at any convenience store, supermarket, or liquor store. They come in little gas vials. They're relatively cheap – only $15 per vial. I better stop talking to myself and stop here to get some gas.

As I was approaching the door to the store, the clerk saw me and immediately pulled out a sign saying, "Naps not welcomed."

"I'm not a Nap!" I said to the clerk.

"You sure look like one." He said.

"What if I told you I am Chinese?" I asked.

"Sorry, we don't serve them either. You guys are all the same!"

"That's an insult! I'm an American!"

"You sure don't look like one, even though you're the first one that doesn't have an accent!"

"Then that settles it. Are you going to sell me gas or not?"

"No!" he replied.

I walked out in anger and disgust. Then I remembered where I can get some gas. I programmed my car to head for Chinatown. Hopefully, I'll have just enough gas to make it there.

As I was on the highway, I became highly anxious and sweaty as I saw my gas gauge swiftly dip from a quarter of a vial, to nearly empty. With luck, I've made it into Chinatown and found an 8-88 store open nearby.

"Hi there! I would like to buy a vial of gas."

"No problem." She replied. "That will be $15 please."

"Here you go. Thank you very much."

"No, thank you," she replied.

I plugged in the vial into the gas compartment and was swiftly on my way to Wendy's.

Wendy owns and lives in a real nice 5-bedroom, 5,300 square foot, two-story, ranch-style house overlooking Eaton Canyon along Pinecrest Drive. It overlooks the Eaton Canyon Saddle between Mount Markham and San Gabriel Peak in the San Gabriel Mountains. Once in a while, we love to go hiking on the trails leading to Henniger Flats that overlook Los Angeles. And on a real clear day, you can see all the way out to Catalina Island.

"Knock, knock!" I said pounding on the door. Her doorbell never worked. "Good morning!"

Wendy opened the slowly opens the door, slowly in her usual manner.

"Good morning," she says quietly. "How's your day?"

"Don't ask." I replied. "My day is starting off terribly!"

"Oh?"

"Yeah. I was running low on gas. So the first place I stopped at refused to sell me gas because I was an NAP!"

"Oh no!" she said. "I can't believe that! What's this city coming to?"

"That's not all. He said that even if I were a Chinese, he wouldn't sell me gas."

"I think you should have called the cops. You could have got him for discrimination!"

"I don't think the cops would do anything. They probably would have arrested me!"

"You're probably right. They're just droids anyway! So what did you do next?"

"I jumped into my car and drove to Chinatown and got gas at an 8-88. At least the girl there was very pleasant."

"I'm sorry you're having such a poor day, Sweetie. We need to do something to cheer you up. I think a good walk up to Henniger Flats would get your mind off this matter. What do you think?"

"That sounds like a good idea." I replied. "But can we eat? I'm really hungry!"

"Sure! What do you want?"

"What do you have?" I asked.

"How would you like an open sandwich with jam, cheese, and meat slices; and cereal and milk? And to boot, I'll make you your favorite Turkish-style coffee – that should give you a good jump-start! What do you think?

"That sounds fine with me!"

So after she gave me a big hug and a kiss, she went into the kitchen to prepare breakfast. I proceeded into her den to watch the television.

"I'm going to turn the TV on!" I shouted.

"Fine!" she replied. "Make yourself at home."

Using the remote buttons, I channel surfed. All the stations interrupted their broadcasts to cover breaking news out of Australia. Apparently, the Chinese had occupied Australia and were moving troops and equipment onto that continent in preparation for a face-to-face confrontation with the Republic of North America.

"Hey Honey," I said, "you'll have to see this. China just took over Australia!"

"No thanks!" she replied. "I'm sick of all this war stuff. If the RNA goes head on against the Chinese, they're going to get their asses kicked back to this continent! Besides, it's not worth fighting over an island the size of a postage stamp! All of this based on false pretenses – like they did with the War of Iraq in 2003! We'll be there forever!"

"I can't argue with that!"

"Besides," she continued. "What's going to happen if China wins and the RNA defaults on all the loans it made from China? Are we going to become a colony of China by default? Are the Chinese going to own us?"

"Hmm," I said. "You pose a good question there."

"Where do you want breakfast? Here in the kitchen? Or, on the patio?"

"The patio, of course!" I replied.

Her patio was in the backyard overlooking the Eaton Canyon, and it was a really beautiful morning, clear, and very warm – that is, if you consider 50 degrees warm.

We took everything to the patio and had a peaceful breakfast. I really have to say, with her beauty and the backdrop of the Eaton Canyon, it was a "sight to behold." It was, indeed, a lovely breakfast.

I have to admit, we both hate to clean up the mess, but it was a necessity. She keeps an immaculate house. Conversely, I'm a rat pack that keeps everything. So when we get married, there are some habits that I'm going to need to improve on.

After we cleaned up, we proceeded on our casual walk on the trail leading to Henniger Flats. It starts with a steep incline down the side of one hill that leads to a bridge across the San Gabriel River bed, then starts the slow, steep, gradual two-mile ascent to Henniger Flats. I hiked this trail several times during my younger days as a Boy Scout. But it was more different with Wendy. With Wendy, it was more of a casual walk up the mountain as we exchanged jokes along the trail. This time, the joke went a little too far for her. While I told her that I needed to stop and take a little rest because I was getting a little short of breath, we actually were at a point in the trail where there is a nice short-cut that I had learned in the Scouts. I told her that I would catch up to her eventually, but that she needed to continue.

"Sweetheart," I said softly and breathing heavily. "I need to stop here and take a little breather."

"Are you okay?"

"Yes." I said. "I'll be fine. Why don't you go ahead without me. I know that you like to run hills. Now would be a good time without me hindering you. I'll meet you at the Flats."

"Are you sure you'll be okay by yourself?" she asked again.

"Yes, yes. I'll be fine."

"Okay. Take your time. But if you really need me, call me and I'll come running back."

"Fine," I said. "Don't worry about me."

"I love you." She said as she gradually began jogging of into the distance.

"I love you, too!" I said as I watched her gradually fade farther away.

As soon as I was sure she couldn't see me, I started my ascent into the bushes and up a steep incline. It was a path carved for and by many generations before me. It really was no secret that this shortcut existed. The shortcut shaved off a mile off the trail. And at the end of the shortcut, you were only 500 yards away from Henniger Flats.

I got to the top of the shortcut in about ten minutes. From the point that I last saw Wendy, it would have taken at least twenty minutes to get to this point. So, I sat and waited.

Eventually, I heard Wendy's footsteps as she was running towards my current position on the trail. Then we encountered each other.

"A. Gordon Sakata!" she exclaimed surprised. "I can't believe you have the audacity of doing this to me! I thought you were back down the trail resting only to find you here having beaten me further up the trail! How did you do it?"

"It's a generational secret." I replied laughing.

"A generational secret like heck!" she said in disgust. "You cheater! On the way back down, you're going to show me that shortcut!"

"But it's much more dangerous going back down than it is coming up!" I replied.

"I don't care." she said. "You're going to show me that way back down or else!"

"Okay, Okay." I said.

"Now, make a promise to me. Promise that you will never leave me again."

"But the war?" I asked.

"Promise?"

"I promise never to leave you again. Satisfied?"

"Yes." she said quietly. "Let's kiss and make up."

We spent a considerable while on that spot kissing, hugging and making up. A couple running on the trail passed us.

"How disgusting," one of them said. "A Nap and a white trash in love!"

"Jeez!" I said. "You can't even get any privacy on a nice quiet trail."

We wrapped our arms around each other and proceeded into Henniger Flats.

On the campgrounds, there is this nice area overlooking the Los Angeles Basin. There are no benches to sit in this area, and the mountainside is known for its red ants. So if you're not careful of where you sit, you can get bitten quite badly. Red ants and I do not get along very well. I remember having been attacked by Texas-size red ants in Houston when I was a teenager. That little episode landed me in the emergency room with a severe reaction from the venom.

But we finally found a nice quiet, private place to sit as we began talking about the possibility of getting married.

"Wendy?" I asked in a hushed voice.

"Isn't the view just beautiful today?" she said softly. "What's on your mind?"

"Last year I asked your hand in marriage and placed that rock over your finger. And we made a promise to each other to get married. How about setting a date?"

"Are you in a big hurry?"

"It's just that ..." then I paused for a moment.

"Yes ... It's just that with all this talk of war, I think something is going to drive a wedge between our relationship ..."

"Like what?"

"Like us being separated by who knows what and how," I answered. "I really don't know. I just have this feeling that something is going to happen if we don't act soon."

"You know," she said in a louder voice, "I really want a big wedding at the First United Cathedral in Los Angeles. You know, the one with the big organ there. I think it would be appropriate since you love to sing with organs."

"I know," I said. "But who's going to marry us in L.A.? They have a ban on interracial marriages in the state. I read that they instructed all the clergy in California not to perform interracial marriages."

"I read that too. Maybe we can wait this out until after the war and the hysteria is over with. I'll still love you then like I do now."

"I think by then, it will be too late. I think we need to do something fast. And then, maybe have a big celebration after the war is over."

"What do you propose we do?" she asked.

"Let's go to Las Vegas tonight. I heard there are still wedding chapels there that will marry us on the fly."

"This is awfully short notice, don't you think? Who we going take as witnesses? Are you ready to go on the fly like this?"

"Hey, I'm willing to do anything on the fly at this moment. I can call my friend Ed. I think he's free today. Let's see, what's today? Monday? How about your friend Bonnie? Is she free? Would she be available?"

"I don't know. I'll give her a call. I know that she likes to do things on the spur of a moment. But this more than doing something suddenly don't you think?"

Wendy instructed her cell phone to call Bonnie's phone. She asked if Bonnie was free and available for a trip to Las Vegas Bonnie was enthusiastic about going and agreed to meet the both of us later in the evening. At the same time, I called Ed who also was available to go on the fly.

We stood up and started our decent down the trail back to Wendy's house and got about 500 yards from Henniger Flats.

"Wait a minute!" Wendy said as she grabbed my arms, I abruptly stopped walking.

"What's up?"

"Remember your promise?"

"Oh yes. I promised that I would never leave you."

"No! Not that one. The promise of showing me that shortcut!"

"Oh… yes. That one! Well …" I said as I walked over to the edge of the steep path that led through the shortcut down the mountain. "We'll have to be real careful! It's steep and it might also be slippery in spots. But, on the other hand, it will save a lot of time. Okay, follow me closely!"

We got about 50 feet down the shortcut where there was a very steep slope.

"Okay …" I said to Wendy. "We can take this little shortcut by sliding down hill for the next 300 feet. Or we can take the detour which will take us about 5 minutes out of our way. What is your choice?"

"Let's take the slide."

So we sat down as if we were in a two-man bobsled and we leaned forward.

"Hang on!" I said as she embraced her arms around my waist and we went sliding down the slope for the next 300 feet creating a cloud of dust as we glided down the dusty pathway.

At the bottom of the shortcut, we stood up and dusted ourselves off as we laughed loudly and continued our walk down the main path.

About forty-five minutes later, we were back at Wendy's house.

"What do we need to do now?" she asked.

"I think we need to book the chapel and a minister. I hope we can get one this fast." I said. "Let me use your phone."

I called several places in Las Vegas only to be disappointed that they were booked for the week and couldn't accommodate our request. Then, eureka! I called the Megasphere and learned that there was a cancellation at 4 o'clock Wednesday, so I immediately booked a "Staircase to Heaven" package.

"Sweetheart!" I shouted.

"I'm right here." She said softly from a mere five feet away.

"I'm sorry. I didn't know you were there. I had a hard time finding a place. But I got lucky and found a place to get hitched twelve-hundred feet above the Las Vegas Strip."

"Twelve-hundred feet above the Las Vegas Strip?" she asked. "Where's that at?"

"The Tower at the Megasphere Hotel!" I said.

"You're going to have to hold me awfully tight!" she said. "I'm scared of heights!"

"We'll get into town tonight. Then we'll have to go to the courthouse tomorrow morning to get a marriage license."

"I really hope we're doing the right thing."

"Everything's going to be just fine. I'm kind of excited about this little adventure. Aren't you?"

"Well… I don't know what's going to transpire in the next few days, but I think it's going to be fun!"

"Okay. I'm going to go home and do a little packing. I'm going to get my concert tux for the wedding so I won't have to rent one there. I'll meet you back here around 5 o'clock."

"Okay my love." as she gave me a hug and a kiss. "Please be careful driving home and back."

"I love you."

"Love you too …"

I programmed my car to drive to my apartment in Whittier. As I was listening to the radio and Antonin Dvorak's *Stabat Mater*, breaking news interrupted with an announcement that the RNA was moving more troops and military equipment to Hawaii, Saipan, and the Marshall Islands. Then another news report announced that spotters off the San Pedro lookout point spotted what appeared to by a Napajanese spy submarine and warned the residents of Los Angeles of a possible impending attack. That was highly impossible because Napajan does not have submarines, let alone a navy.

Upon arriving at my apartment I was greeted by my landlord. She is a very nice Italian who gave me my best recipe for spaghetti sauce.

"Hi Gordon!" she said while waiving and watering the flowers. "It looks like your fans have been leaving you a lot of messages while you were gone!"

"Oh really?" I said. "Thank you. I'll have to take a look."

I finally got to my front door and paper was tacked all over the door. At the base of the door was a Styrofoam food container with a yellow note on top.

As I read the notes and messages, they were all but welcoming. One note said: "Nap – go home!" Another said, "Dirty Naps not welcomed here!"

"I'm starting to get the message." I mumbled to myself. "What does this one say?"

"Traitor!"

I read the message on the food container and it read: "Bon Appetite!" I really couldn't have imagined what was in the box itself, but it probably wasn't nice. But I opened it anyway. It contained dog excrements.

I tore everything down off the door and window of my apartment and tossed them into the trash container at the side of the building. On the way back up to my apartment, I decided that it was time to pack everything. The first thing I did was to find my checkbook and write a check to Mrs. Belcher, for my last month's rent which I would give to her on my way out.

Then, I proceeded to pack everything in the apartment that will fit in the car. Most of the stuff in the apartment was trash anyway. What I left behind, Wendy had at her house anyway. So, essentially all I needed were my clothes, my music, and my financial records – that was a lot in itself.

As I finished loading the car, I ran into Mrs. Belcher in the carport. "Mrs. Belcher!"

"Yes, what is it my son?" she asked. "I see you have a lot packed in your car. Are you going somewhere?"

"Yes, as a matter of fact." I said, "I've decided to move out. Here's my last month's check and a little extra for the cleaning fee."

"Why so soon?" she replied. "You know you have to give thirty-days notice."

"I'm getting married to Wendy on Wednesday, and I'll be moving in with her when we get back from Las Vegas."

"Oh! Congratulations!" she said joyfully. "And may you both have a long and happy life together."

"Thank you very much, Mrs. Belcher." I said. "But now I have to get back to Wendy's."

"God's blessings to both of you!"

I programmed the car to go back to Wendy's house. News on the radio was talking about the possibilities of evacuating all the Napajanese on the West Coast – from California to Washington in the United States portion of the RNA. They said it was for our "protection and safety."

I got to Wendy's in relatively short time. I was greeted at the door by Bonnie and Ed.

"Hi Gordon!" said Bonnie.

"Hi Bonnie!" I said.

"Hey, Gordie," said Ed. "What's up?"

"A lot!" I said.

"Like what?"

"It's a long story." I replied. "I'll tell you on the way up to Vegas."

"Where's Wendy?"

"Here I am! I was upstairs packing."

"Hi, Sweetie" I said as I wrapped my arms around her to hug and kiss her. "You don't mind if I drop off a few things here do you?"

"Not at all … What do you mean a few things?"

"I moved out of the apartment."

"Oh my God!" she said. "What brought this on so suddenly?"

"You might say, 'I got the 'message.'"

"I'm sorry. Exactly what happened?"

"Like what?" asked Ed.

"I really don't care to say. But it was gross!"

"Come on guys." Wendy said. "Let's help Gordon unpack the car."

The four of them started walking out to the car.

"Leave my garment bag and my blue suitcase in the car, thanks." I said.

After we unloaded the car and put everything into Wendy's bedroom. We packed the car with the other's belongings for the trip. Wendy locked up the house and was the last to get in the car.

Then, I programmed the car for Las Vegas and we were on our way for our vacation.

] Logout.
Good-bye A. Gordon Sakata. Come back soon.

CHAPTER 11

In Las Vegas

] Login, A. Gordon Sakata
"Welcome A. Gordon Sakata. Please enter today's date."
] Date: 08/28/2208
"Today is August 28, 2208. Please enter the time."
] Time: 08:00
"The time is 8 o'clock. Welcome to the Cyberspace living room."

We stopped off briefly at Best Burger's in Barstow for a quick bite. But we wanted to get into town as soon as we could. As we were being seated at our table in the restaurant I remembered that I was going to tell the three of them my little episode at the apartment.

"Okay. This is what happened back at the apartment. After I left Wendy's to pack up my stuff for this trip, there were all these messages on my door and windows that weren't too inviting." I said.

"What did the messages say?" asked Ed.

"Some accused me of being a traitor … others said NAP go home. Then I had a box lunch sitting at the door way."

"What was in the box?" said Bonnie.

"Dog excrements."

"That's disgusting!" she replied

"What sort of sick person would ever do that?" said Wendy.

"That's when I decided to pack everything up – or mostly everything, and move out. What the heck, I'm starting a new life today anyway, right?"

"That's right, Gordon. I think you did the right thing!" said Bonnie.

We finished our little snack there and decided to make one more stop at the Barstow Super Stop nearby to pick up several vials of gas for the trip to Vegas and back to LA. In the Super Stop, there are several gift shops and food service areas. There was also a liquor store that sold gas vials. It used to be manned by a human the last time we passed through here going to Las Vegas. But that person was replaced by a droid – a very rude one as well.

"I would like to purchase these 8 vials of gas," I said to the droid.

"We don't service Napajanese," it said.

"Then I would like to buy these vials," said Wendy.

"Sorry, Ma'am. We don't service interracial couples."

"I thought droids didn't discriminate." I said.

"We are programmed not to discriminate."

Then mysteriously, Wendy went into a trance as if she were communicating with the droid.

"Droid 2150, may we please buy these vials of gas?" she said.

"Yes, this will be $120."

"Thank you 2150," said Wendy. "We'll make sure that gets reflected into your records."

"What did you do to that droid?"

"Nothing. I just spoke to its 'inner soul.' Besides, I have my way with computers – especially with stupid robots!"

"Do you have magical powers that I don't know about?"

"They say I have some special gifts," she said.

After returning to our car we were finally on our way to Las Vegas. We arrived in town around 11 p.m. that night and checked into our rooms at the Megasphere Hotel and Casino. Ed and Bonnie had their own rooms. We were given a really nice bridal suite. And after a restful night, which we all needed, we are about ready to go out to the Clark County Courthouse to get our marriage license. But business first – no, not playing the slots or the card tables, it was breakfast time. So we got in the car and headed for the Florence Hotel for breakfast buffet. I was starved.

So, after our grand feasting at the Florence that morning, we went to the Clark County Courthouse and took out our marriage license without any problems – no hassles, no strange looks, nothing unusual at all. It was a very pleasant experience.

After that, we decided to go to back to the Florence to do one more item of business – to buy matching wedding bands at the Blue Diamond. This is was here where I got her engagement ring. So I thought it would be appropriate to find something that would be nice and fitting for the two of us. It took a while and we spent a long time. Ed and Bonnie went to the casino to gamble for a while. Eventually we found a set that we really liked, and it was amazing that each ring fitted us perfectly as – if they were already made for us.

We shopped around for a little while longer. Wendy also had to look for a nice, but simple, wedding dress. She did that on her own because she wanted to surprise me for the wedding.

We eventually got back together and went searching for favors for both Ed and Bonnie. Eventually we accomplished everything that we needed to do on this spur of the moment adventure.

Later that evening, we decided to go out to Paul's Supper House for a pre-wedding dinner and had Italian cuisine and several bottles of imported wine. It was a good thing my car has auto-drive on it. At the restaurant, we had a grand little party among the four of us.

"Here's to the newly-weds to be," Bonnie said. "May you both have a happy and fruitful life together filled with a lot of joy and happiness!"

"Here! Here!" replied Ed. "Gordon, are you sure you want to go through with this? You know, I can put you in the car and take you back home if you want. We can even go to Laughlin on the side!"

"Yes, Ed…" as I looked and kissed Wendy. "I am absolutely sure I want to go through with this?"

"Wendy?" asked Bonnie. "When the minister asks you if you will take Gordon to be your lawfully-wedded husband, da ditty dada, are you?"

"I don't know …" said Wendy. "I'm scared of heights!"

We all laughed.

"So …?" asked Bonnie to Wendy. "How many kids are you going to have?"

"I haven't thought about that," Wendy said. "One … no more than two perhaps."

"And you Gordon?" asked Bonnie.

"I want a traditional Napajanese family!" I said. "At least ten kids!"

"TEN?" said Wendy. "What do I look like? A baby-producing machine?"

"Just kidding," I said. "Besides, I know the law says you can't have more than two or else they'll tax you for each additional child over that limit. Can't afford any more taxes than what they're already collecting!"

We continued to laugh, drink, and exchanges stories until closing time.

We got in the car. I was so toasted that I couldn't even remember how to tell the car how to get back to the Megasphere Hotel.

"Car …" I said.

"Destination?" the voice asked.

"Megersfrer? … Mergersfar? … Megersfurry Hotel!" were my instructions to the car.

"Sorry, destination does not compute. Do you mean Megasphere Hotel in Las Vegas?"

"Clo…clo…close 'nough," I said.

"Sir, my sensors indicate you are intoxicated. Please press the emergency auto-drive button now!"

When the car senses that I'm drunk, the emergency auto-drive button flashes alternately in red and yellow lights. I pressed that button.

"Please sit back and I will prepare you for your trip," said the voice in the car.

So I sat back at the auto-prep system went into immediate action which strapped the four of us in our seats. As the car shifts into auto-drive, a protective shield rose over the windows so that the glass wouldn't break in case there was an accident or a collision with another car. However, all cars in the 23rd Century are equipped with collision avoidance systems and are designed to maintain a 100-foot distance between vehicles.

"Driving," the voice announced. "The estimated time of arrival is 5 minutes. I shall call ahead and arrange to have you all assisted to your rooms."

"Thank you, Car…" I said.

Upon arrival at the hotel, we were greeted by hotel staff who assisted us on these people transports that glided each of us back to our rooms. We didn't even have to walk! All we had to do is sit down on these pods, and it automatically knew where to take us. I was really impressed! I only wished that it were flexible enough that I could have stopped to play a couple of rounds on the slots. I felt pretty lucky today.

Back in our rooms we got into bed. But we couldn't fall asleep right away.

"How was your day?" Wendy said.

"I enjoyed it very much being with you all day, my love." I replied. "I hope this will never end."

"I loved this day, too," she said. "I think tomorrow is going to be even more special for the two of us."

"I agree. Are you excited?"

"Yes. Very much so."

"Are you tired?"

"No. Not at all! I'm just anxious for tomorrow."

"It will be here soon, my love." I said.

"And I'm glad it will be with you, dear." We drew nearer in bed and intimately kissed the night away.

Oh, Computer –

] Logout.

Good-bye A. Gordon Sakata. Come back soon.

CHAPTER 12

Wedding Day

] Login, A. Gordon Sakata
"Welcome A. Gordon Sakata. Please enter today's date."
] Date: 08/29/2208
"Today is August 29, 2208. Please enter the time."
] Time: 09:00
"The time is 9 o'clock. Welcome to the Cyberspace living room."

Today is our big day, Computer. I got a special wakeup call from the wedding coordinator this morning, and she wanted me and Ed to go up to her office to take care of the financial arrangements before the ceremony at 4 o'clock this afternoon. She also said that she prepared something special for us this morning. No sooner after I hung up the phone with her, there was a knock at the door.

"Who is it?" I asked.

"Room service, sir." replied the voice on the other side of the door.

I peeked out the little port in the door and it looked like hotel staff. So I opened the door very cautiously.

"There must be a mistake," I said. "We didn't order room service."

"This is compliments of Ms. Blake, your wedding coordinator."

"Oh, this must be the surprise that she told me about."

"Yes, sir!" said the attendant as he rolled the cart to the window overlooking the strip. "Eggs Benedict, O'Brien potatoes, fruit basket, muffins, coffee, and orange juice. Enjoy!"

"Thank you very much." I said as I slipped him a tip and closed the door behind him as he walked out the room.

Wendy was taking her shower while all of this was happening.

"What was all of that about?" inquired Wendy as she dried her hair.

"We've just been treated to breakfast – err, room service!" I said.

"Oh, by whom?"

"Compliments of Ms. Blake."

"Who's Ms. Blake?"

"She's our wedding coordinator. I have to meet with her in 90 minutes."

"How thoughtful of her! Please thank her when you see her."

"Will do."

We both sat down and enjoyed the view over a lovely breakfast. I was tempted to turn the television on, but elected not to. There has been too much news about the impending war that I didn't want to ruin this day.

"Well, I need to get along," I said to Wendy as she sat at the breakfast table sipping her coffee.

"Okay. I can't go very far looking like this. I'll catch up with you a little later on."

"Okay, honey," as I bent over to kiss her. "Take your time. I'm going to swing by Ed's room and then we'll go to see Ms. Blake. I'll see you in a little while."

"Good enough. Ciao!"

"Love you," I said as I went out the door.

Ed's room was four floors down, so I hopped on the next elevator going down.

As I got off the elevator, I ran into Bonnie who was also on the same floor.

I came to Ed's door and knocked. Ed opened the door.

"Hi, Gordie!"

"Good morning, Ed." I said as he walked out the door. "Hey Ed, we have a little time before my meeting with Ms. Blake. What say we gamble a little in the casino?"

"That sounds good to me."

We got on the next elevator going down to the ground floor where the casino was located. I only had $20 on me to gamble with.

"How long we going to play?" he asked.

"Probably not that long" I said. "I only have $20 bucks to deposit in one of these one-arm bandits."

"So, five minutes at the most?" he asked.

"Yeah, I'd say around that much time. I'll meet you back here."

"Okay." he said.

We separated and went in different directions. He liked playing the card tables. I set out to search for a good progressive slot machine.

"Ah! Here's one." I said to myself looking at the sign. It was a Megabucks slot. The progressive jackpot was $25 million. I inserted my bill and hit the "max button" and the wheels started spinning. With the five spins – like usual – no luck. Then on the sixth spin. The wheels started spinning unusually fast.

The first wheel stopped on a megabucks symbol. The other two continued to spin very fast. Then the second wheel stopped and gave me my second megabucks symbol. All I needed was a third one to win the progressive jackpot. It seemed like eternity. The third wheel kept spinning and seemed like it would never stop. Then, bang! It was all over … A THIRD MEGABUCK SYMBOL.

I sat on that stool stunned and starring at the slot machine with amazement. This had never happened to me in my life. It was a miracle! $25 million! What was I going to do with all this money? The slot's alarm was screeching loudly as attendants and security personnel came rushing to my assistance.

"OH MY GOD!" I shouted. "What has happened? What have I done?"

"Congratulations, sir!" said one of the attendants. "You have just won $25 million!"

"Sir, you'll have to come with us," said one of the other attendants. "This machine can't pay you that kind of money here."

"Oh. Oh, sure." I replied. "Where do I go?"

"This security guard will be happy to escort you to the personal banker here in the hotel. Just follow him."

"Just follow me, sir," said the security guard.

"Wait a minute!" said one of the attendants. "We need to take his picture!"

As stunned as I was, they posed me in front of the slot machine and took several pictures.

"Okay!" said the attendant. "Go get your money!"

So I followed the security guard to an obscure private office.

"Ms. Norris," said the security guard. "This is…"

"Oh. Err, Gordon. Gordon Sakata."

"I'm very happy to meet you Mr. Sakata." She said. "How may I help you?"

"Here's his winning voucher," The security guard said.

"Oh! Congratulations! Only people who have won a sizeable prize are sent to this office. And I see you have won a considerable prize! Please have a seat."

"And you are?"

"I'm a personal banker. I handle the high-level accounts. Coffee, tea, or water? Is there anything I can get you? You're going to be here a while."

"But … But, I really can't." I said. "You see, I have to meet our wedding coordinator, Ms. Blake in twenty minutes."

"Oh, Sharon? I'll call Sharon right now and tell her that you're going to be a little late. In the meantime, please fill out these papers."

She picked up the phone and called Sharon Blake.

"Sharon said just to come on up when you're finished here."

My cell phone rung – it was Ed wanting to know where I was. I told him it was a long story, but to keep playing the tables and that I would call him back as soon as I was done here. I continued filling out all of the papers that she gave me. There were several of them that asked for the same information.

"Here you are." I said to Ms. Norris. "I hope these are in order."
She glanced over the papers.

"Now, I'll have to scan your right eye for identification purposes."
She takes me to the eye scanner and placed my chin on the scanner's platform.

"Now, open your eyes wide open and be very still" she instructed. A few seconds elapsed. "Good, now I'll just transfer your personal information to the other terminal. You may go to back to the desk."

She pressed a few keys on the keyboard and a few beeps were heard as the data was transferred to the other terminal.

"Let's see what we have," she said. "That's odd. Your address is not the same as the mailing instructions on the paperwork. Is there any reason for this?"

"Yes," I said. "I just moved to my fiancé's house yesterday. We're getting married this afternoon. I would like all future payments sent there."

"No problem … And congratulations on your marriage. May the both of you have a long and wonderful life together."

"Thank you very much!"

"So I assume that you know that you asked for your winnings to be distributed in twenty-six annual payments and not in one lump sum. Is that correct?"

"Yes." I replied.

"And, we are obligated to withhold federal income taxes" she added.

"I understand that also." I said.

"Then, how do you want your first payment, by check or direct deposit?"

"By check please."

"Very well. Please wait a few minutes while I get the check."

I sat there waiting for about fifteen minutes. Then she returned.

"Okay Mr. Sakata. We're almost done. Here are two checks. Actually, one is not a check. This one is only a souvenir commemorating this event. It's your souvenir check for $25 million. You can frame it, but you can't deposit it – the banks won't accept it. Here is your real check – you can tell the difference. It's much less because this is your first installment less the withheld taxes. After this, you will be getting twenty-five more checks like this annually to your house. At any time, you may request to have these funds deposited directly into an account of your choice. I strongly recommend that you do that. Do you have any questions?

"No, Ma'am," I replied. "Thank you very much for all of your help."

"It was my pleasure, Mr. Sakata. Good luck to you and may you have a wonderful life."

I walked out the door tucking the real check in my wallet and the fake check in my shirt pocket. Then I picked up my cell phone and called Ed.

"Hey, Ed," I said over the phone just barely hearing him because of all the noise from the surrounding slot machines. "Meet me at the designated meeting place."

In just a few moments, I met Ed near the elevators.

"We need to go see Ms. Blake right now." I said to Ed. "How did you do?"

"I did okay." he said. "I only won $500 playing Blackjack."

"How did you do? Where were you? What took you so long?"

"I won a few bucks. AND, I had to see a personal banker."

"A PERSONAL BANKER?" he replied. "They're only for high-rollers! How much did you actually win? A hundred thou…?"

"More!"

"Five-hundred K?"

"Keep going!"

"Wait!" he said. "Hold on! You didn't win a mil did you?"

"No!" I replied. "More!"

"How much more?" he asked.

I pulled out my fake check and pulled out the picture that they took of me in front of the slot machine.

"MY LORD!" he said. "I CAN'T BELIEVE IT! What are you going to do with all this money?"

"It's going to be my wedding gift to Wendy."

"All of it?"

"Well, maybe not all of it — most of it. She always wanted a big wedding."

"I'll tell you this much, when she sees this, she's going to get her big wedding even if it's just between the four of us!"

"Yeah, I guess your right!"

Ms. Blake's office is a very small office at the base of the tower where the wedding ceremony was scheduled for.

"Hello, Ms. Blake?" I asked as she was seated behind her desk.

"Hello, Gordon. I've been expecting you. I understand that you had quite an exciting morning today."

"That is, perhaps, and understatement."

"So, Mr. Sakata," she continued, "you have ordered the 'Staircase to Heaven' package. Is that correct?"

"That's correct."

"As you know, this package includes a wedding on our indoor or outdoor observation deck located on the 120th or 121st floor, a professional photo package, admission to the tower observation decks for you and your guests, complimentary passes to the Romance Lounge on the 107th floor for your entire party, pop music played on the observation deck, and a bottle of champagne. Is there anything else you would like in addition?"

"Yes, Ma'am. I would like to order a grooms' rose boutonniere and a 6-rose hand-tied bridal bouquet."

"No problem. Just one last thing — what floor would you like your service on?"

"The 121st floor please."

"Indoors or Out?"

"Oh, outdoors for sure."

"Very well … Let me calculate your bill and you will be all set. How do you want to handle the invoice? Cash? Check? Credit card? Debit card?"

"Debit card — if that is okay with you?" I asked. "Money now is not a problem."

"Very well, I'm glad to hear that you are doing well. Here is your invoice."

I gave her my bank card, and the funds cleared instantaneously.

"I think we're all set. Be here by 3:30 this afternoon at the base of this tower and our staff will escort your party up to the chapel at the top where you will be getting married. Do you have any questions?"

"No, I don't think so." I said.

"Very well then, I'll see you in just a little while."

After all the excitement of the morning, I was feeling not only a little exhausted, but also a little gamey. So, I decided to go back up to the room to rest for a while and take another shower before I changed into my tux. I rode the elevator back up with Ed and we agreed to meet at three-thirty at the base of tower as we were instructed by Ms. Blake.

As the doors closed behind Ed on his floor and the elevator continued up to my floor, I couldn't help but think of what our new life was going to be – especially as new multi-millionaires. It was a good time for me then. I was alone in the elevator with no one there but myself to ponder. Yet, an impending war weighed heavily on my mind as the doors opened on my floor and I stepped out walking slowly to my suite.

Historically in the past, Napajanese were always sent to relocation camps during the last several wars. I couldn't help think that they would do the same. If they repeated history, would that mean that we would be separated? Would they force Wendy into relocation camps? What would these new camps look like? Would they be the same as other "relocation camps" or would they be more like "concentration" or "prisoner of war" camps? These matters continued to haunt me as I walked towards my suite.

I opened the door to my suite and sought out Wendy's presence. She wasn't there and it was around 1:30. So I debated on either staying awake, or taking a little nap. I was a little hungry and there was muffin and a banana left over from breakfast on the cart so I consumed that. Then, laid down on the bed.

Suddenly, I was pleasantly startled around 2:30 with a kiss.

"Hi dear," I said in a softly and groggy voice. "I didn't hear you come in."

"I know…" she said. "You were sawing logs! Time to get ready, honey."

I hopped out of bed and took a quick shower and changed into my tux making sure that I had that souvenir check in my left pocket. Wendy was in another part of the bridal suite getting ready, so she was out of my sight temporarily. Then, there was knocking at the door.

"Who is it?" I asked.

"It's me, Bonnie."

I opened the door. Bonnie was dressed to the hilt. She wore a long purple satin gown with purple shoes and a white, double-stranded pearl necklace. She was gorgeous.

"My, my!" I exclaimed. "You look absolutely beautiful!"

"Oh, thank you very much. How's the bride to be coming along?"

"Come in here quick!" shouted Wendy. "I need your help!"

So Bonnie hustled into the next room as I continued to wait. It was almost 3:15.

"Honey?" I said. "It's time to go."

"I'm almost ready!"

Then, there was absolute silence. The faint sounds of small footsteps, and the most gorgeous sight I have ever seen in my life.

"My love." I said to Wendy. "You look absolutely stunning!"

"I love you." She said in a soft, faint voice. "Shall we?"

"Yes!" I replied in a whisper. "Take my hand."

She beheld my arm and we walked out the door with Bonnie following and closing the door behind. It was a magical moment for me. It was like escorting a princess to the ball while servants were unrolling the red carpet in front of us.

We caught the next elevator down. Four floors later, the elevator stopped, coincidentally on Ed's floor. It was Ed who came in and joined us.

"Hey, you two look absolutely stunning together!" remarked Ed as he stepped into the elevator. It was the only the four of us in there. It was almost as if it had been planned that way all along.

We got to the elevator at the base of the tower at 3:34 where the wedding staff was there to greet us as planned. Then, we entered into the elevator for our 1200-foot ride to the top of the tower.

As we stepped out of the elevator, I was given my groom's rose boutonniere and Wendy was given a 6-rose hand-tied bridal bouquet which complimented her wedding gown really well. As we proceeded to the platform outside, Wendy grabbed me tightly as traditional wedding music played in the background. We looked over the railing. It was a long ways down. Then, we were greeted by the minister.

"Dearly beloved…" said the minister. "We are gathered here this afternoon to join together Wendy and Gordon in holy matrimony…"

The minister continued on with the ceremony. But it seemed like the world was silent as I continually fixed my eyes on Wendy. I was eternally happy for this occasion and for being blessed with a wonderful companion. I really couldn't help but think what she was thinking about as she continued to gaze into my eyes. I knew she wasn't exactly listening to the minister either. Then, came the questions of the moment.

"Gordon?" asked the minister. "Will you take Wendy to be your lawfully wedded wife? Will you love cherish her, in good times and bad, in sickness and in health, poor or rich, sadness and happiness till death do you part? If so, say 'I will.'"

"I will." I said.

"Wendy?" asked the minister. "Will you take Gordon to be your lawfully wedded husband? Will you love cherish her, in good times and bad, in sickness and in health, poor or rich, sadness and happiness till death do you part? If so, say I will?

"I will." She said while still holding to my hands very tightly.

"Then by the powers vested in me by the State of Nevada, I pronounce you husband and wife. You may kiss the bride."

We kissed. And kissed again. And what the heck, I thought one more time for the road wouldn't hurt would it?

"Lady and gentleman," said the minister. "I present to you, Mr. and Mrs. A. Gordon Sakata."

The music in the background rose as the four of us hugged each other and received their well wishes. Then we proceeded indoors to complete the marriage certificate and it was official. Then, I thought it was the right time. I reached into my left tux coat pocket and pulled the check out.

"Wendy? I have a special gift for you."

I handed her the souvenir check, her opened wide, and she suddenly looked stunned.

"Where? How did you get this money?" she asked.

"This is truly my lucky day!" I said. "I won it this morning playing a progressive slot. I hit it big on my last spin. I couldn't believe it myself!"

She wrapped her arms around me tightly and gave me the biggest kiss of her life. It was the biggest kiss I ever received from her.

We went back down the tower and back to our rooms to change. Then we went back out on the town and partied and danced all night into the wee hours of the morning. But when we got back to the room at the Megasphere, the partying wasn't over. It continued in the bed until well into the middle of the next morning.

We woke up later in the afternoon and agreed to leave Las Vegas in the evening when the weather was a little cooler. We got back home to Pasadena around 2 in the morning. Ed and Bonnie stayed over until the following day.

The next morning, we thanked Ed and Bonnie for their company during the trip and for serving as best man and maid of honor. Then, it was time to begin our new life together as "husband and wife."

] Logout.
Good-bye A. Gordon Sakata. Come back soon.

CHAPTER 13

Start of a Brand New Life

] Login, A. Gordon Sakata
"Welcome A. Gordon Sakata. Please enter today's date."
] Date: 08/30/2208
"Today is August 30, 2208. Please enter the time."
] Time: 09:00
"The time is 9 o'clock. Welcome to the Cyberspace living room."

I was excited to get going on this first day. I actually had a lot of work to do for my upcoming performance of *Lincoln Portrait* on National Napajanese-American Day next year on April 1, at the Whittier Civic Auditorium at Whittier International University with the National Napajan Symphony Orchestra. But, this could wait for a while. First things first!

I had to go to the bank, open up a new joint checking account and deposit this first installment check from Las Vegas. Then, it would be nice to get a whole new wardrobe, I thought, since I left over half of it at my old apartment. Oh, there's just so much to do today, Computer, that I really don't know where to begin.

"Wendy, dear? Where are you?" I asked in a loud voice since I was alone in the bedroom.

"I'm here in the kitchen" she said.

I walked into the kitchen and saw her sitting casually drinking some coffee and reading the newspaper. I gave her a light kiss.

"Good morning, dear"

"Good morning, my love!" she said. "How are you today?"

"Just fine, thank you." I replied. "Do you remember my promise at the top of the mountain at the beginning of the week?"

"You made a couple of them." She said. "Which one are you referring to?"

"The promise I made about not breaking apart?"

"Verrrry clearly. What's up?"

I opened this little compartment in my bionic arm which contained a back-up tracking module. There were two of them. There was one for the manufacturer which was permanently built into the arm. Then, there was another which was a mobile backup unit which could be used remotely with a range that spanned the continent. I pulled the little module out and shut the compartment.

"Here… Put this on your key chain."

"What's this?" she asked.

"It's my tracking locator. It will tell you anywhere I'm at. Just plug it into any tracking or locating device and it will lead you right to me anywhere on the continent."

"Anywhere?"

"Anywhere! I have a permanent device in my arm. In case of an emergency, you can call the manufacturer and they can tell you where I'm at also."

"Wow!" she said. "This is really neat! I really didn't know you had this in you! Was this there all the time?"

"All the time!" I said. "I kept it especially for this occasion."

"I will keep it with me forever. Will it work in with my GPS navigator in my car?"

"Yes, in any device."

"Super!" she said. "I'll never lose you. What are your plans for today?"

"Well, I really didn't have anything particularly planned out. I thought we'd play it as the day goes on. What do you think?"

"That sounds good to me."

We both jumped in the shower together, got dressed, then got in the car and headed for the bank. After we opened our joint checking account together, we headed to new-town Pasadena where we shopped around for some new clothes for me.

It was a wonderful day. After doing a little shopping around, we went to the park and had a little picnic and played around for a while on the swings. Then, the clouds started to come in rapidly. It didn't rain. It just became really dark and overcast suddenly, and very cold. We decided to go back home to cozy up near the fireplace and have a couple cups of tea.

Besides, I needed to get back to work building my new studio in Wendy's house. Wendy had an abandoned, unoccupied guest cottage in the backyard that I planned on converting into my writer's/rehearsal studio. That in itself was going to be our master project for a while. It had a lot of really nice possibilities. The structure went all the way to the edge of her estate. Then, the yard dropped into the canyon below. There was a spectacular view of the San Gabriel River basin. On a good day, there would be water gushing through the riverbed. But most of the time, the riverbed was dry.

Once in a while, we would go down to the riverbed and collect rocks. I got lucky one day and ran across some really nice gems – rubies just to mention part of my find. I found some other interesting treasures down there that I'll somehow fit into the scheme of things in the studio somehow. Otherwise, I'll just take them to the nearest rummage sale at a local church.

] Logout.
Good-bye A. Gordon Sakata. Come back soon.

CHAPTER 14

A Meeting in the Oval Office

Author's Note: This portion of Gordon's story is not contained in his recorded diary, but were received through a written accounting from Gordon and White House Archives in the 23rd Century.

A meeting with President Henderson was held in the Oval Office of the White House with Vice President Buckley, the head of the Central Intelligence Agency, and the Joint Chiefs of Staff.

"Gentlemen," said the President. "We need a strategic plan to capture Napajan for their oil reserves. Our oil supply is practically gone and California remains stubborn by not letting us drill off its coastal waters. How do you propose we acquire this island?"

"By force, sir?" said Admiral Carpenter. "Our joint forces can take that little postage stamp in a matter of a day or less. Back in World War II, the Japanese took it in five-hours."

"But," responded Vice President Buckley, "the Chinese are moving military personnel, equipment and droids onto Napajan. The rock is going to be hard to take! I don't think it's going to be as simple as you think. The Chinese have a big force. Do we have allies supporting us on this?"

"We can do it ourselves!" said General Gomez. "Our military forces have better equipment and more advanced technology than the Chinese."

"Are your droids capable of fighting in the jungles of Napajan?" asked Air Force General Brooke.

"Well…" responded General Gomez "no, not at this time. They are field ready, but they can't fight guerrilla-style or jungle warfare very well. I'd say we need to give this technology at least another 25 more years."

"Then what do you propose we use?" asked the President.

"We'd draft and recruit people, sir," replied General Gomez.

"People? Real people?" the Vice President responded.

"Yes, sir!" said General Gomez. "People are out there unemployed, being laid off by the millions and replaced by droids anyway and being displaced as if they were paper plates or throw-aways. Back in the 20th Century, there used to be 'recycling programs.' Why not recycle people for warfare? It will give them something constructive to do. They would be doing a great service to the country."

"But," said the Vice President, "people are going to get seriously hurt – even killed. That's going to take a heavy burden on the economy. We don't even have the funds to cover for their medical care when they return. What is going to happen to those who lose their arms and legs? Who's going to pay for their continued health support? The taxpayers?"

"Gentlemen," said the President "we're getting off track here. Right now we don't even have a reason for going to war."

"We can stage one, sir!" said Admiral Carpenter. "The Japanese will have a cargo ship that will arrive in South Beach on December 6 or thereabouts. The contents of that ship will contain brand new SUV's that will be unloaded off on the docks. At that time, we can stage an attack and make it look as if the Napajan Navy launched an attack from one of their submarines off the coast of South Beach. The damage will be horrendous but realistic."

"Wait a minute …" said the President as he paused to think about this scenario. "Are we talking about a wag the dog scenario here?"

"Yes, sir!" replied the Admiral.

"Then I can go to the Congress and ask them for a declaration of War?" asked the President.

"Yes, sir!" they all said.

There was a moment of silence in the room.

"Let's do it!" ordered the President. "Admiral Carpenter, carry out your plans and report back to me with a plan of attack in five days."

"Yes, sir!"

CHAPTER 15

Big News

] Login, A. Gordon Sakata
"Welcome A. Gordon Sakata. Please enter today's date."
] Date: 11/26/2208
"Today is November 26, 2208. Please enter the time."
] Time: 07:00
"The time is 7 O'clock. Welcome to the Cyberspace living room."

I thought I'd get an early start this morning and go to Manny's to pick up some supplies to finish painting the studio. It's almost finished. Wendy has been a little lazy getting up lately. She seems more tired and easily fatigued. In fact, she's also very moody. When we'd paint, she would paint a few square feet, take a long rest, the paint again, then take more rests. I'm not really bothered by it very much. But I know her behavior changed a little since our wedding day.

"Honey?" I asked Wendy as we were painting my office. "Have you been feeling Okay? You just don't seem to be yourself lately?"

"I've been feeling fine, dear. What makes you think that?"

"Well, you've been rather moody lately. In fact, I think you should take a break and go down to the drug store, and get one of those self-examining pregnancy tests just for the fun of it."

"What? Do you think I'm pregnant? I don't think so!"

"Come on! I'm just asking you do it just for the fun of it. Here's $30. I'll pay for the kit."

"Well, I can use something with a little carbonation in it right now. I'll be back!"

She got in her car and went to the drug store. Upon her return home, she went straight into the bathroom. Suddenly, I heard a loud call.

"Honey!" she shouted from the closed door of the main bathroom.

I ran running out of the studio office, through the living room and up the stairs to the master bathroom in our bedroom.

"Are you okay?" I shouted through the closed doors.

"Yes!" she said. "I have something to show you!"

She opened the door very slowly and holding a small white tray with a cup-like cylinder.

"See the blue circle?" she said.

"Yes" I replied.

"That means I'm positive!" she said joyfully and in tears. "You were right all this time!"

"Do you mean we're …" I paused in excitement. "We're going to have…"

"A baby …" she said softly as we embraced, hugged and kissed each other in joyful bliss.

"Now," she said, "this box says that the test can be inaccurate and the only way to tell for sure is to see a doctor."

"Well, call the doctor."

She immediately called her gynecologist to make an appointment. The day was slow for him so Wendy was able to make an immediate appointment that afternoon. We had a quick bite to eat for lunch and went to the doctor's office and sat patiently in the waiting room.

Eventually, Wendy was called into the examination room while I stayed in the waiting room. An hour later the nurse came out to give me the report.

"Mr. Sakata?" asked the nurse.

"Yes." I replied. "Is she Okay?"

"Yes, she is. Congratulations, she is pregnant."

I was allowed in the examination room where I met the doctor and was informed that Wendy was three months pregnant. The baby and mother were just doing just fine. And I was elated. I'm going to be a father!

On our way back home, I had to stop off at the market. It was the day before Thanksgiving and it was my turn to cook the bird. I know, Computer, you're probably laughing internally. But, I'm a serious cook! I like to cook and can do it quite well. You will be surprised how well I can fix a meal – especially during Thanksgiving.

Anyway, we have a lot to be thankful for – we have a bundle of joy coming our way in March or April of 2209! That's something to really look forward to.

] Logout.
Good-bye A. Gordon Sakata. Come back soon.

CHAPTER 16

The Start of War

] Login, A. Gordon Sakata
"Welcome A. Gordon Sakata. Please enter today's date."
] Date: 12/07/2208
"Today is December 7, 2208. Please enter the time."
] Time: 07:00
"The time is 7 o'clock. Welcome to the Cyberspace
living room."

This day started out like any typical day in the life of any middle-class family. The news was also typical of the day as well – millions more around the world were losing their jobs and being replaced by more droids, people being displaced from their homes and kicked out into the streets. Shanty-towns were increasing in numbers all over the world. In Los Angeles, it wasn't atypical to find tin shacks and cardboard houses where strip malls once stood. Mega shopping malls were turned into centers for the homeless. For example, there was a large mega shopping complex in Arcadia that had elegant shops, department stores and fancy restaurants that served the area well up until the middle of the 21st century. Then as people lost their homes and became homeless, the center was converted into a regional center to house the homeless.

Don't get me wrong, there are still outlets where you can find good stuff. It's just that one has to drive a little farther to get them. Especially, getting things for the baby's room that I'm working on, it has become one of my projects. After all, Wendy has to really take it easy for the time being. At least until after the baby arrives. She has, however, been a tremendous help assisting me in designing and planning out the theme of the baby's room.

It was about 9 a.m. as I was assembling the baby's dresser and changing table when I heard a massive explosion. I couldn't tell from what direction it came from. Then, it was followed by four more out explosions after that.

"Honey! Did you hear that?" I shouted to Wendy as she was lying in bed resting.

"Yes! What do you think it was?" she shouted back.

We both ran into the den and turned on the news. All the local stations interrupted their regular programming to show a massive ship on fire in harbor of South Beach. It had apparently exploded while unloading vehicles on the docks. The SUV's that were already on the docks were on fire as well. But the ship appeared to be leaning towards it starboard side as if it were sinking.

I channel surfed for a little while, but finally decided to keep in on KLFT, Channel 9, which apparently had the best coverage. Their airship overhead seemed to have the best angle, and they were the first at the scene on the ground.

"We are getting unconfirmed reports –" the reporter said, "that a Napajan submarine was sighted off the coast of California in the South Beach Harbor. People dressed like Napajan commandos stormed in and raided the docks from the water and set explosives to the ship. That set off the first big explosion that was heard for miles. Then, four torpedoes were launched from the submarine and struck the side of the ship. The commandos were seen fleeing back out to sea towards the waiting submarine."

"That's peculiar," I said.

"What's that?"

"Napajan doesn't have a submarine, let alone a navy." I replied. "This had to have been an inside job."

"Could it have been the Chinese?" she asked.

"I seriously doubt it. Although the Chinese have a huge military force, they never used it for offensive purposes until recently when they occupied Australia. And even then, that was only to gain a foothold for moving forces and equipment to defend Napajan. Otherwise, their military is used primarily for defensive purposes only. In never was known as a country of aggression except in the ancient days of Genghis Khan."

"Then who could have committed this act of aggression?" she asked.

"Quite frankly, I wouldn't put it past this current administration for wanting to start a war. After all, Napajan is sitting on top of a lot of oil."

"Ah! Do you think anything is going to happen to us?"

"I hope not. But I wouldn't put it past this administration."

] Logout.
Good-bye A. Gordon Sakata. Come back soon.

CHAPTER 17

RNA Declares War on Napajan

] Login, A. Gordon Sakata
"Welcome A. Gordon Sakata. Please enter today's date."
] Date: 12/08/2208
"Today is December 8, 2208. Please enter the time."
] Time: 08:00
"The time is 8 o'clock. Welcome to the Cyberspace living room."

I woke up this morning and went through my usual routines – had breakfast, took a little walk down to the bridge and back. Wendy and I thought about getting a dog, but then had second thoughts, although a dog would be a good companion for me – especially keeping me company in my office. Quite frankly, it was getting too expensive maintaining a house pet anyway – especially with the pending arrival of a new baby. In the news, there were often reports where people were abandoning their pets as they lost their houses or giving of their pets to the local kennels or county pounds where they were eventually euthanized because people simply could not afford their upkeep. That would have been an issue for our family. Winning that prize in Las Vegas certainly helped out quite a bit.

I needed some inspiration for a book that I was writing, so I decided to turn the television on for a while before I got started in my studio. Wendy eventually joined me in the den as I was casually scrolling through some electronic magazines. Then, suddenly, the programming was interrupted once again. This time it was a broadcast from Washington. President Henderson was about to make a speech before the joint houses of Congress.

"Yesterday, December 7, 2208" said President Henderson. "- a date which will live in infamy – the Republic of North America was suddenly and deliberately attacked by naval forces of the Empire of Napajan.

The RNA was at peace with that nation and, at the solicitation of Napajan, was still in conversation with the government and the Monarch of Napajan looking toward the maintenance of peace in the Pacific.

Indeed, one hour after Napajan naval squadrons had commenced bombing in Long Beach, the Napajanese ambassador to the RNA and his colleagues delivered to the Minister of State a formal reply to a recent RNA message. While this reply stated that it seemed useless to continue the existing diplomatic negotiations, it contained no threat or hint of war or armed attack.

It will be recorded that the distance of California from Napajan makes it obvious that the attack was deliberately planned many days or even weeks ago. During the intervening time, the Napajan government has deliberately sought to deceive the RNA by false statements and expressions of hope for continued peace.

The attack yesterday in South Beach has caused severe damage to RNA commerce. Very many RNA lives have been lost. In addition, RNA ships have been reported torpedoed on the high seas between San Francisco and Honolulu.

Yesterday, the Napajanese government also launched an attack against Malaya.

Last night, Napajanese forces attacked Bora Bora.

Last night, Napajanese forces attacked Guam.

Last night, Napajanese forces attacked the Philippine Islands.

Last night, the Napajanese attacked Wake Island.

This morning, the Napajanese attacked Midway Island.

Napajan has, therefore, undertaken a surprise offensive extending throughout the Pacific area. The facts of yesterday speak for themselves. The people of the RNA have already formed their opinions and well understand the implications to the very life and safety of our nation.

As commander in chief of the Army, Navy, Air Force and Marines, I have directed that all measures be taken for our defense.

Always will we remember the character of the onslaught against us.

No matter how long it may take us to overcome this premeditated invasion, the Repblic's people in their righteous might will win through to absolute victory.

I believe I interpret the will of the Congress and of the people when I assert that we will not only defend ourselves to the uttermost, but will make very certain that this form of treachery shall never endanger us again.

Hostilities exist. There is no blinking at the fact that our people, our territory and our interests are in grave danger.

With confidence in our armed forces – with the unbounding determination of our people – we will gain the inevitable triumph – so help us God.

I ask that the Congress declare that since the unprovoked and dastardly attack by Napajan on Sunday, December 7, a state of war has existed between the Republic of North America and the Napajan[i]

"Can you believe that?" I asked Wendy. "Now we're really at war."

"I'm really afraid now. I hope that we don't lose this house."

After news commentaries with other journalist, local stations started covering events in Los Angeles and other parts of the country. Anti-war demonstrations sprang up all over the world. It was not just the RNA against Napajan. It was the world against the RNA. Some nations elected to be neutral about the whole issue, others assisted Napajan with military assistance and weapons. Napajan had no facilities for producing biological or nuclear weapons of mass destruction. It was all a ploy. Napajan had only a small defensive army. No navy and air force, nor the military technology that the RNA had. Yet, to the defense of the Napajanese was its primary ally, China, which had the military equivalence of the RNA and did not hesitate to use it.

Discrimination against Napajanese-Americans was at a all-time high. The FBI and Homeland Security Forces rounded up key Napajanese-Americans, all of whom were American citizens, and detained them for an undetermined period of time. Many are still detained today and are falsely being held as spices and war criminals. A curfew was placed on Napajanese-Americans. No Napajanese could be out of the house past 5 p.m. without the fear of being arrested. That curfew just about applied to all Asians since we all "looked alike."

A popular Napajanese restaurant in Whittier was closed for good because they received death threats against the owners. I guess people say that they are tolerant of things, but when it really comes down to it, you really cannot be too sure what they are tolerant of. In some cases, they don't practice what they preach.

This really made things difficult for me. I couldn't go out partying with my friends in the evening anymore for fear of being arrested if I were out past 5. Nevertheless, we decided to start our own organic garden in the backyard to supply us with some essentials during the course of the war.

I used this time to run out go to Tom's Club and stock up on sugar and flour. I knew that back in World War II, these commodities were hard to get. And there, they sold them in restaurant size, or bulk supplies.

I'll be back.

] Logout.
Good-bye A. Gordon Sakata. Come back soon.

] Login, A. Gordon Sakata
"Welcome A. Gordon Sakata. Please enter today's date."
] Date: 12/08/2208
"Today is December 8, 2208. Please enter the time."
] Time: 14:00
"The time is 2 o'clock. Welcome to the Cyberspace living room."

"Hi, Honey!" Wendy said as I came driving back from Tom's Club. "How did it go?"

"I did okay. But it was tough over there!" I replied. "They had nine check-out lines for regular customers and just one check-out line for all Asians!"

"Is that why it took you so long?" she said.

"Yes! It seemed like it took forever to pay for all this stuff." I said as I began unloading the car.

"You have quite a bit of stuff there," she said. "That should last us through the war."

"Not if the war lasts for a hundred years like the War of Iraq!" I said.

"I hope they have the common sense of having a plan to get us out of this war very quickly."

"It could be disastrous for us! We can get our butts kicked by the Chinese!"

"You have a good point there!"

] Logout.
Good-bye A. Gordon Sakata. Come back soon.

CHAPTER 18

Battle of the Pacific Islands

] Login, A. Gordon Sakata

"Welcome A. Gordon Sakata. Please enter today's date."

] Date: 02/02/2209

"Today is February 2, 2209. Please enter the time."

] Time: 09:00

"The time is 9 o'clock. Welcome to the Cyberspace living room."

Since my last entry, thousands and thousands of men and women were called to serve the military. It was a little strange; they rejected everyone who was Asian or looked Asian. There were advertisements (propaganda) encouraging people to enlist. Otherwise, they were forced into the military otherwise. They especially took the people out of the overcrowded prisons and sent them into the Pacific all in the name of "civic and patriotic duty."

Many people outright opposed the war and resisted going into the military. These people were often chastised, removed from their homes, and some often mysteriously disappeared.

On the war front, the RNA military was no match against the

superior Chinese army – especially in jungle warfare. The RNA infantry, many of whom were ill-trained and ill-prepared for jungle warfare, often did not put up a fight against the superior Chinese droids. Of the brave men and women who did fight, many came back maimed. The government was ill-prepared in supporting these brave soldiers who gave the ultimate sacrifice of a limb. Often, the expense of bionic limbs was borne by the families and friends of the soldiers. If the soldiers died in combat, they were typically cremated rather than buried and the ashes turned over to the families in a cost-saving effort by the government. Soldiers with post-battle mental disabilities and injuries were often abandoned and left to their own devices. Many soldiers never returned home. Many of them were displaced out into the streets – into the shantytowns of America, left to fend for themselves. No, they wouldn't even get support from the corporations – not even the ones who manufactured the equipment and machinery that they operated in the theatre of battle – a good number of which malfunctioned in the field. They were all simply abandoned – like "paper plates" – thrown away like trash.

It was reported that the RNA was taking on unusually high casualties and losses. Immediately after the war started, the country lost Guam, the Philippines, Wake and Midway Islands in head-to-head combat with the Chinese. They claim that it was the Napajanese – but that was a false assumption because the Napajanese didn't have a military of that size to match the might of the RNA. The only force on the planet that was capable of doing it was China.

It was reported that RNA forces drew back and dug in on the Hawaiian Islands. The Chinese were in swift pursuit. That was going to be the next biggest testing ground for the RNA.

] Logout.
Good-bye A. Gordon Sakata. Come back soon.

CHAPTER 19

Battle of the Hawaiian Islands

] Login, A. Gordon Sakata
"Welcome A. Gordon Sakata. Please enter today's date."
] Date: 02/18/2209
"Today is February 18, 2209. Please enter the time."
] Time: 10:00

"The time is 10 O'clock. Welcome to the Cyberspace living room."
Soon after the four Pacific Islands fell to the Chinese earlier in the month, fighting broke out on the shores of Hawaii. This was actually the first combat the RNA has ever experienced on its own soil since it was attacked by terrorists on September 11, 2001.

The Battle of Hawaii was fierce. The RNA fought well. After all, there was a huge military base in Hawaii already. Again, the RNA forces suffered huge casualties. China temporarily captured Maui and held a stronghold there for a week. Then the Province forces fought back and took the island over.

You're wondering what happened to the Mexican contingency? Those forces were held back to defend the RNA continent and deployed throughout the continent.

In Hawaii, it was a see-saw battle. The Chinese would capture Lanai and Molokai, but eventually, those would be taken back by States-led forces. States' forces were successful in holding off the Chinese on Oahu, big island of Hawaii, and Kauai.

In two weeks, when the dust settled. It was a turning point for the RNA. The RNA held off the Chinese and from there, was able to go on a short offensive.

Some theorized that the final battle would be for Napajan itself. Both sides retreated to neutral territories to rebuild for the next big push.

] Logout.
Good-bye A. Gordon Sakata. Come back soon.

CHAPTER 20

National Napajanese-
American Day

] Login, A. Gordon Sakata

"Welcome A. Gordon Sakata. Please enter today's date."

] Date: 04/01/2209

"Today is April 1, 2209. Please enter the time."

] Time: 06:00

"The time is 6 o'clock. Welcome to the Cyberspace living room."

Tonight is my big night. I here in the new Whittier Civic Auditorium on the campus of Whittier International University to perform *Lincoln Portrait* by Aaron Copland with the National Napajanese-American Symphony Orchestra and I'm very nervous, anxious and excited. I never have done anything like this before. Although I have spoken in public at conventions and workshops before ...

But I'm even more anxious because Wendy is due anytime now. And, SHE IS BIG! I really wouldn't be surprised if she is carrying twins! You're wondering why I'm out past 5 o'clock? That's because the government declared NN-A Day a special day and waived the curfew just for this day. We have to be back home soon after the concert is over with and we have to go straight back home – no side stops permitted. In fact, we had to get special permits to be out this late.

Excuse me Computer, I'm being called to the stage ...

]Pause

The music to *Lincoln Portrait* began. Eventually into the piece, I received my cue from the conductor:

"Fellow citizens, we cannot escape history."[ii]

The music softened as I continued to speak.

"Fellow citizens, we cannot escape history. We of this Congress and this administration will be remembered in spite of ourselves. No personal significance or insignificance can spare one or another of us. The fiery trial through which we pass will light us down in honor or dishonor to the latest generation. We, even we here, hold the power and bear the responsibility."[iii]

I talked about where Lincoln was born and where he lived. Then continued to tell about another of his speeches.

"The dogmas of the quiet past are inadequate to the stormy present. The occasion is piled high with difficulty and we must rise with the occasion. As our case is new, so we must think anew and act anew. We must disenthrall ourselves and then we will save our country."[iv]

I described Lincoln's physical characteristics, then described his attitude towards slavery in another speech.

"It is the eternal struggle between two principles, right and wrong, throughout the world. It is the same spirit

that says 'you toil and work and earn bread, and I'll eat
it.' No matter in what shape it comes, whether from the
mouth of a king who seeks to bestride the people of his own
nation, and live by the fruit of their labor, or from one
race of men as an apology for enslaving another race, it is
the same tyrannical principle."[v]

I described Lincoln as a quiet man with big ideals about democracy.

"As I would not be a slave, so I would not be a master. This
expresses my idea of democracy. Whatever differs from this,
to the extent of the difference, is no democracy."[vi]

As sixteenth president of the United States, Lincoln was noted for delivering great speeches. To highlight the work of the piece, I talked about a speech which he delivered on the battleground of Gettysburg.

"That from these honored dead we take increased devotion
to that cause for which they gave the last full measure of
devotion. That we here highly resolve that these dead shall
not have died in vain. That this nation under God shall
have a new birth of freedom and that government of the
people, by the people, and for the people shall not perish
from the earth."[vii]

The music came to a grand finale.. The audience rose for a thunderous standing ovation. After I took my bows to acknowledge the audience's response, As I started my return backstage, I was called back on stage for another round to acknowledge the audience with more bows. I finally returned to the dressing room backstage.

]Computer Resume

Computer, that was quite a workout. I'm exhausted and Maestro McMasters came in to congratulate me on a grand performance. A knocking at the door was heard.

"Who's there?"

Wendy just came in and gave me a big hug and a kiss.

"Sweetheart, you were fabulous!"

"Oh, thank you my dear." I replied as I struggled to get both arms around her waist. "You know, you're getting so big that I'm having an awfully hard time trying to give you a hug."

"Oh, that's Okay." She said. "But I appreciate the thought anyway."

"You know," I asked.

"What?" she asked.

"I sure hope the kid doesn't come now." I said.

"What do you mean by that?" she asked.

"I mean," then I hesitated, "I would not like to get arrested at the hospital while helping you deliver your baby."

"Oh, they wouldn't do that. Would they?"

"You never can't tell in today's crazy world!" I replied. "We better get you home."

"Yes. I think with all the music, the baby's emotions have been stirred a little."

"Are you sure you're not carrying twins?"

"Well …" As she paused to think about it more. "You know, I have been feeling the baby kick in different places more than once at the same time. And it feels like there's been more than one baby in there moving around."

"I think this would be a good time to get us home. What do you think?"

"That sounds good to me. The sooner the better."

] Logout.

Good-bye A. Gordon Sakata. Come back soon.

CHAPTER 21

Arrival of Twin Peaks

] Login, A. Gordon Sakata

"Welcome A. Gordon Sakata. Please enter today's date."

] Date: 04/10/2209

"Today is April 10, 2209. Please enter the time."

] Time: 20:00

"The time is 8 o'clock. Welcome to the Cyberspace living room."

Today was rather an uneventful day, Computer. I did some gardening work out in the back most of the day. We kind of grazed for meals most of the day. Wendy was having a hard time keeping things down. Then rolled around 8 o'clock in the evening.

"Sweetheart, please call the hospital," she said in a soft voice. "I think it's time."

As I gathered her necessities I got on my cell phone and called the hospital. I was told that they would be waiting for or arrival. I took Wendy out to the car and secured the house. I instructed the car to go to the hospital only to get a rude message by the car's voice.

"Warning!" the car's voice said. "Cannot secure passenger in seat. Please use seatbelt extension."

Great, I thought, where was I supposed to get a seatbelt extension at this time of day? I'm already taking a risk of being out here this late at night after curfew anyway. Then it dawned on me.

"Wendy," I said. "I'll have to recline your seat another 30 degrees back."

"Are you sure this is going to work?" she asked.

"I'm not positive. But, it's my only chance to get the car to move. Car, recline passenger seat 30 degrees back."

"Reclining." The car said.

"Car, go to hospital."

"Securing all passengers." said the car. "All passengers secured. Now driving."

The car finally went into motion. I instructed the car that it was a medical emergency. The car started to go faster. We eventually arrived at the hospital where staff was waiting for us. The nurses sat her in a wheelchair that took her to one of the birthing rooms where they connected her and the baby to monitors. "You know," said the midwife. "You are going to have twins!"

This was the start of a long, long night. At first, there was an aura of excitement in the air. Then, that aura turned into hard work.

Wendy's doctor came to the hospital around 1 o'clock the next morning. Between contractions, Wendy managed to get some shuteye. As for myself, the adrenaline was running rapidly. I couldn't go to sleep. But when she did wake up during a contraction, she would squeeze my hand so hard, it felt as if my fingers were going to break off – including the fingers on my bionic arm! In fact, the fingers on my bionic arm often sent shock waves up my arm every time she squeezed my hands. I don't even think she remembered squeezing my hands every time she had a contraction – she was too zoned out!

The highlight came around 3:40 a.m. as the first major push started. We coached her through her pushing and breathing during each contraction. It was difficult for Wendy, and I would imagine for the first baby also. By 4:20 p.m. my first child was born – an 8 pound 14 ounce healthy boy! I was elated and it dawned on me. It was April

11. My birthday, exactly the same time I was born. Anyway, his name is Byron Gordon Sakata.

Then, the second push for the next child started. But by comparison, this one popped right out. She was a 9 pound, 3 ounce healthy girl! Her name is Beverly Katherine Sakata.

What was unusual about the two of them, not only were they identical, but they both had very Asian complexions. Neither one of them had the same skin color as Wendy. But that didn't matter, my birthday gifts were both beautiful.

I hugged Wendy in bed as she laid there exhausted.

"They're beautiful!" I said to her as I gave her a big kiss. "I love you."

As the babies were cleaned and wrapped in blankets, they were both given to Wendy as we both enjoyed our new family together.

After a few days, mom and babies were allowed to come back home. It was a good thing that they kept them there for a few days. I had to run out and get a matching crib since there was an extra person to attend to. As for the theme of the babies' room, we designed it to be neutral anyway since Wendy wanted to be surprised at the time of delivery. I would have to say that's pretty close to what has happened. We got one of each.

Bonnie came over frequently to help Wendy. I took care of the kids a lot when they came home. But during the day, there was a lot that I had to do in the studio. So, Bonnie's presence and assistance was a blessing to say the least. Wendy, in the meantime, spent a lot of time recuperating and slowly returning to a normal life.

] Logout.
Good-bye A. Gordon Sakata. Come back soon.

CHAPTER 22

The Great Roundup

] Login, A. Gordon Sakata
"Welcome A. Gordon Sakata. Please enter today's date."
] Date: 05/03/2209
"Today is May 03, 2209. Please enter the time."
] Time: 09:00
"The time is 9 o'clock. Welcome to the Cyberspace living room."

This morning, Bonnie came over early at Wendy's request to help out with the laundry since the diapers were being used rapidly, day in, day out. I haven't been watching the television lately, so I thought it would be a good time to catch up on some news. So I walked into the den with Beverly in my arms while Wendy followed with Byron in her arms. The four of us sat down together and I turned on the television quietly as the two infants slept.

There was a special press conference by General Gomez in front of the Pentagon.

"I have," General Gomez said as cameras and flashbulbs were flashing, "just issued Civilian Exclusion Order Number 3346 ordering people of Napajanese ancestry, whether citizens or non-citizens, to report to assembly centers, where they would live until being moved to permanent relocation centers."

"What does that mean?" asked Wendy. "Are they going to take you away? They can't do that!"

"You're right!" I said. "I have my constitutional rights as a RNA citizen!"

"What are we going to do? Are they going to take us all? Or are they going to take just you?"

"They can't do anything." I said. "They just can't expect us to pick up and leave our houses and go to these 'assembly centers' willy-nilly!"

Bonnie entered the den. "Hi guys!" she said. "I just finished putting the diapers in the dryer. What's going on?"

"The government wants all Napajanese and Napajanese-Americans to report to an assembly center starting today." I said.

"What? That's impossible! They can't do that to you! Could they?"

Then there was an abrupt knocking at the door. I gave Byron to Bonnie.

"Here, take Byron for me, Bonnie." I asked.

Then there was more knocking at the door.

"Just a minute! Who is it?"

"FBI!" as a gruff male voice shouted. He rushed through the door with five other colleagues and local police officers.

"What's this all about?" I said.

"We have orders to take you to headquarters for questioning." He said. "We ask for your cooperation to come with us peacefully."

"What have I done?"

"Nothing, just come with us."

"But if I have done nothing, why am I being interrogated?"

"Don't ask any questions," he said. "Just come with us right now."

"But, I am a RNA citizen with rights. You can't arrest me without cause."

"The Office of Homeland Security has announced that all Napajanese-Americans must register with the federal government no matter what the citizenship status is. Besides, you're not being arrested. We're taking you in for questioning."

He continued by saying that they are doing this for our own "safety." I find that hard to believe.

Wendy and Bonnie rushed to the door.

"Sweetheart? Is there anything wrong?" asked Wendy.

"These gentlemen want to take me downtown for questioning."

"What has he done?" Wendy said.

"Nothing at all, Ma'am," the agent said. "We just want to ask him a few questions in our offices. Now, sir, if we can get your cooperation?"

"Bonnie, take care of Wendy while I'm gone!" I said.

"Yes, I'll do all that I can."

"Sweetheart, I love you!" I said to Wendy.

"I love you too!" said Wendy. "Take extra care of yourself!"

"You know where to find me!" I said as I pointed to my bionic arm. She got the message.

That afternoon, the agents escorted me to their offices in Los Angeles. They didn't say that I was being detained for anything, but I was hand-cuffed. They just said that they wanted to talk to me about the ship's sinking in San Pedro. At their office, they put me in a room with a two-way mirror. I said that I didn't know anything about it or who the perpetrators were. But they persisted in asking about my whereabouts on that morning of December 7. I said that I was out on in my house with Wendy and that they could verify that by calling her up. They refused to do so.

Then they wanted to know about all my activities with the Napajanese-American community in Los Angeles. I told them that I rarely have anything to do with them or any of the organizations associated with Napajanese, foreign or domestic. They persisted that I was very active in the Napajan community. The only thing I did as a Napajan was perform Copland's *Lincoln's Portrait* at the Whittier Civic Auditorium. I'm proud of the fact that I come from a race of people who are genuinely concerned for humanity and live out their lives in respect for each other as humans. That's been my philosophy throughout my life. I told them that Napajanese would never sink a ship, especially if it doesn't belong to them, let alone their own ships. Napajanese do not have an offensive, "special forces" commando unit like the RNA. They have no need for one. They have been a peace-loving, neutral country for centuries!

I asked them when I was going to be released. They replied, "Never!"

I said, "What do you mean by 'never'?"

They informed me that I was going to be sent to the Santa Anita Race Track for detainment and processing.

"You can't do that! I am an RNA citizen!" I said.

"That's all irrelevant now. Civilian Exclusion Order Number 3346 specifically says that all Napajanese are to report to regional assembly centers. You'll have to go to Santa Anita for processing," the agent said. "From there, you'll probably be sent to a relocation camp in Manzanar, Tulle Lake, or Heart Mountain."

"You already did that to the Japanese-Americans in World War II and had to pay a big retribution price for it after!" I said.

"That's not going to happen this time." said the agent. "You can't get blood out of a rock. Especially when the government is broke!"

"If the government is broke, who's paying for this? Who's paying for your salary? Who gave the government an unlimited line of credit on their charge card?"

"That's enough questions for now." said the agent as I was escorted away into a parked bus along with 50 other "detainees."

Once we arrived at Santa Anita, there must have been at least 80,000 Napajan-Americans in line waiting to be processed. The population of Napajanese in America was estimated at about 800,000. I don't see how they are going to put all of us in relocation camps. On the outer gates of the race track, there were signs saying that races were being temporarily cancelled because "Naps" were being processed here.

As I stood in line to get processed into the detention center, I often wondered what it was like to be a Japanese-American during World War II. Stripped of your dignity, pride and possessions, and forced into temporary housing customarily designed for race horses. Well, the truth came to fruition, as I was finally processed passed the detainment admissions area. I was assigned to this horse stall along with 20 other men as we had to sleep on hay on the ground. The only things we received were blankets and a toothbrush.

"How generous of them!" I said to myself.

By coincidence, I was assigned to the same stall as my cousin Glen Sakata whom I hadn't seen in ages. While single men and women were separated into different stalls, families had to share facilities with other families. I understand that one stall had 10 families in there at once.

We talked a while since we didn't much feel like sleeping. Mainly, we discussed the inhumanity of man towards other men and how cruel people could treat other people were not only primitive but sad. It's again like the paper plate-syndrome, many people are treated as "trash" or "throw-aways." I guess in this world there would always be the problem of "paper people" unless we change the system and society, not only as a country, but as worldly need.

The next morning, they woke us up to do some exercises near the race track itself. People were allowed to run the track as if we were horses on a tether. Then, they escorted us back into the stalls where we fed breakfast. No utensils were provided, nor paper bowls even. We were fed just a spoonful of oatmeal with vitamins and a shared a bucket of water. That didn't go over too well with the 20 of us.

After "breakfast," they marched us over to the detainment processing area where we were assigned relocation camps. I was assigned to Manzanar while Cousin Glen was sent to Heart Mountain, Wyoming. We said our parting good-byes as we boarded separate school buses for our destinations. The buses had curtains all around the windows so you couldn't see out.

While sitting in the bus. I heard my name being called.

It was Wendy's voice, but I couldn't see her because the windows were pulled up, shut closed, and covered in black.

"Gordon!" she said. "I know you're in there! I love you, and I'm going to get you out soon!"

I started weep profusely. I really missed her as tears began flowing like a raging river down my face. I was glad my tracking module was working. I had hopes of seeing her and the children again, sooner rather than later.

]Logout.
Good-bye A. Gordon Sakata. Come back soon.

CHAPTER 23

First Day at Camp

] Login, A. Gordon Sakata
"Welcome A. Gordon Sakata. Please enter today's date."
] Date: 10/01/2208
"Today is October 1, 2209. Please enter the time."
] Time: 09:00
"The time is 9 o'clock. Welcome to the Cyberspace living room."

This had to be about the roughest ride I ever had. The insult of the matter was being forced onto yellow school busses that took over five hours to get from Arcadia to Manzanar over night. The bus driver didn't even stop for a "personal business" break. It didn't matter to the driver, it was a driod anyway. And, sitting towards the back of the bus, it was very bumpy ride!

Then, as soon as we got off the buses, they had us form into two separate lines, male and female. I don't know where the ladies' line went to, but they led the men into what was like a warehouse separated by a curtain that went from one end of the building to the other. The interior of the building looked very much like an old gymnasium – something like what they had during World War II when the Japanese-Americans were relocated here. In fact, it just might be that same building. I didn't think a building that old would still be around in 2209.

Nevertheless, they had us disrobe down to nothing! They made us take our shoes off and throw them in one pile. Then shirts, trousers, and underwear when in their own separate piles. They claimed the clothes were being donated to charity. After we were done they marched us into the freezing cold. Snow still covered the mountains to the west of the camp. There we were, in two lines once again – men and women – all of us naked as jaybirds! We were first processed through a medical examination area where we were given a variety of shots. Then they marched us into a common shower area. No stalls, not even walls. It was just a covered area surrounded by chain-link fencing.

After we were done showing, the dusted us off individually with some kind of white powder and gave us bright orange jump suits and sandals, but no underwear.

Then a guard approached me.

"Sir, you have to remove that watch!" he said.

"I have medical clearance to wear this watch." I replied. "Without this watch, my arm won't work!"

"Rules are rules! He argued. "Do I have to confiscate that watch or force if from you?"

"I demand to see your commanding officer!"

"Sergeant Ochoa!" screamed the guard in a deep, loud voice.

"What's the problem, Corporal?"

"We have an uncooperative prisoner."

"A Prisoner?" I said. "Is that it? What crime have I committed?

"This man will not surrender his watch." The guard said to the sergeant.

"Well, take it off of him!"

"Yes, Sir!"

"Don't you dare take my watch! There's a medical reason for wearing it!"

The guard pulled the watch off, and the right arm went immediately limb and hung lifeless.

"What happened?" said the sergeant. "Medic!" he yelled.

The doctor performing the physicals ran over. "What's going on?"

"I just pulled off his watch and his arm went lifeless!" said the guard."

"You idiot!" said the doctor. "This is an exempt watch! It's actually a computer that runs his bionic arm! It has a medical insignia. See!"

I put my watch back on and rebooted the computer. It was a good thing I was able to keep it, however, or else I wouldn't have been able to document my "adventures" in this jungle of fenced-in blocks. I guess they didn't want anyone to assemble privately and hold "community meetings." Maybe they thought that if we congregated behind walls, they would think that we were scheming on a conspiracy of some sort. These "blocks" were so opened that we didn't even have the luxury of having anything to break the cold draft that came down from the Sierras.

Later in the afternoon, once we settled down on our concrete beds. They made everybody gather in the administrator's assembly hall where we were informed of our "rights" – which basically meant that we didn't' have any rights as RNA citizens and that we were all classified as "enemy combatants." What an honor! Reciting the lyrics to Copland's *Lincoln's Portrait* one day, and being classified as an "enemy combatant" the next. Such is the life in the Republic of North America!

We demanded our rights as citizens of the country but it was ignored. If the government was so "compassionate, they really didn't demonstrate it – especially towards Napajanese-Americans. They felt they were doing us a favor by "protecting us" from the people of the country. If we were being "protected" they why did they have laser cannons pointed inward instead of outward?

If you ever been to an animal shelter, that's what these stalls were like. We were each partitioned off by chain-link fences with a little portal where they served our meals. It was like having dry cereal – more like dog food – 24/7. Once in a while, if we needed to drink water, they would give us some in a stainless steel bowl.

What about doing our personal business? There was this concrete block with a hole full of some chemical and a stainless steel toilet seat. Yes, we were given toilet paper – but, we were instructed to ration the toilet paper at each use – limited to only one square per sitting. They said it was necessary for the war effort and that we needed to "save the trees." What trees? Most of the forests were destroyed back in the 21st Century at the same time the world's oil supply was depleted to nearly nothing. Oddly, however, I did notice some big trees just to the west of here in the Sierras.

In fact, at one point, America was forced into using hemp as a cash crop. It was about time; they just about depleted every other natural resource that was available in earlier times. Oil these days was mostly that synthetic junk that is still polluting the atmosphere. But unlike global warming in the 21st Century, we are now in an ice age like I said before. Yes, October is exceedingly cold! Like about 10 degrees below zero on the average. In the summer, it's only a paltry 20 degrees above zero in the nation's warmest zones like, California.

There's absolutely nothing to do here in camp for entertainment – not even television. I guess they wanted us totally isolated from the world. They let us out of our pens once in a while for our daily exercises, but mainly it's a very controlled activity. The only excitement we get around here is when the guards entertain themselves by shooting off the laser cannons onto the roof tops just to see how many inmates will jump out of bed.

From what I understand of history, the Japanese-Americans had it rather luxurious when they were here during World War II. They had enclosed barracks, planted gardens, had cots to sleep on; community mess halls and even a school system here. Not the case this time around! We're treated like those people who were penned up in Guantanamo Bay in the days of the Iraqi War during the early 21st Century. Even then, I understand they had some kind of material to break the wind and give them a small degree of privacy. As of now, I don't even think we have legal representation. There are cameras all over the place – even lenses pointed downward on your toilet seat!

I'm frankly so incensed right now that I'm going to log off and try to get some sleep.

] Logout.
Good-bye A. Gordon Sakata. Come back soon.

CHAPTER 24

Three Days at Camp

] Login, A. Gordon Sakata
"Welcome A. Gordon Sakata. Please enter today's date."
] Date: 10/03/2208
"Today is October 3, 2209. Please enter the time."
] Time: 04:00
"The time is 4 o'clock. Welcome to the Cyberspace living room."

I had a hard time passing the night and finally dozed off very early in the morning. I was startled by a finger tapping on my shoulder by April who was in the next pen next to mine. All the prison complexes were coed.

"April, you know if they see us talking they're going to take us out and shoot us." I said.

"That's the risk I'm willing to take. At least it will get me out of here." She said.

"What's up?"

"We're going to storm the guard barracks today when they let us out for our morning walk."

"But we'll get killed. They have weapons. We don't."

"We need to stand up for our rights. It's not right that they treat us like animals here. Did you hear that they're using some of us as human guinea pigs for laboratory experiments?"

"No." I said.

"They have been injecting experimental drugs in some of us. Several people in camp have already mysteriously disappeared without explanation."

"Really? But how are we going to fight back?"

"Leon will give the signal at the time we're walking past the security towers. Then we'll storm the guard barracks. Are you in?"

"I'm in!"

Around 10 o'clock, the inmates were released from their pens to walk around the campgrounds. We all headed towards one section of the area where it was heavily secured by guards. The guards took note of the gathering and commanded the prisoners to return to their cells.

"Return to your cells," commanded Major Connors.

But hundreds of the inmates ignored the commands and gathered at the designated assembly area. The guards were seen scrambling to get organized to counter an offensive.

Then the signal was given.

"Go for it!" shouted Leon.

All the inmates stormed the guard barracks and rushed the unprepared guards.

"Open fire! Fire at will!" commanded Major Connors over the loudspeakers as the guards began shooting at the inmates. There were more inmates than guards. But the guards had the advantage of laser cannons and rifles. It was a blood bath.

Some of the inmates managed to make torches and were able to set the barracks on fire. The barracks built to a roaring inferno. With all the hysteria and commotion, there was no way of saving the building. Other inmates were successful in bringing down the main guard tower where they often played games shooting off its laser cannon over the prisoners.

Guards were severely injured as inmates fell to their death in droves.

I was rushing alongside April towards the main entrance to the guard barracks when one of the guards stepped out and shot April through the heart.

I reached for April as she was going down. I was slightly grazed by a shot to my left arm.

"April, are you okay? April, talk to me!"

She laid on the ground lifeless. I was horrified and saddened. Blood was gushing out as I was trying to stop the hemorrhaging without success. I tried to hug her, but two guards picked me up by both arms and dragged me back a holding cell along with other survivors of the riot.

After the riot subsided, the survivors were forced to gather the dead prisoners and stack them in an open area of the camp grounds. The deceased guards were placed in coffins and transported back to their families.

The lifeless bodies of those who made the ultimate sacrifices for their freedom were cremated in an open area as camp officials made all the survivors stand in witness to the affair. We all stood in silence and in mourning, grieving over the lost ones. It could have, and should have been us. They are now freed. We, however, are still imprisoned.

] Logout.
Good-bye A. Gordon Sakata. Come back soon.

CHAPTER 25

Five Days at Camp

] Login, A. Gordon Sakata
"Welcome A. Gordon Sakata. Please enter today's date."
] Date: 10/04/2208
"Today is October 4, 2209. Please enter the time."
] Time: 06:00:00
"The time is 6 o'clock. Welcome to the Cyberspace living room."

These jump suits don't keep us very warm. Camp staff says that the suits are designed to maintain a constant body temperature of 98.6 degrees. But I really don't know how they tested that out. They must have tested these out on laboratory animals instead of humans. My bionic arm keeps my body temperature consistently warm, but with the wind chill, it has been colder than usual. And, with average nightly temperatures at around 15 degrees below zero, I think I was coming down with a rather severe cold or even the flu.

I called for the guard to take me to the infirmary. At first he hesitated, then seeing me with severe coughing spells, runny nose and a red face, he opened the pen and escorted me to the infirmary at a short distance.

The doctor examined me and said I had a severe case of the flu and ordered the guard to place me in solitary confinement so I'd be separated from those who were healthy.

So there I lay, on a pile of hay and given nothing but water. No, not even aspirin or some kind of medication to relieve my misery – just water. It was like I was put on death row just for being sick.

I would have my moments of feeling better. But most of the time, I felt very ill. Sometimes I wished I would just pass out.

Computer, I'm going to log off and get some more sleep. After all, there's nothing else to do since I'm confined to this pen like a dog in the pound.

] Logout.
Good-bye A. Gordon Sakata. Come back soon.

Author's Notes: The following are based on camp's archives.

"Doctor," said the sergeant as he entered the infirmary. "You requested to see me?"

"Yes," he replied. "Please have a seat."

Major Connors was also requested to join the meeting in the infirmary.

"Sorry, I'm late, doctor," said Major Connors."

"That's quite alright Major." said the doctor. "The reason why I asked you all in here is because I did a little more research on Inmate 5502's bionic arm. As it turns out, that watch/computer of his is capable of doing much more that running his arm. It is capable of keeping his life's diary. He can keep a recorded history of everything that goes on in this camp and expose it to the rest of the world!"

"But this is a top secret installation." Said Major Connors. "He can be a breach to Republic security."

"Yes," said Dr. Jones. "We can't let our experimental projects leak out to the public."

"We need to get rid of him!" said the Lieutenant. "What if we kidnapped him and took him up to the hills and left him to rot in the cold forest of the Sierras. He'll never find his way back down."

"I can get three of my men to help," the sergeant said.

"Very well," said the Major, "carry out your plans as soon as possible."

"Yes, sir!"

CHAPTER 26

Two Weeks at Camp

] Login, A. Gordon Sakata
"Welcome A. Gordon Sakata. Please enter today's date"
] Date: 10/14/2209
"Today is October 14, 2209. Please enter the time"
] Time: 22:00:00
"The time is 10 O'clock. Welcome to the Cyberspace
living room"

It's been almost two weeks after coming here into camp and I am still in solitary confinement. Inside this box it must have been 25 degrees below zero. Outside the box, it must have been around 15 degrees below. Through the peepholes I could see the guards moving about wearing their nice warm snow suits. The guard dogs looked like they were more prepared and better dressed for the freezing cold weather better than the prisoners.

Today, there was a blizzard roaring through the camp. Snow and high winds were prevalent and it was evident as the prisoners were let out their pens for their daily exercises that it was hard to move around against the forces of the hard wall of air.

I was feeling somewhat better that I had two weeks ago, but still was not at full strength. The guards came to my pen to escort me out – but I was not going back to my original pen. In fact, they blindfolded me and tied me up.

I was carried by two men and thrown into the back of what I think was a pickup truck. All I remember was driving around for a while. It was cold and probably dark since it was about 11 at night. I remember smelling the scent of pine as we probably we were riding around in the middle of a forest full of pine trees. The air was not only very cold, but very crisp. I never smelled air so clean in my life. Back in the city, air pollution was prevalent 99.8 percent of the time. I don't think Los Angeles ever had a day of clean air since the 21st century.

We must have been riding around for a good three hours, then I remember the truck going over some kind of rocky surface. No, it wasn't gravel, it was more like going over large rocks. After we got off the main highway, the ride was very rough for about 5 minutes. Then, we came to an abrupt stop. I was untied, and the guards removed my blindfold. It was still dark. It must have been around 2 in the morning.

I asked the guards where we were. The told me, "That was for me to figure out. Have a nice life." Then they hopped back into the truck and drove off. There was a bed of pine needles piled under a large tree and since I was tired and exhausted, I decided to sleep until daybreak.

Daybreak finally came at around 6:30 and I got up to get my bearings. I didn't exactly know which way was north, south, east, or west. But one thing for certain, wherever I was, the landscape was absolutely gorgeous. There was this quiet lake right in front of me with what appeared to be a thin layer of ice. Just around the bend I saw a pile of rocks that I decided to explore a little later on.

But I was hungry. I didn't have any matches to start a fire with so going fishing was out of the question – at least for now. I knew that pine nuts were a good source of food. There were a lot of pinecones around, I'll picked on those for a while and then scouted around for some wild berries. My training as a scout always told me to stay put! Eventually, rescue parties will find you.

But, that seemed rather remote since I doubted that I was reported as a "missing person." After all, I was only dumped here by prison guards to fend for myself. It didn't immediately look like I was near a major road. In fact, this place looked like it was in the middle of nowhere. Although, in a way, it did look very much like paradise. Especially after being "freed" from the Manzanar kennel. Maybe, just maybe, I should take up temporary residence here – like Ralph Waldo Emerson did in the 19th century. I could build a small shelter with bark and pine leaves under the tree or, perhaps near that pile of rocks. The sun seemed to strike there most of the day and will probably be the warmest spot in the area. I guess I should see what those rocks are all about.

I drew nearer to the rocks and noted that the rocks weren't piled like that naturally. It was definitely a work of man. It almost looked like a long lost grave. It fact, that's exactly what it was. After examining the pile a little closer, there was a skeleton of a left hand sticking out from under the rocks. Oddly enough, there was this ring on a finger. I wondered why they didn't take the ring off when they buried this person here.

There was some kind of emblem and inscription on the ring, but since it was full of mud and dirt, it was hard to make out the details, so I went down to the lake to wash it off. To my utter amazement, it was an exact replica of the ring I was wearing – or, was this actually the original lost ring.

There was an engraving inside the ring which read – "A. Gordon Sakata." I put the ring back on the skeletal bones and gathered up a few more rocks and placed it over the exposed hand. Gordon Sakata, I finally found you!

It was like having a family reunion of sorts. I exchanged stories.

What? Am I kidding? I was just talking to myself! But actually, if I was really quiet, I could almost hear voices talking back to me in the silence of the forest as if they were telling me stories about the past, present, and future. One of the stories that came to mind was when I was camping at Fillbrook.

"Gordon, there was this time when I was at Fillbrook in one of the campsites that was surrounded by barbwire. It was supposed to have kept the bears out." I said.

"As I slept, suddenly I heard scratching and clawing outside my tent." I continued. "It definitely wasn't a human. Then, I heard heavy breathing as if this creature was standing right outside my tent."

"I grabbed my laser hunting knife and crawled deeper into my sleeping bag and zippered it shut. I was cold and shaking nervously as I thought for sure I was going to be breakfast for some beast."

"After a while, I heard the creature move a little further away from the tent as he began to munch on something crunchy. It wasn't me, fortunately."

"I waited through the night until daybreak. Then I crawled out of my sleeping bag and got out of my tent. A visiting bear apparently had a meal off of one of another patrol's food supplies that were left on the ground. Fortunately, we stored our food in an inaccessible area – on the roof of the latrine."

Then, as if the spirits were talking back to me, I had unbelievable visions of my own. I looked up in the dark clear sky and saw an earth-like planet revolving peacefully before my eyes. There were images of people enjoying themselves on the beaches, in restaurants, in the parks, and during picnics, people laughing and enjoying themselves. Suddenly, there appeared frightening images of wars, mass destruction of cities and villages, famines, people starving, people in the streets without homes. I heard voices crying for help, desperation and great helplessness. Then I heard small voices of other people laughing as if it was a joke, a big game. Then suddenly, this earth-like planet burst into a massive fireball. The sky returned to total darkness with the glimmering of the stars. Once again, there was total silence.

This was the start a series of messages from Heaven.

] Logout.
Good-bye A. Gordon Sakata. Come back soon.

CHAPTER 27

An Introduction to
"Sermons on the Mount"

] Login, A. Gordon Sakata

"Welcome A. Gordon Sakata. Please enter today's date."

] Date: 11/15/2209

"Today is November 15, 2209. Please enter the time."

] Time: 09:00

"The time is 9 o'clock. Welcome to the Cyberspace living room."

It's a good thing they didn't confiscate my watch. As long as my batteries last, I would be able to record my experiences at a place that I couldn't even point to on a map. Strangely, the place looked familiar, as if I've been there before. There was this beautiful lake, tall trees, an open meadow, and a pile of rocks.

Thank goodness for scouting. You know, they said a lot of bad things about scouting for many years – but, one of the greatest things about the scouting program is that it teaches you how to survive – especially if you have been on a survival trip to the Fillbrook Scout Ranch in New Mexico. I've managed to survive on my own for about a month since

I was hustled out of camp. One of these days, I'll figure out how to get out of these mountains. But I should say, it's beautiful up here – a little chilly, but beautiful.

I found some large logs and build a bed of pine needles as a mattress. Then, near the lake, I found some weed to make fabricate rope so that I could tie some other large pieces of wood to make a frame which I made into my overhead shelter that protected me from the elements during my stay on the mountains. Especially when it rained or snowed.

I finally found some flint nearby so I managed to start a fire to keep myself warm during the night and to cook my daily catch of trout from the lake. Oh, yes, that was story in itself. It took me a while to figure out that part of the survival puzzle, but I found some long branches one day that I was able to carve a sharp tip at the tips. I was then able to use these branches as spears. I was surprised to find out that the lake was plentiful with very large trout. I guess they ate well in this particular lake. My typical meal was trout, pine nuts, and wild berries. There were a few herbs that I was able to use also and that helped to break the monotony.

You know, people would go through a lot of different ways to gain power. Most people are satisfied with just what they have. A few people seek ways to get ahead – usually at the expense of others. You'll find this a lot in corporations and government. I guess they think the higher they get, the more "enlightened" they become. Then they start to worship the "enlightened" ones – the ones that made it to the very top – and try their hardest to achieve the same status no matter how many other people are expended because of their ambitions nor how miserable it is in their personal life.

People always had the false assumption that you had to do something to attain enlightenment. Throughout history people have tried their best by doing various things to have attained enlightenment. Many have failed in their journeys. Why? Probably because they tried too hard in doing so. There is a saying worth remembering: "Be still and know that I am God."

As the saying goes, "be still." How can you expect God to communicate with you if you are constantly moving around while constantly being distracted by other things? Up here in the mountains, it is very simple to be still and listen to God's voice. Buddha is the greatest example of being still. He did absolutely nothing but meditate under the bodhi tree, then attained enlightenment.

I have attained enlightenment. No, not because I stepped on other people to get to this level. As a matter of fact, I've done nothing at all! All I had to do was to declare my enlightenment. There are different levels of enlightenment. But the enlightenment of God's universe is not gained by man's materialistic ways, but by communicating with God at a higher level than that taught by most religions of the world. And surviving up here in the mountains has made that possible. I was able to attain enlightenment by being still and doing absolutely nothing on this mountain but listening and meditating. Be still for once and let God communicate to you.

I am going to attempt to document what I have learned spiritually in this journal as long as the batteries last and as long as I am able to last. Hopefully, someone will find this Computer, and be able to upload it and share my experiences with the rest of the world long after I'm gone. Of course, Computer, that's hoping that someone will come along and find us here in these mountains.

] Logout.
Good-bye A. Gordon Sakata. Come back soon.

CHAPTER 28

Thought One from the Mount

***"One Mind, One Body, One
World, One Universe"***

] Login, A. Gordon Sakata
"Welcome A. Gordon Sakata. Please enter today's date."
] Date: 12/10/2209
"Today is December 10, 2209. Please enter the time."
] Time: 10:00
"The time is 10 O'clock. Welcome to the Cyberspace
living room."

I was down at the lake fishing early this morning and I really don't know what brought this along, but the fabled story of the *Three Musketeers* entered my mind. God had a message to tell me and he reminded me about the motto of Musketeers is, "One for all, and all for one."

People say that I may be out of my mind. Some people may say that what I am attempting to talk about is heresy. They may even consider me as a schizophrenic. They may call me and this memoir of mine all sorts of negative things. But the truth of the matter is: I talk to and with

God *(period)*. God is in me and I in God. We are one. I can truthfully say this and so can you!

I know that some with say that there is no God. That's perfectly fine. Some will be surprised to find out that God does not require He be worshipped. It's a choice that he has given to each individual. As for myself, I can declare his existence because I communicate with God daily. What else are you supposed to do all alone up here in the mountains? God is keeping my sanity and hopes alive.

The irony is that those who launch negative comments about me really don't know who they are, nor where they have come from. It is prior to birth, upon their spiritual arrival here on earth, that they have forgotten that they too are of God and God is in them. The fact is, God is everywhere. Not only in me, but in you, in trees, in the water, in rocks, in flowers, in the wind, in the rain – I do mean, everywhere. God is everlasting and in constant motion. Yes, even rocks are in motion, too. To God, there is no backward or forward, up or down, left or right, male or female, right or wrong. God is God – the all in all, the Alpha and Omega. God inspired the Bible. But he also inspired others to write the Torah, the Koran, and yes, the teachings of the Buddha (Prince Siddhartha) – and for that matter, all other forms of earthly and universal religions. Rather than criticizing one another, or saying that "my way is the only way," truly compare each religion with an open mind and you will find similarities and commonalities in all religions. Why? Because, all religions are a creation of God. And the universal truth of the matter is, you have the choice to believe it or not.

Our mind is a wonderful creation and an evolution of itself. Now some will say that creation and evolution cannot coexist – that it's either one or the other. I say it can be both! The human being was created by God, but has evolved through time. As humans evolved, so has the brain. In modern days, like in the 20th and early 21st centuries, computers were developed that were extensions of the mind. Central processing units (CPUs) and hard disks were very much like the human mind – capable of processing and storing information. But unlike the riddle of the "chicken and the egg," the human mind, of course, came first. Like humans, computers have also evolved through time – becoming smaller and smaller through each decade. Now, and entire book can be stored in a computer, the size of a wristwatch.

Like the computer's brain, so must the human mind be programmed. All religions teach us the basics of living – in peace and harmony. Yet, there are inconsistencies in all religions that teach violence, right and wrong, and just about everything else. I tell you that that which is God's lives on. That which is influenced by man are only doctrines that can live or die. God has no doctrine. In God's universe, there is no right or wrong. That which is right or wrong is only a perception of man. Hence, that which may be right in one country, may be wrong in others. These choices are left up to man. Therefore, I tell you, that the "end of the world" will not be that of God's choosing, but that of man's. Why? Because, man has not learned how to master the "intellectual" part of his mind. That part of the brain which leads us to higher levels of thinking and civilized behavior. We still act on the primitive parts of our mind which is very "animalistic" and very childish – those parts which rely heavily on instinct and past behavior. And more ironically, it's also very selfish.

Unlike animals, humans have the capacity to reason. In primitive times, if we didn't like something, we destroyed it. How do we know this? Because, we all have experienced this in one life or another. Yes, we all have been on this Earth more than once – some of us more than others. Yet, some of us are relatively new to the experiences here on Earth. This is a universal truth, we are all traveling throughout this universe. Earth is only a stopping point in our journey. Some call it a vacation spot. Others may call it something else. Nevertheless, you are not only a citizen of your municipality, state and country, but you are also a citizen of the universe.

There is one earthly misnomer about the soul in relationship to each person. Many believe that the soul resides in a person or resides in a person's mind. That's totally false. The soul envelops the physical body and is not a separate matter or entity. The soul is so large, that it truly spans the universe. It is the soul that enables us to travel forward and backward in time, and to and from civilizations of other planetary places. However, this wasn't truly realized until the late 22nd Century.

Until the late 22nd Century, the public of the world had been kept in the dark about visitors from other celestial planets through government secrecy and cover-ups. Towards the end of the century, the truth began to surface as people began to discover that visitors from other worlds have been actively visiting the planet since the beginning of time. It was getting harder to contain the truth. Yes, Aunt Mabel, we have been visited by beings from "outer space". Not only that, we have been visited by humans from other time periods as well as from other civilizations.

But let us get back to the mind. Humans have a peculiar way of programming the mind. Programming is done by way of educating the mind. Some are programmed better than others. We have seen that throughout the time of modern man. That man has chosen who will be better educated than others. In fact, if it were up to some, others would not be educated at all. Hence we have segregation, racism, differences in educational systems and philosophies amongst nations, ageism, and just about every kind of "ism" that you can believe. God has designed us to be equally educated not only within one country, state, or municipality, but equally as planetary citizens of this world. The mind is a very powerful organism. It is through this intellectual and highly educated mind that we can know how to harness that of our animalistic mind and truly promote peace and harmony throughout this earth without having to resort to wars and weapons of mass destruction in order to resolve our differences. It is through our means of thinking on a higher level of reasoning, can God's power truly be revealed through every being. Why? Because we all have a measure of God residing in us – we all are children of God. Only by realizing this, can God's power truly be revealed.

God wants us to be in a continuous state of re-creation. That is, we should be recreating ourselves, not only as individuals, but collectively for the sake of mankind. Unfortunately, as children, our minds are still at that which exhibits child-like behavior – such as, sibling rivalry. Our minds have yet to grow from infancy or toddler-like thinking to that of a mature adult. That is, nations still exhibit child-like behavior – fighting amongst nations, having more than others, not sharing the wealth and property, intellectual knowledge, greed, and corruption and the craving for power. Corrupt nations have gone to the extent of using a variety of means of controlling the mind through false propaganda, lying and cheating.

In the early 21st Century, the United States had a two-party political system. There were actually more political parties than that, but really, only one party dominated the governance of the country. The political party was known as the "Conservative" party whose mascot was an elephant. The rival party was called the "Labor" party, whose mascot was a donkey. For the longest time in the nation's history, these two parties were the dominating political entities until that latter part of the 21st century. The Conservative party was the first to go after it had a streak of corruption, lying, deceit, mismanagement and an abuse of power of the nation's economy. In fact, the party almost was successful at dismantling the Social Security system between 2004 and 2008 while spending hundreds of billions of dollars trying to spread "democracy and freedom" around the world for the sake of corporate greed and corruption. Social Security was a means of serving those less fortunate that was a genuine eyesore amongst the Conservatives. In fact, they gave "fancy" titles and labels to just about everything they intended to dismantle under the guise of "reform." Everything that they wanted to do was sold to the American public in one form of a package or another. One of their pet projects was "Operation Iraqi Liberation" (OIL). The leaders of the nation then sold a propaganda package to the American public that was supposed to protect them from terrorism and the false Iraqi goal of building weapons of mass destruction. It was later discovered that there were no weapons of mass destruction, but the invasion cost both nations thousands of innocent lives. Yet, the administration claimed that it "valued life." The truth of the matter was they sought Iraq's oil reserves for their own greedy self as a "nation" and it more benefited corporate executives trying to make bigger profits for themselves rather than benefiting the average citizen who suffered through higher gasoline prices while salaries and wages continued to decline. That's also to say that salaries of corporate executives and management continued to rise. The government fashioned itself after big corporations that constantly denied their employees the freedom of speech and expression. Management in these companies were notorious for stealing ideas from others and claiming credit for themselves and not recognizing the originator(s) of the idea. Companies were also notorious for controlling and manipulating the press.

There were two entities in American society that the Conservatives and corporations had a great hatred for – National Public Radio and the Corporation for Public Broadcasting. Neo-conservative interest and corporations did not control these publicly funded organizations. They claimed that their affiliates were too "liberal." Fact of the matter was, they had a more balanced program than the commercial networks who were controlled by conservative management. They, the neo-conservatives, went as far as appointing an ultra-conservative as chairman of the board for the Corporation of Public Broadcasting. Then the neo-conservative dominated legislative branch of the government proceeded to cut funding for these agencies while still funding a war based on false information and lies.

Then there was the matter of pre-emptive wars itself. While bankrupting federal and state services to the less advantaged, they continued to amass a huge arsenal of "modernized" nuclear weapons, all of this under the cover of what they termed as the "Patriot Act."

The Patriot Act was sold as protection from terrorists. But rather than protecting the country from terrorism, the act secretly took away rights and freedoms from the citizens. This left the door open for the government to establish concentration camps in times of peace and war.

The "Leave No Child Behind Act" meant exactly that. That is to say it left no child behind from forcing military service upon each child. Provisions in the act forced schools to surrender private, confidential student information to the government for the purpose of a military build-up. Yet, it failed to provide funding for a successful educational program. Instead of educating children on the basics of reading, writing, and mathematics, the arts, and ethics of life, and learning how to make money and investing, they developed minds only how to take and pass exams and withheld funding to school districts if they weren't successful. God's mind was never meant to be tested, but meant for life- long learning. What was this build-up for? One-world dominance!

Eventually, the public got the message after the nation became involved in two more conflicts in Iran and North Korea. America then, like the RNA is now, just couldn't resist the temptation to stick its nose into other nations' business. It was because of the Conservatives' arrogance, stubbornness, mismanagement, tyranny, greed, disregard for the Constitution and abuse of power that the American public permanently banned the party from ever gaining public office again. But unfortunately, by the time the American public realized their misgivings, the country went bankrupt.

Perhaps the biggest mistake of the Conservative Party was that it laid claim of ownership of Christianity. God never gave Conservatives a "license to own" Christianity. In fact, the things that Conservatives did were in total conflict of not only the Bible, but that of God's desires as well. Christianity cannot be owned – it was meant to be shared freely. But the Conservatives always argued that "you're either with us, or against us. My way or the highway." They couldn't tolerate criticism very well. They always interpreted "criticism" as being an "attack." This was especially true for rich "Christians" who often lined their pockets with millions of dollars in bonuses after laying people off which in turn affected their livelihoods. Back then, and also true today, is that people are treated like paper – discarded and thrown away.

Rather than effectively educating all of the nation's people, regardless of race, color, creed and religious beliefs, executives elected to develop ways to stupefy its employees and the rest of the American public by less effective means of education (automation, computer-based, and "help-desks") rather than encouraging people to read more through books and human instruction. Human minds can only educate other human minds. Computers cannot educate minds because they only have the capacity of that which has been programmed into them by human minds – and that's not very much! The human mind is capable of reasoning and imparting information millions of times more than a computer. Humans can offer more effective feedback than computers. That will happen once we have learned how to use the whole brain rather than just a fraction of what it is capable of doing. But the power behind this is to educate everybody – not just a few. God has a plan for each individual to contribute in his or her own way to mankind. We each hold a piece of the puzzle in God's never-ending jigsaw puzzle. Make use of this invaluable resource for the world depends on it. Don't look abroad for your cheap labor and educated minds and call this "globalization." If you really want to globalize the world, do it for the sake of mankind and not for your personal wealth.

Jesus and Prince Siddhartha (Buddha) gave up their worldly possessions in order to truly understand the needs of common man. They even sacrificed their lives for the good of mankind. You can only know God by giving up your worldly possessions. The world's wealth and resources was meant to be shared equally amongst all. There is no true "ownership" of anything because you came into this world with nothing, so shall you leave this world with nothing. Materialism is impermanent. Life is impermanent be it before, now, and/or hereafter. Those who travel light will enjoy the privilege of moving on to other celestial cultures of higher thinking. Those who travel with heavy luggage may very well return back here to earth to do it all over again.

Some say that education is a dangerous thing – I say, no education is even more detrimental. The lack of education leads to violence, crime, hatred, bigotry, wars and the destruction of mankind. An educated mind leads to higher levels of reasoning, logic and understanding of the values of life. But, we cannot continue to evolve our minds if we continue to live in the past.

Like I said before, God is in constant motion. Because we are of God, so are we in constant motion. Our objective is to re-create ourselves – to better ourselves and the quality of life, not just for a few, but for many. If we worship a doctrine or only a book, then we are refrained from continuing to press forward. As God lives, grows, and continues to learn, so should we. But we cannot do this if continue to live to the standards of the past without modifying our way of living for the future. God is ever changing – so should we. We are often reluctant and afraid of changes and therefore unwilling to adapt to new way of living. We often refer to the Bible, Torah, and the Koran as a way of living. But in order for these precious teachings to truly live, it must also be allowed to grow. I am not advocating abandoning your faith, belief, or religion. I am encouraging you to enhance your spirituality by ridding those matters in your books that aren't applicable in today's world. Discard the things that don't work and enhance the things that do. This should also hold true for a living and evolving Constitution of any nation. Rid yourselves of matters that are irrelevant and don't work and continue to write legislation and policy for the betterment of man and not corporations, businesses or political parties. For it is the role of government to enhance and improve the quality of life and for the common good of its people. Not as that as a servant for the elite few. For it has been said, "Man was created equal."

We are not paper – things to be thrown away at will. Since our mind is of that of God's and God is in us, so are we related to each other through God. Therefore let us treat each other – Christians, Jews, Muslims, Buddhists, and everyone else – like brothers and sisters as if we are of one body. The body lives in harmony as one being – in peace. Let us not view ourselves as citizens of any one nation – but citizens of the world and of this universe. And since we are of one body, so should we treat each nation as a community, living equally as one world. For this one world is only a member of a vast community of other celestial worlds in one universe – God's Universe.

] Logout.
Good-bye A. Gordon Sakata. Come back soon.

CHAPTER 29

Thought Two from the Mount

"The Universe's Answer to Poverty, Starvation, Homelessness and Lack of Abundance"

] Login, A. Gordon Sakata
"Welcome A. Gordon Sakata. Please enter today's date"
] Date: 12/15/2209
"Today is December 15, 2209. Please enter the time"
] Time: 11:00
"The time is 11 O'clock. Welcome to the Cyberspace living room. Warning! Your batteries are low!"

I was gazing at the stars this evening and was amazed at God's universe. It was as if each star had a story to tell – a message to impart to everyone that listened.

Okay, so you know that I'm already of a different mind at a different level than the average person, now, you're going to get a mindful of boggling information. But you'll have to understand, cold weather can do some strange things to one's mind.

First of all, there is intelligent life in the universe. Many societies on other planets have higher levels of thinking and are more sophisticated than humans on this planet, unfortunate to say. There are some societies that live by war alone and constantly migrate from one stellar system to another creating war against other civilizations. Other civilizations are more sophisticated and intelligent enough to use reasoning and logic in place of war – especially where there are major differences between nations and societies. As a matter of fact, each and every one of us has come from one of those two kinds of societies. And, this type of behavior is common in all countries on planet Earth. Some believe that war is the answer to all dilemmas and disagreement between nations and societies. Others favor, and are very gifted in using diplomacy, logic, reasoning, and wisdom in solving problems. The latter type of behavior are those individuals who have come from civilizations of higher thinking. And, it is from these civilizations and societies that comes the answer to the world's problems of poverty, starvation, homelessness, and lack of abundance. That's because in these civilizations, there is no such thing as starvation, hunger, and homelessness. In fact, for each individual, there is unlimited, unbounded life of abundance, peace, and prosperity. In the early 21st Century, there was a movement called "The Secret" that taught that each and individual can live an abundant life by incorporating the "Law of Attraction." While it goes into much more detail than that, it is a universal truth. But, in other societies of abundant living, you don't have to incorporate or call the Law of Attraction very hard. In fact, all you have to do is will it – and it will be so. Remember that I said in my previous thought that God is in each individual, and each individual is God. Therefore, the power that is in you is greater than that which is in the world. Yes, when you are broadcasting your wants and desires to the universe, unlike in other civilizations, there is a lot of static interference here on Earth. Some of that interference is very powerful – and, unfortunately, these are the type of people who hold on to the world's wealth and influence government to legislate policy and laws in their favor. A lot of the world's corporations are like this. These people only make up 1 percent of the world's population but are more influential in government than the rest of the 99 percent of the people in the world. If you really want to end poverty, hunger, and homelessness – then WILL IT SO! You have the power to do so just as much as the measly few that dictate the direction of this world. There is power in numbers! It's time for the people to take control of the direction of the world – not by just a few wealthy individuals who hold on to the world's riches. And, this kind of revolution in society doesn't have to be violent. Changes can be brought about non-violently – It can and should be a very peaceful transition. But the power of the process lies in intelligence, logic, courage, and action. If you want the world to live in abundance, then be bold and courageous about it. Take necessary actions to make it so! It is possible for 100 percent of the world's population to live in equal abundance.

How you ask? Adopt the model of higher thinking civilizations. Ask yourself the question: What is more valuable – gold, oil, or human life? If you ask someone from another civilization of higher thinking, gold and oil or some precious metal that we consider as "valuable" has very limited value. That person would conclude that human life is far more valuable that any precious metal or substance that the Earth has to provide. Some civilizations have absolutely no currency at all and people live very abundantly. Other societies base their currencies on the value of life which is – unlimited and priceless! Yes, many warring civilizations have currency systems that are based on some material substance that they perceived as "valuable." But like in currency systems on Earth, nation's currency and values are inconsistent and incompatible with other nations. What one country considers as valuable may be perceived as something totally worthless by another nation. In general, there is no uniform standard or agreement. The immediate action to take is to unify the world's monetary system – rid yourselves on the basis of oil or precious metals, and turn to a standard of human life. Of course, some people would think that human life is worthless. But the truth of the matter is, every individual has something to contribute to society and is highly valuable to the world. People were born to be equal. Many national doctrines have already stated this. Yes, there is a price on human life – especially if someone's life has been taken away by unnatural means. Then, the issue is settled in courts where millions of dollars are paid to victims of the deceased individual.

Since human life is precious – so is the matter of living in abundance precious to each individual. Therefore, make it worthwhile! Give each individual universal credits where one credit equals one dollar. Let each individual earn at least $50,000,000 Universal Life Credits a year for life. After all, we know that life is precious, so why not shoot for the stars?

This will solve a multitude of problems. With people making $50 million ULCs a year, people will be able to afford life's basic needs and the world can rid itself of poverty, hunger, and homelessness. With people equally given the same amount of credits – this will open up the opportunities for those who were less fortunate, to live in abundance equally with everyone else. Furthermore, it solves additional problems that the world commonly experiences.

Think about it, with a unified monetary system, people will not have to worry about exchanging money either for lesser value or greater value depending on where they travel to. There will be no need for currency exchanges.

Corporations of the world do not have to worry about laying off people for they will not carry the burden of paying their employees. Employees will work for pure enjoyment since their pay is already given to them. Therefore, companies will have to develop other forms of incentives.

The world's problem of lack of health insurance will be solved. In fact, people will no longer need insurance since $50 million ULCs a year will enable people to pay directly for their own medical needs without having to depend on insurance.

A lot of court and litigation issues between disputing parties can be settled out of court and individuals will not have to worry about sacrificing anything in order to come to a settlement.

On the flip side of the coin, rich billionaires will have their annual earnings drastically reduced. $50 million ULCs may be dramatically less than their customary living styles require. However, for the good of equality of all mankind, this is a sacrifice that must be made. Of course then too, we can increase universal credits to $50 billion a year since life's value is limitless.

No, I am not advocating that people would be implanted with some kind of electronic device like a memory chip or something like that. In this century, that's an obsolete way of managing your account. All you have to be is just you – like, just sign for it or whatever you are trying to purchase!

But as I have said before, this cannot happen unless you take bold and courageous action – not by yourselves. Do it collectively and cooperate with other nations of the world – regardless if they be friendly or hostile. In fact, by doing so, you may develop more friends than enemies and a greater understanding of each other since you would be working towards a common cause – abundance for everyone. So, don't just sit there and read about it – go out there and do it!

] Logout.
Good-bye A. Gordon Sakata. Come back soon.

CHAPTER 30

Thought Three from the Mount

"Making War Obsolete – Being Good Stewards of People"

] Login, A. Gordon Sakata

"Welcome A. Gordon Sakata. Please enter today's date."

] Date: 1/1/2209

"Today is December 20, 2209. Please enter the time."

] Time: 11:00

"The time is 11 o'clock. Welcome to the Cyberspace living room. Warning! Your batteries are very low!"

The tall magnificent trees in this forest appear to coexist peacefully with the smaller trees, shrubs and other vegetations around them. In the distance, I could see that a behemoth monster could have disastrous effects when it falls on the little tress nearby. Here, there were probably more little trees, than the tall giants. But when you added everything together, it made for a very beautiful landscape – each element depended on each other in contributing towards the scenery.

Since the beginning of man, there has always been a matter that always differentiated different species of mankind whether it was race, nationality, and even among citizens which were commonly known as "social classes." It was among these social classes that one class considered itself to be more "superior" than others. They were usually referred to as the "ruling" or "upper class," which normally made up of about one-percent of the population. Yet it was this very small minority that often had a profound influence on other people of "lesser" stature. These people were more affluent. Members of ruling classes often treated people differently. People in the more affluent societies treated people in the "middle" and "poverty" classes as more expendable. This was common in the 20th and 21st Centuries where it was typical to lay off mass numbers of employees while top executives were rewarded with millions of dollars in bonuses. Yet the people that were laid off often lost their retirement pensions and health benefits. Laws were passed that blamed individuals for their ill-fortunes when it was actually society's fault for causing one's personal problems. Yet, corporations never assisted in giving these individuals a helping hand, but moreover, recorded permanent derogatory remarks and comments on national databases that reflected their inability to make payments on their credit card bills just after losing their jobs. And for many, a lot of individuals were never able to obtain gainful employment again.

The government in the 20th and 21st Centuries were also of no help. The 34th President of the United States was probably one of the biggest embarrassments in U.S. Foreign policy – besides its history. He started a war with Iraq based on false intelligence and never completed "his war" against the terrorists in Afghanistan. In fact, the government in Iraq had nothing to do with the destruction of the World Trade Center in the first place. So, basing his justification to go to war against "terrorism" against a country that had nothing to do with the cause in the first place, he sent thousands of young soldiers to their deaths for an unjustified war. What a demonstration of using expendable people at one's personal ambition! The President came from the "upper" class of American Society and the family was very affluent. Yet soldiers were recruited largely from struggling areas of society, out of families that were struggling to survive – you know what I'm getting at – those types that were largely considered as expendable as paper plates. They were people like us – the throw-aways! After all, we didn't come from a line of fine china.

But, that will soon change. Because when the world starts to demand a change its monetary standard from the "oil standard" to the "human standard," it will be awfully difficult to send someone to war who is valued at $50 million as opposed to a paltry $25 thousand or less. Furthermore, when each individual in the world is given $50 million ULCs a year, the world of banking will certainly change. There will be no need to maintain credit records on people who cannot pay their bills in a timely manner. This will eliminate the need for loans and credit cards all together!

But more importantly, since everyone will be given an equal living expense, each and individual will be equals – no one being less or greater than the other in power or influence. Yes, there might be a few "billionaires" who might lose some of their fortunes. But the world, as a whole would be a better, more equal place to live.

God never meant there to be different classes of people. People were created equally and were meant to be treated as equals. That is why there is a degree of divinity in each one of us –- as individuals – who possess a unique answer, a "piece of the puzzle" to the mystery of this universe. To destroy this by sending people to war to be killed as "sacrificial lambs" for the sake of political, societal, and religious differences is wrong. Each one of us is a thread, a part of the fabric of the universe that was meant to be intertwined in God's grand tapestry. That is why there are different religions. We are all part of God's master artwork. To God, there is a whole rainbow of colors in this universe. On this earth, he likes to use white, black, brown, yellow. He even likes to augment the populations of the world by accenting it with like sexes such as gays and lesbians. Yes, these people are also part of God's grand mosaic, and each carries a piece of the grand puzzle. And like that of a great artist, he likes to mix and create new colors. After all, he is the maker of this Universe!

Just as God has given us to make changes in society such as in a universal monetary system that is equitable for all and guarantees prosperity for all, he has also given us the power to change our way of thinking and reasoning. We have power not to destroy each other, but to also reason with our enemies. Life is not only precious – and soon to be more valuable than ever – but it is sacred and not an expendable commodity like paper plates! We should therefore use our senses and intelligence to diplomatically find solutions to our differences so that we can mutually respect each other's divinity on this earth.

How do we ensure that this can become a reality? By being in a constant, continual state of change and forward motion. By ridding ourselves of things that no longer work or hold us back and continue to support, maintain, and improve those things that still work and continue to benefit our lives. We must choose wisely leaders that will support the cause of peace and tranquility among all nations and eliminate their weapons of mass destruction – including the "super powers" of the world. We must find ways that will benefit and profit mankind as a whole and not as individuals or as profit making corporations. And, we must also find ways to preserve our lives by preserving the environment in which we live so that we can ensure that the quality of our planet will be preserved for the benefit and enjoyment of generations to come.

Like that of the forest, if we were to cut away the smaller vegetation, in favor of the tall green trees, there would be large gaping holes in the picture. There would be barren empty spaces in a landscape. As well in society, if we rid ourselves of common people by sending them to war and left only the affluent to stand, there would be empty spaces in this picture as well. The support and human infrastructure would collapse and so would society as well.

In the ancient days of nobility, kings used to fight the battles along side with their armies. If men are truly "created equal," then leaders of nations should fight their own battles first before sending others off to war on their behalf. After all, that would be the only noble thing to do.

] Logout.
Good-bye A. Gordon Sakata. Come back soon.

CHAPTER 31

Thought Four from the Mount

"An Unforgiving Society"

] Login, A. Gordon Sakata
"Welcome A. Gordon Sakata. Please enter today's date."
] Date: 2/5/2210
"Today is February 5, 2210. Please enter the time."
] Time: 12:00
"The time is 12 o'clock. Welcome to the Cyberspace living room... Warning! Your batteries are extremely low! Please recharge me at your earliest convenience."

I was on my mattress of pine needles meditating and debated hard about the thought of forgiving the society for sending me to prison camp, let alone, bringing me up here to this location in the mountains to die. But I have to keep positive thoughts about me and within me. It's the only thing that is keeping me alive. I know that things will get better, not only for me, but for the rest of the world. Therefore, I have forgiven the people who have performed these acts against me. Strange things can happen to people's behaviors during a time of crisis.

Unfortunately, some people have to suffer for their inadequacy and ignorance.

Computer, you know that society is basically built around the premise that we should punish those who make mistakes – even if it's not their fault or they had absolutely no control of over their circumstances.

God has always been a forgiving divinity. We, as children of God, have never been of the forgiving kind. We would rather punish someone rather than forgive someone of his or her mistakes rather than rehabilitating the person or offering assistance or correcting one's behavior in a constructive manner. Rather, we seek punishment by incarceration and often forget about the person behind prison cells. Then files are created that permanently follow a person and everlastingly reflects on the individual's history and reputation. Thus, society appears never to forgive a person for his/her past actions or circumstances no matter how innocent they may have been.

Take for example people who are laid off and unable to pay their bills because they have no means of income. Employers will not hire them for a variety of excuses like "they are too old, or, they have nothing to offer, or they are too expensive." These same people offer absolutely no means of assistance to a displaced employee to get rehired in another company or organization and is often put out on the streets left struggling to survive on his or her own.

While is still happening, bills continue to incur and other companies expect payment on bills as if everything was "normal." These companies also do not care about the "well being" of these displaced individuals who are displaced not because of their own free will but forced out because of someone's "business decision." Where is the humanity in all of this process? Are we more concerned about the bottom line rather than the good of mankind? After all, if it were not for mankind, you really would not have a bottom line to begin or work with.

There is an example of the irony of all of this where some people are more concerned about saving money for corporations rather than saving the well-being of a fellow human being. It was reported on the news several people were denied the cost of emergency medical transportation cost from their insurance companies because at the time they were being transported during their "emergencies" the procedure was not "pre-authorized." The insurance response was that they were denied coverage because they, the insurance representatives, were "saving" money for the insurance companies. In some cases, people have even died because they could receive timely medical care because of insurance company denials of coverage.

Some hospitals in big cities in the 21st Century used to discharge patients in their gowns onto the streets after they were treated because they were not able to pay for their services. Yet, rather than sending them to a place of warmth and comfort, they were dropped off by taxicabs out into the cold with nothing to wear but a medical gown.

People who were attempting to rebuild their lives often encountered roadblocks and barriers when they could not qualify for re-employment because they had a "bad credit history" or were deemed as a "bad credit risk." Yes, in the RNA, when one is down, society loves to keep you down for as long as it can. Even if you tried to resurface, they would make every attempt to knock you right back down again. Like it or not, someone is always keeping a record of you, not matter who you are or whatever you do. There is always information about you on a database somewhere in this world, whether it would be for positive, constructive purposes, or for destructive purposes. In short, like it or not, the North American Society is not a very forgiving society, even thought the Great Master commanded "Forgive one another as I have forgiven you." We have still not learned how to forgive one another.

We truly haven't learned to treat and respect each other as equals. People are always playing the game of "one-upmanship." Many people are always trying to gain the upper hand. People think they were treating other people fairly. Truthfully, when we think we're providing other people enough or when we thing that they are making or earning enough, they really are not making or earning enough. Not even close to making ends meet. That's because people keep raising the stakes even higher. Take for example the oil crisis in the 21st Century. Salaries and jobs declined while oil prices continued to soar to record prices and oil companies made sinful profits. Yet, the people were often told to "live within their means." How can we truthfully expect people to live within their means when the bar continues to rise at an ever changing rate so people cannot keep up with the changes? Yet, governments do absolutely nothing to govern nor control these changes. It's like asking the question, '"who's ruling who?"

We live in a world of fear. People fear that their property will be taken away because they cannot pay their bills and often wonder how to make ends meet. At the same time, there are rising health issues associated with these fears like high blood pressure, diabetes and heart diseases which I personally believe are caused largely by societal pressures and the cure can be solved by removing societal issues from one's life. In the RNA, the life span is known to be a lot shorter than those in other nations. In the 23rd century, the average life span in the RNA continent has fallen to 57th in rank among the nations of the world. I believe it was much better in the 21st century. But starting in the 20th Century, government had done nothing to fix the failing health system in America and the problems only compounded through the ages. Where a lot of nations enjoy free health care or medical care at a minimum cost, health care both in Canada and in Mexico where it was once very affordable, is now very expensive due to profit-mongering insurance and pharmaceutical companies.

Inhalers, which cost about a dollar in Cuba, now cost, on the average $500 in the Republic of North America. Yet, people say that we have one of the "best" medical systems in the world. The fact of the matter is, more people are dying off at an earlier age than ever before. The average life span in, the 23rd century is now 59 years for men, and 62 years for women.

On another subject, people are still expected to pay their bills or corporations are allowed to seize their properties – not the government. Back in the 22nd century, a federal law was passed to allow any institution to seize personal property without warning for failing to pay bills on time. Unemployment was no excuse even though people were losing their jobs every hour. All the government did was to assist the corporations in evicting the people from their properties and placing them out into the streets. Oh yes, the government couldn't send people to their graves – but they had no problems putting people out into the streets and often left it up to the benevolence of charitable organizations to care for these people – like, churches and synagogues who were losing members in their congregations very rapidly and rapidly losing federal funding to support their charitable causes.

We have always lived in a world where we lived by the philosophy: "An eye for an eye, a tooth for a tooth." We weren't very good at forgiving each other. And unfortunately, Corporate America really wasn't into the business of forgiving either – but was truly more concerned about its "bottom line" rather than for the good of mankind.

My right arm feels a little weak right now. My battery must be running low. I'm finding it much more difficult to carry firewood with it so I better give it a little rest to conserve the energy.

Just as a final thought for now, it's about time that we not only forgive each other, but it's time for the meek to take its rightful place in the society to inherit the world. Let us take the fear out of living for all.

] Logout.
Good-bye A. Gordon Sakata. Come back soon.

CHAPTER 32

Logging Off for Good

] Login, A. Gordon Sakata
"Welcome A. Gordon Sakata. Please enter today's date."
] Date: 2/5/2210
"Today is February 5, 2210. Please enter the time."
] Time: 14:00
"The time is 2 o'clock. Welcome to the Cyberspace living room... Warning! Your batteries are extremely low! This is an urgent reminder. Please recharge me at your earliest convenience."

I've been on this mountain for over three months. It's snowing and still no sign of a rescue party. As soon as the snow breaks, I will begin to seek my way down the mountain.

I was thinking about famous biblical passages and during this time of war, the passage that comes to mind is from the great prophet Micah (4:3). It says, *"Nation shall not lift up a sword against nation, neither shall they learn war anymore."* One would think that after all these centuries that civilizations would have learned their lessons and not make war against one another. Yet, they continue to make more sophisticated weapons of destruction, designed to cause harm to other fellow humans. If we are truly sisters and brothers, why then do we continue this sibling rivalry and continue in our obsolete and violent ways of living?

Then there was a sudden whirl of air swirling around the lake. There was thunder and lightning, yet there wasn't a cloud in the sky. Suddenly a feminine figure stood before me.

"Hi Gordon!" said this familiar voice as she wrapped her arms around me and gave me a big hug and a kiss. I couldn't see her very well because of the glare but it definitely was a feminine figure and the voice was very familiar.

"Wendy, is that you?" I asked.

"Yes, my love. I missed you soooo much. I'm really sorry it took me so long to find you."

"That's quite all right. I'm glad you found me at last!"

"But what is this thing? How did you finally find me?"

"Your tracking signal became weaker by the day. I tracked you to the base of this mountain by my car. Then I had to call for my mother ship for additional assistance."

"Your mother ship?" I asked. "What are you talking about?"

"I have a personal secret to share with you, Gordon?"

"A personal secret? What secret is this?"

"My name is not Wendy."

"No? Not Wendy? Then who are you?"

"My real name is Princess Kathy Kusumatsu from the planet Xychron."

"Princess Kathy Kusumatsu? Not Wendy? What am I supposed to do?"

"Watch closely and I'll show you my real identity."

The magically she transformed into this stunning Asian beauty.

"Wait a minute!" I said. "That's why the children look so Asian and not Caucasian?"

"Exactly!"

"But why the disguise?"

"It was for my protection and your's. Other Xychronians are here on Earth also. I did not want to give away my identity."

"What about our marriage? What will become of that?"

"We will still be married. But now, you will be my prince!"

"Prince Gordon Sakata?"

"Exactly!" she replied.

"The kids?" What about the kids? How are the children?"

"They're just fine. My assistant Christine has been helping me all along."

The children appeared with another woman named Christine. I embraced both Byron and Beverly, then turned to the woman.

"I can't thank you enough for helping my wife take care of the children. Your name again?"

"Hi Gordon!" she said. "I missed you. My real name is Christine. But you knew me as Bonnie."

"Bonnie? Don't tell me you're also from Xychron?"

"Yes. I came here with Kathy to help her look for a husband. And I think she's found gold in you!"

"But Your Highness? How can you and I be biologically compatible? I mean ..."

"That's because, we are biologically the same. On Earth's time many centuries ago, the Monarch of Napajan, in the ancient city of Kamanpura, sent a colony into the space in search of celestial civilizations beyond Earth's hemisphere. That exploration led to a planet just on the other side of the Sun, mirroring Earth's orbit. We are humans just like you."

"But," I asked with great amazement, "Why hasn't your planet showed up on celestial maps or through telescopes?"

"That's because the Sun acted as a natural curtain from your view. Our presence could have never been detected by your scientific equipment here on Earth."

"Then," I asked. "Has Earth been visited by creatures from other civilizations before?"

"Longer than you think. Remember, we have learned to travel through time. Inhabitants of Earth have yet to learn how to do that.

As for people on my planet, we have visited the Earth frequently. It's been like a vacation destination for us until now."

"I can't believe it!" I said.

So, I followed them into this grand inter-terrestrial craft as we prepared to depart.

Now, I know that in today's times, we do have inter-galactic vehicles. But this one definitely does not look anything that is of this world. It was a massive sliver ship. We took off from earth and after a few hours in flight, there was what was said to be my new destination, a new "earth," Xychron.

As we set course and were on our way to Xychron, I looked out a large window. Suddenly, Earth burst into a huge fireball. I don't know exactly what caused it but it must have been something serious and devastating to have exploded into little fragments. Kathy stood by the window besides me as we both watched the destruction of Earth.

"You know," she said. "The RNA lost the Battle of Napajan and eventually had to surrender to the Chinese."

"You're kidding?" I said. "What happened to the RNA after that?"

"The RNA went bankrupt and defaulted on all of its loans to the Chinese."

"Wow!" I wonder what happen to the country after that?

"A peace treaty was signed between China and the RNA under the condition that the RNA became a territory of China."

"A territory of China? Would they have agreed this?"

"With all the loans the RNA took out from China, the Chinese literally owned the RNA. It was their next best hope for survival. But rather than facing the fact of becoming a Chinese territory, the RNA literally committed nuclear suicide. It took the planet and the people of the world with them. All this could have been avoided. We might be able to save the planet." She said.

"Really? How?"

"This ship is capable of time travel. If we go back in time, you can give your story to someone in an earlier time period. Maybe someone can influence the way people and nations behave through your story so that they can change their ways before the 23rd Century even begins."

"The 23rd Century was influenced a lot by what happened in the 21st Century." I told her. "You know, as I was doing my research of Gordon Sakata I, I came across a friend of his who was a struggling writer by the name of Jason Shohara who also lived in Whittier. He had an old URL coded: www dot jasonshohara dot com. People used to write to him through a thing called "email" at <u>jasho1967 at live dot com</u>. Or that's what I recorded in my cell phone here. He lived during Gordon I's time and I think he would be a good one to drop off the diary. It says he was good at using technological devices. Maybe he will be able to figure out how to download the data off of this device."

"I'll instruct the commander to go to the 21st Century," said Kathy. "First or second half?"

"To be safe, at the turn of the century, between the 20th and 21st centuries, should be safe." I said.

"Very well," she answered.

The starship gradually picked up speed and made course in reverse orbit around the former Earth's rotation. As we were "spinning around," Earth came back into pieces in dizzying fashion. It took a while, but after several hundred rotations around the Earth, the ship started to slow to a hover over Whittier in the cover of night. Kathy came back into my quarters.

"We're here." She said. "Are you ready to be transported down?"

"Yes," I said. "I won't be long."

"Don't be," she warned. "You can't afford to be seen — especially in that bright orange jumpsuit."

As soon as I knew it, I was transported down in front of the house of Jason Shohara. I quietly walked up the path to his front door, s opened the mailbox and deposited the memory chip from my bionic arm. Then I walked to a clearing on the front lawn and signaled the hovering starship.

"I sure hope for the sake of mankind, this works out. If it doesn't the end of the Earth would have been the demise brought about by man and not by God. Alright..." I whispered and waited for a car to pass by. I think I've been seen by the driver. I hope not. But he stared at me as he slowly drove passed me.

"Okay, pick me up."

] Logout.
"Logging you off. Your batteries are dead! Shutting down now..."

PART II

CHAPTER 33

The Journey Home – Making Automobiles Obsolete

] Login, A. Gordon Sakata
"Welcome A. Gordon Sakata. Please enter today's date."
] Date: 0/0/0000
"Please enter the time."
] Time: 00:00
"Welcome to the Cyberspace living room"

I finally got my arm charged and it really feels good. But we've been travelling for a while en route to Xychron and I'm really at a loss as to what date and what time it really is. Since we went back in time, we've spun forward into present time, just short of when Earth blew up, and we're now on our way to Kathy's world.

I'm really excited about my new life on a new planet, a new world. From what they've told me, things will be much different there than it was on Earth. I knew that, by and large, it was going to be for the best for our children. I am just really amazed at how big the kids really grew in just a few short months! I was in the ship's nursery playing with the twins as Kathy entered from her briefing.

"Hi dear! How did your meeting go?"

"It went well. They wanted to know my whole life's story while I was on Earth. I spoke to mom and dad and they wanted to know how you were doing and that they are looking forward to meeting you. How are the kids?"

"I think they've had it for the day. Byron and Beverly will surely sleep well when we put them to bed."

"That's good! There's something I need to show you."

We picked up the kids, one each, and prepared them for bed, fed them, and put them to bed. I haven't done this since they were infants at the old house.

"Gordon," Kathy said, "The reason why were travelling in the royal cruiser is for yours and the children's convenience."

"What are you getting at?"

"Customarily, we don't travel like this."

"What?"

"Yes. We can travel without the use of a space vehicle or even a car!"

"But how can you do that"

"Watch, I'll be right back."

She closed her eyes, then disappeared as if she was vaporized.

"Where did she go?" I mumbled to myself.

Seconds later, she reappeared eating an apple from the tree apparently from our backyard.

"Wait a minute! How in the world did you do that? Are you some kind of magician?"

"Earthlings have been notorious and overly dependent on gasoline that they never bothered to explore the powers of their brains."

"Are you saying it's all in the mind?"

"Yes. Earthlings only use a small portion of their brains. They know that they have a soul, but they never use it."

"What are you getting at?" I asked.

"There's a lot to be said about the complacency of Earthlings. People had become so depended on material resources, that they've often raped the natural resources of Earth without replenishing the supply. Humans were always taking, but never giving back to Mother

Nature. Such as, oil. You have become so dependent on oil for profit that you never bothered to tell the world that the best way of transporting yourselves were for free! It wouldn't have cost anybody a cent, but to develop people's skills in using their brains for transporting themselves from one place to another.

"Exactly how much of the brain do you use?" I wondered.

"All of it!" she replied. "Not only that, we have learned to harness the powers of the soul. Some of you call it the 'Holy Spirit' within you. Even you, yourself, Gordon said on Earth, that the soul envelops the body. This is absolutely correct! The soul is as large as the universe! This is why you too can travel from one planet to another without using any type of vehicle."

"But how is this possible?" I asked."

"People often turn this switch on unconsciously. When people sleep, they go into REM sleep. At this stage of sleep, they can freely travel out of their bodies from one world to another and return instantaneously to 'base.' Have you ever wondered or remembered in your sleep about being in a distant land that wasn't anything like Earth? Reading signs on buildings that weren't in English or a familiar language?"

"Yes! Quite often!"

"That's because you were adventuring into other lands in your sleep. And, you didn't even use a car to get there. But, we can do this at the conscious level — while we're awake. And this requires more brain usage. Try it!"

"Nah! I can't do that! There's no way I can do that."

"That's because you haven't learned how to completely focus on just one thing. That is getting from one place to another."

"But how do you do that? When I think I'm concentrating on something, another thing comes into mind."

"That's the problems with Earthlings! You always have too much on your minds. Now try it."

I sat down and tried doing what she asked me to do. I concentrated and concentrated.

"No, I just can't do it. It's impossible." I said.

"That's the other problem" she said. "You just said it yourself, that you 'can't do it.' Empty your mind and focus, or concentrate on just one thing. Think of just that one place where you would dearly love to be … some place beautiful. And keep your mind's eye focused on that destination."

"Yes, I think I know what you're saying." I told her while shutting my eyes tightly.

"Now, tell your soul," she instructed, "take me there!"

No sooner after she said that, I was immediately mentally teleported back to the lake on the mountain where I was rescued. Oddly enough, I landed near Gordon I's grave where I retrieved his ring, then shut my eyes, concentrated again, and focused my destination on our quarters in the starship where I left. Magically, as soon as I entered the thought, "take me there," I was transformed back into the cruiser standing in front of Kathy.

"You did it!" she said. "Congratulations! What's that you have in your hand?"

"It's the twin ring that I got from Gordon I. I'm sure he would want it passed along to the next of kin – especially when I have the other ring."

"That would be lovely." she said. "Now we have a matching set."

I put the extra ring in a safe place, but as I did so, I still wondered about the magical or mysterious powers of the rings. What did these rings have in store for me? Or was it only a family myth?

"We will be arriving on Xychron in one day." said the captain. "Please prepare for arrival."

We actually came into Xychron's orbit at that moment, but it took a few orbits to slow the ship down to land. As I looked out the window, I saw several continents separated by large crystal clear oceans that were deep blue with polar ice caps much like that at the North and South Poles. There were many beautiful mountain ranges like the Rocky Mountains on the continent of the RNA with snow-covered peaks, tall green trees and crystal clear lakes. There were also open plains but I didn't notice any major areas of barren land like desserts.

From the air, I noticed several large rivers and tributaries which fed into the oceans. All-in-all, the planet was very similar to Earth.

There were clouds that lofted over parts of the planet like on Earth and moved gently across the planet in an easterly direction. Xychron very much had a similar atmosphere to Earth. The atmosphere was much better than Los Angeles. There was a definite absence of air pollution as well as water pollution. Just before we landed, Kathy informed me that she would have the royal medical staff look at my bionic arm. On Xychron, there is an accelerated stem cell program that may give me a brand new, live real arm altogether. Wow!

I have to prepare for landing.

] Logout.
"Good-bye A. Gordon Sakata. Come back soon."

CHAPTER 34

A New Home – A New Life

] Login, A. Gordon Sakata

"Welcome A. Gordon Sakata. Please enter today's date."

] Date: 0/0/0000

"Please enter the time."

] Time: 00:00

"Welcome to the Cyberspace living room."

That was the smoothest landing I've ever experienced in such a large craft. The doors flung open, and there was a massive crowd gathered on the landing pad. Kathy and I gathered the children and we followed Christine, the Captain, and crew out the door as the cheers from the crowds rose to a deafening roar.

To meet us were Kathy's parents, His Majesty the Emperor Gabriel and, Her Majesty the Empress Juliana. It was my first time being in front of royalty besides Kathy and I really was beside myself. I really didn't know how to behave so I followed Christine's lead.

"Gordon," said the Emperor, "It's a pleasure meeting you my son. Katherine has told me all about you. May I present my wife, Empress Juliana."

I bowed and kissed the hand of the Empress.

"I am extremely honored to meet you your majesty." I said to the Empress.

"The pleasure is mine, Gordon," said the Empress. "Thank you so very much for taking care of our daughter, Katherine."

"The honor is mine, my Lady."

"Ladies and Gentlemen!" said the Emperor in a raised voice. "Welcome home Princess Katherine and Prince Gordon Sakata!"

The cheers of the crowd grew even louder and louder as we were escorted off the landing pad and into transport vehicles that made absolutely no noise. As we left the air facility, we drew nearer to the city I could see skyscrapers taller than the tallest buildings I've ever seen on Earth. In fact, these buildings dwarfed the tallest ones in Manhattan. Then there was some green clearance. It was a huge estate with a lot of trees and open space, which was unusual within a typical city boundary.

Then the motorcade turned up a gradual sloping hill and there stood a palace. It was rather odd, I said to myself, as the vehicles circled around the plaza to the main entrance. There were no gates, not even armed guards!

"Kathy? Back on Earth, in a place like this, there would be armed guards and soldiers crawling all over the place. Do you have any here?"

"No. We have no need for weapons here. We don't even manufacture weapons on this planet. There's no need to. Only a planet that lives in hostility, rules by the proverbial sword, creates borders amongst them, and lives like animals, have weapons. Only creatures of lower level thinking need weapons. Here we live in absolute peace, harmony, and tranquility."

"I guess there's a lot I'm going to have to learn — an awful lot in my new life."

"Come on. They're asking us get out and to follow them into the palace."

We followed the royal staff through several large room and hallways. I was really amazed with the classical-style paintings, murals, and tapestry that adorned the walls and the hallways. The ceilings were artwork in itself and I was caught breathless at the masterpieces in each panel that was in the ceiling of the Emperor's living room.

"How do you like our living room, Gordon?" asked the Emperor.

"I like it very much, Sir." I said. "It reminds me of some of the palaces I've visited on Earth. Yet, in a way, some parts of it remind me of a hotel I stayed in downtown Los Angeles. It was the Biltmore Hotel."

"I've stayed there on several occasions also!" Emperor said.

"You have? When have you been there?"

"On Earth's time, it was during the early 20th Century. That is where I got some of my ideas. If course, I didn't go there looking like royalty. I went looking like a typical travelling businessperson."

"Yes," I said, "Katherine told me about your amazing abilities for intergalactic travel. I only wished people on Earth had known about this a long time ago."

"Yes. The problem with Earthlings is that they're too busy fighting each other. Nations there need to do like what had happened during the turn of the 20th and 21st Century."

"Really? What that might be?"

"There was this wall in Berlin that divided East and West," he said. "That was a turning point in Earth's history momentarily. It was the will of the people that brought down that wall that separated them. That's what needs to happen amongst all nations. Here, we do not have that problem. Xychron is one planet, one nation – we all have a common cause and a common interest."

"Amazing!" I said. "Utterly amazing!"

"Dinner is served," a staff member of the Emperor said.

"Very well," Emperor said. "Let us proceed into the grand dining hall."

As we proceeded into the grand dining hall, I was surprised by the change of décor. It was a huge change from the classical style design in the living room to a more casual, contemporary look in the great hall. In fact, dress was very informal. The hall was so large that it appeared that the entire population of the city could fit inside. And that's exactly what had happened. Everyone was invited to a grand dinner.

"Katherine, Gordon," asked the Emperor. "I hope you don't mind, but I've invited the residents of the city to join us on your homecoming."

"Oh sure," said Kathy. "That's perfectly fine with me."

I was taken back for a moment. I had never been to such a huge celebration before. I felt as if I was some kind of celebrity – which I guess being a prince I was exactly that. But, somehow, it didn't get to my head. I felt as if I belonged to the people and that's the way it should have been and as long as I'm living, always will be. I think Kathy felt exactly the same way. As a matter of fact, I really don't have the impression that her family is into all the pomp and circumstances like royal families were back on Earth. This is truly a different kind of royalty.

It was a simple, but elegant dinner. The beverage was something that I've never had before and there was definitely the absence of alcoholic beverages – not even wine or beer.

"Kathy?" I asked.

"Yes, Sweetheart?" she replied.

"Do you have any alcoholic beverages on this planet?"

"No. We have a similar substance that is similar but it's mostly frowned upon here." She explained. "We don't have large brewing companies or distilleries like that back on Earth. Alcohol-like substance typically destroys brain cells, and it's not good for clear thinking, especially when you're traveling from planet to planet. If you're toasted, you can miss your target just by being off by a mere tenth of a degree."

"So you do sell these kinds of beverages here?"

"We don't sell anything here." She said. "I'll tell you more about this later when I take you around the town. Anyway, please meet my friend Shahab."

"I'm very happy to meet you."

"The pleasure is mine."

"Shahab's ancestors came to Xychron aboard the original exploratory space expedition from Earth. It is said that Shahab's ancestors were Iranian."

"What do you do?" I asked.

"I am an actor."

"Really?" I responded, "I do some performance myself."

"Is that so?" he said. "What are your talents?"

"I sang in a large choral ensemble."

"That's great!" he said. "Xychron has a great choral program. The princess is going to have to introduce you to their music director."

"How about it Katherine?" I asked.

"All in time," she said. "All in time. The night is growing old. I think it's time that we retire to our quarters. We have to take a trip to our own house tomorrow after a good night's rest here."

"You mean," I said, "we're not staying here?"

"Oh no!" she said. "Our place is on the other side of the 'pond.'"

"Exactly how big is this 'pond?'" I asked.

"Well," she responded. "Do you remember flying over that huge body of water before we landed?"

"Vaguely, yes." I said.

"We have a castle in the mountains on the other side of that ocean" she said.

"Way over there?"

"Yes. Good evening, Shahab."

"Have a nice night to the two of you"

"It was a pleasure meeting you." I said as I shook his hand.

We went to our temporary quarters to retire for the night.

] Logout.

"Good-bye A. Gordon Sakata. Come back soon."

CHAPTER 35

Moving Day

] Login, A. Gordon Sakata
"Welcome A. Gordon Sakata. Please enter today's date."
] Date: 0/0/0000
"Please enter the time."
] Time: 00:00
"Welcome to the Cyberspace living room."

Computer, I am going to reprogram you since your date and time format is really incompatible to what's here on Xychron.

] Deactivate Date Sequence
"Date Sequence Deactivated"
] Deactivate Time Sequence
"Time Sequence Deactivated"
] Reboot
REBOOTING

]Login, A Gordon Sakata
"Welcome A. Gordon Sakata"

We had breakfast this morning with the Emperor and the Empress in the family dining room, and we casually talked about our plans for the future of the children's education. When the twins grow older, they will return to the palace to receive their education under the supervision of the Emperor and Empress. We decided on Xychron, as I found out from Kathy, the grandparents are responsible for educating the children during their adolescent years until they are teenagers. Kathy explained that the Palace staff had an outstanding educational program, and children from the community were often sent to the Palace school for their early and elementary education.

We prepared for our departure in the Kathy's starship that brought us here since I still have to do a little more practice in travelling using the technique of mental teleportation. As Kathy said, if you are off by the slightest degree, you'll be off course by thousands of miles. Kathy's castle was more like a semi-palace. She had her own staff, and I guess it would be safe to say, "our" staff of assistants. Christine was one of them, but she was the personal assistant to Kathy. So, as we were preparing for departure, I was really excited about living in a castle. The twins, however, had their own opinions. And, I think the long enduring journey from Earth to Xychron was catching up. They were getting a bit cranky, and Byron wanted a lot of attention. Beverly wasn't that far behind. But she definitely was mom's girl.

We said our fond farewell to the royal couple as the ship lifted off the landing pad. It was only a ten minute flight from one side of the sea to the other side. And I guess the analogy of a "pond" was pretty accurate.

We loaded the caravan of transports and travelled through several winding villages. But unlike the shantytowns on Earth, people here lived in dwellings the size of mansions. There wasn't a "single family" home, condo, townhouse, or apartment, to speak of anywhere in sight. They were all very large complexes. As we passed through the streets I also noticed the absence of private motor vehicles. I guess that's because Xychronians travel by mental teleportation.

"Kathy?" I asked.

"Yes, Dear?"

"Are most vehicles large transport vehicles like trucks, busses, and transports?"

"That's a good observation. Most vehicles here are large because they carry merchandise or equipment that you can't carry if you're commuting mentally. Or, if you are traveling with a group of people, like we are."

"Yesterday, you said that you don't sell things here."

"That's correct. There's absolutely no use for a monetary system here. We are not on a gold or some kind of precious metal standard or oil standard like they used on Earth. That's because we don't have very much of these metals here. Besides it's useless to us. People are our most valuable assets. Our, so to speak, 'monetary standard' is based on people, not metals."

"So, how much are people worth on this planet?" I asked.

"People are priceless!" she said. "You really can't put a price tag on people. What we have done is give each individual universal life credits. On Earth, these credits would be worth well over $25 million a year.

"Twenty-five million a year?" I said. "That's incredible."

"Not really. Each individual is eligible for this amount once he or she is born. The 25 million universal credits are placed into a trust. When the individual turns adulthood at 18 years, then he or she is eligible for 25 million universal life credits each year for life. That is, each individual maintains balance of 25 million universal credits per year. The amount renews automatically at the beginning of each year."

"So what about our children?" I asked.

"The children now have 25 million universal life credits each into their own accounts." She replied. "We are the executors of their estate."

"And me?" I asked.

"The same," she replied. "Except, your account renews automatically each year. It replenishes each and every year for life."

"So, what you are saying, is that I would not have to buy a thing for the rest of my life."

"All you have to do is just ask for it."

"But do people have different amounts in their accounts? Is there a social class system here like there was on Earth?"

"No, everybody here is treated equally no matter if you are of royalty or if you are a commoner. We are all the same. Therefore, we're credited the same – no more, no less."

"But why the need for palaces and castles?" I wondered.

"That's because we have to host people from other celestial systems frequently. They need somewhere special to stay."

"Talk about castles," she said, "here we are. Welcome home, Dear."

I got out of the transport vehicle and stood in absolute amazement and astonishment. This castle was huge! It wasn't a medieval castle like that of the ancient earthly times, but the grounds were enormous, the buildings were huge! I was really afraid of becoming lost in this place. Around the castle's grounds were tall trees, a lot of grass, and the most beautiful flowers I have ever seen in my life.

"Kathy?" I asked as we were walking into the castle. "Am I in Heaven?"

"No silly! This is Xychron. It's not a perfect place. From what I've heard, Heaven is much better. But I think you will like it here better than Earth."

] Logout.
"Good-bye A. Gordon Sakata. Come back soon."

CHAPTER 36

Time for Rest & Relaxation

] Login, A. Gordon Sakata
"Welcome A. Gordon Sakata."

It was a gorgeous day. It's about 75-degrees and unbelievably clear. After breakfast, we put the kids in wheel-less strollers and Kathy took me for a tour of the castle grounds. My favorite part of the tour was a lake with what looked like to be a weeping-willow. In the distance were twin waterfalls that ever so gently poured water into the lake. We sat under a weeping-willow and decided that that place was going to be our "official" picnic spot.

"Sweetheart?" asked Kathy as we sat, leaned up against the trunk of the tree. "You really haven't missed the meat during meals have you?"

"You know? Now that you come to mention it, I didn't really notice its absence."

"We're vegans here. We don't consume meat like the people did on earth."

"But you ate some down on Earth. Didn't you?"

"I had some on occasion. But only on rare occasions, like when it was with you. Do you think you'll have a hard time adjusting to the absence of it here?"

"Nah! Besides, I wasn't supposed to have very much of it anyway. Though the many years that I had uncontrolled high blood pressure starting when I was about eighteen, I gradually developed chronic renal failure. As long as I keep my blood pressure under control, I won't need dialysis for a while."

"Speak about your health," she said, "I'm going to send you to the Royal Physician about your arm. I think she can replace your bionic arm with a real one."

"For real? I mean, I thought you were kidding when we were coming here in the starship."

"No, I'm not kidding. Remember back on Earth, they were still debating as to the value of stem cell research?"

"Yes. The debate started in the turn of the 21st Century and kept on going through the 23rd Century."

"Well, on Xychron, it's common practice. It's not a debated issue. We discovered its importance and benefits eons ago. I think it will help you regenerate a new arm."

"That would be lovely!" I said.

We stood up and walked the babies back to the nursery where Christine and another assistant took care of them for the remainder of the afternoon while we went and toured the village.

"Driver," said Kathy, "stop here."

"Where are we?"

"You'll have to see this place." said Kathy. "This is a typical example of an elementary school."

We walked inside the school room.

"Good afternoon, Prince and Princess Sakata," said the classroom.

"Good afternoon, children," we said simultaneously.

"Typically, older adults will teach the younger children of elementary school levels the basics of reading, writing, and mathematics, as well as basic social skills such as interpersonal interaction and creative thinking."

"Are they tested?" I asked.

"No. We don't have standardized testing like that of Earth. We have very high standards and expectations of performance and each individual student is evaluated on those standards. Those who fail to meet those standards are given special attention. By and large, most children either meet or exceed those performance standards. Their parents are expected to participate in their child's development at every step of their lives – especially, during their early developmental stages. For that matter, so are the grandparents. The grandparents of the children have just as much a responsibility for the development, discipline and well-being of their grandchildren. The entire family must participate actively in the development and education of the children. It is not just the responsibility of the educational system. Back on Earth, parents were too busy with their careers that they left the children to the care of day care facilities, schools, and other institutions for their development. A strong family bond in these households never effectively developed."

"What if the parents and grandparents fail to meet that responsibility?"

"Then they are sent to mandatory remedial parenting camps. Some say it is like the boot camps of the militaries on Earth."

"I am genuinely impressed."

"Wait until you see our next stop."

"Where are we going to next?"

"Were going to a typical, but representative high school."

We got in the transport vehicle and resumed our tour. As we continued to drive, I had even more questions about life on Xychron.

"Tell me something." I asked. "Are people paid to work?"

"No." she said. "That's why people here seem so contented. They work because they for the enjoyment of it. It's not like on Earth where people worked because they had to earn money for a living, to pay the house rent, the bills, and so on. This makes it convenient because employers do not have to pay salaries or benefits. All employers have to do is invest in facilities, research, and provide a place to work."

"And banking?" I asked. "Do you have banks here?"

"It's really not like the banks that were on Earth. There's a universal bank that manages all the life credits. If you pass away, your funds are deposited into a common pool and redistributed. It's automatically willed to the world. And since everything is under one currency, there's no need for currency exchanges like there was on Earth."

"Where does the money come from?"

"The Universe," she said. "The Universe has an unlimited supply of what you call 'money.' All Xychron has to do is tap into that resource. Many planets have utilized this invaluable resource."

"But why hasn't it been made known on Earth? Why do nations on earth not know or use this resource?"

"It has been kept a long dark secret by the leaders of your planet for generations. Utilizing this resource is not mandated by the Universe. But some found that they can control their people and economies better if they created their own monetary systems even if it meant that only a fraction of the population would benefit from it. They would say the people are getting enough of what they need, but in reality, it's a struggle for the majority of the population to make ends meet, let alone survive sufficiently. You often heard of stories on Earth where royalty often kept the real money while the peasants got only the pennies. That's not the case here."

"What about immigration? Back on Earth, there were border patrols, customs agents, military, and everything you can think of just to secure the borders from undesirable enemies."

"Not here. We have no enemies here. Like dad said, we have no borders between countries and nations like that on Earth. We are all equals as citizens of one world, one planet. That's what makes us different than your former world. We don't even have spies or espionage agencies. If we have something technologically to share, we share it with the whole planet. We're not doing it for the money; it's being done for the best interest of the people – not for any singular individual, company, or government. The whole planet is one nation"

"Wow! This is so mind boggling. It's very hard to comprehend."

"It's really a simple form of managing the planet — at least for Xychron, that is. Earth has only made it complicated because of all the different forms of governments that were created on the planet. Nations couldn't come together as one. They never could come to an agreement. There was always a degree of mistrust among them. That's why there were frequent wars among nations."

"That's a good point." I said. "Have others made this observation about Earth?"

"More than you think. And, there have been many warnings sent to Earth by God and others that were never heeded."

"Others?" I asked. "What others?"

"A lot of Earth's visitations came by way of what Earthlings called 'unidentified flying objects.' Many of these vehicles attempted to send messages to your governments but were unsuccessful because your governments often attempted to block their signals while trying to cover up their presence. There were many skeptics on Earth that said that they simply did not exist. They were blind to the fact to say the least. They called themselves 'scientists' but they, themselves, often worked on faulty scientific premises. Science that was of the lowest types in the universe — that which was highly flawed. Yet, they often passed themselves as 'experts' in their fields."

"I'm afraid I even asked. That's quite an observation!"

"On Xychron, It's not unusual for people to speak directly to God. You will see them speaking directly to Him frequently. I do it all the time. Remember the weeping-willow tree? That's where I like to talk to God. The problem on Earth is that there was too much harmonic distortion and interference — especially as technology took over the world. There were more things to distract people. People just didn't take the time out to listen to God anymore. They went ahead and did things on their own and claimed that they were being 'guided by God.' In reality, they never got his messages."

"Okay. We have arrive at our next stop. All out!"

We got out of the transport to look around of what appeared to be a college campus.

"So is this one of your typical college campuses?" I asked.

"No. Our colleges and universities are much larger. This is a typical high school."

"You're kidding! This doesn't look like a typical high school to me."

"That's because, our high schools are more equivalent to your community colleges on Earth. Students here are allowed to choose and customize their curriculum to meet their own individual goals, needs, and objectives. Here, we encourage the continuation of the basic skills of reading, writing and mathematics to a higher level. And by the time they get to this level, they have been prepared for higher levels of education. But here, we also encourage, like we do in the lower educational levels, the creative arts — instrumental music, choral arts, dance, acting, the performing arts, visual arts, as well as sports. Our educational system attempts to develop the whole individual — not just a part of him or her. Back on Earth, and especially in the RNA, there was a continuous movement towards standardized testing. That didn't really assist developing better, well-rounded students. In fact, they often eliminated the arts and sports all together. That would be going against the Emperor's policies here on Xychron."

"So, I assume that the arts in education are well funded?"

"It's not that they have to be funded. Remember that we don't pay for anything here. Arts education is a mandate from the Universe. Educational systems and school districts will provide arts education. And they have to show proof that they are doing it through concerts, festivals, and grand international competitions, like the ones that the Emperor himself, hosts near the Palace. I'll have to take you to a few of them."

"I would enjoy that very much."

"You were in the choral arts back in Los Angeles. Let's see if the choir here is rehearsing. There is a festival coming up soon."

As we drew near the rehearsal hall, I could hear sounds of voices singing. The work that they were rehearsing was well familiar to me. It was the sounds of Ralph Vaughan Williams' *Dona Nobis Pacem*.

"Kathy? That piece was written by Ralph Vaughan Williams centuries ago back on Earth. How did it get here?"

"We imported it. Remember, we visit there a lot. Travelers do bring back souvenirs once in a while!"

"I guess so."

The sound was beautiful. This didn't sound like an ordinary high school choir. It sounded more like a well rehearsed professional or university ensemble.

As we walked out the choir's rehearsal room, brass blared and percussion drumming in the background. I was fascinated by the sounds and drawn towards what appeared to be like a soccer field.

"Does Xychron have soccer teams?"

"We have some very good ones. But on Xychron, they are called football teams."

"But what you're going to see on the field is not a football team."

"It's the equivalence of what is called a 'drum and bugle corps' on Earth."

"I've heard of those. I had an ancestor that performed in one."

"The one that you are going to see is called the 'Royal Emissaries.' They are rehearsing for the Xychronian World Championships in Augre."

"When?"

"Oh, that would be like in August on your calendar. The Royal Emissaries is one of the most successful corps in the world. They have won numerous world championships."

"Are they professional?"

"No. Everything on Xychron is amateur — voluntary. We do not have professional sports or music organizations like on Earth. Shall we watch them rehearse for a while?"

"Yes, please. I would be very interested in that."

] Logout.
"Good-bye A. Gordon Sakata. Come back soon."

———————

CHAPTER 37

The Royal Hospital

] Login, A. Gordon Sakata

Kathy made good on her promises today. We left the kids under Christine's care while I was taken to the Royal Family's physician given a complete physical examination. Dr. Mitra Howard was the attending physician that looked at my arm and assessed my renal failure.

"The bionic arm," she said, "was a little antiquated and will not serve you very well here. You can't get replacement batteries here because we don't manufacture them, and we don't have the technology to replace your arm the way it is presently constructed. Don't get me wrong, we can give you a new arm, but it will be a real arm, not a mechanical one like the one you have right now. As for your kidney failure, we can easily remedy that with no problem. It will take a couple of weeks. But by and large, when treatment is over with, you should feel like a new Xychronian."

"But Ma'am," I said in response. "I'm a former Earthling."

"That would explain for the bionic arm and the kidney failure. You see, kidney failure here on Xychron has been non-existent for almost eighty centuries! The last time someone had a bionic limb was well over ten centuries ago!" as she turned to Kathy.

"Princess Katherine. I'm sorry, but we're going to have to keep the Prince here for at least two weeks or more."

"That's fine doctor. Please take good care of him. Gordon, they will take very good care of you here. They might put you to sleep for the next two weeks. But when you awake, you'll be a completely new person!"

"I know I shouldn't feel that worried. But I really am scared as to what's going to happen."

"Don't worry. Everything is going to be just fine. When you awake, I'll be right here."

"Promise?"

"I promise."

Then she departed from the hospital and left me to my own devices with the doctor. I was taken to a ward at which time I was shown a hologram of a place very beautiful. It had a hypnotic effect. In fact, it put me to sleep for the next two weeks.

The team of physicians drew blood to harvest stem cells from my body and did something to make them multiply in the laboratory. There were essentially two sets. The first tray contained cells for the regeneration of my arm. The second tray contained cells necessary for reversing the kidney damage.

About a week into the process, they injected the new stem cells into both my failing kidneys which immediately took effect on reversing the damage.

As for the bionic arm, I was taken into the operating room where the arm was removed. Stem Cells from the other tray were injected into my shoulders as the cells rapidly started to regenerate a new arm. This took a week longer than expected. All the while, I was still a sleep. (When they referred to as an "accelerated stem cell program," they really were serious.) By the time I awoke, I realized that I had a brand new, real arm. It reacted much faster, more naturally, and it was even my own skin tone — even real flesh! Amazing! I actually had feeling and strength going down my right arm.

That portion of my brain that was also bionic was also changed to real flesh. The only thing extra that they did was implant Xychronian components which included a tracking module and added memory capacity. Now, instead of being able to be found anywhere on a continent, I can be found anywhere in the universe!

The other thing now, is that I can't log either on or off.

When I came out of the recovery room, Kathy was there to greet me.

"How are you doing, Sweetheart?" she said in a soft voice. "I was very worried about you. Mom and dad send their regards and hope that you're feeling better."

"Thank you, dear," I said. "Really, I feel like a new person. There's so much different about me now that I really don't know what to do."

"Just do what the doctors say and rest. With a little bit of therapy, you'll feel like a new Xychronian!"

"I guess it's going to take some time healing."

"The doctors said you're doing well enough to go home today. How does that sound?"

"The sooner we get home, the better. But I still don't know how they put me to sleep without any anesthesia!"

"Oh! I forgot to tell you, we don't use that here. We use guided imagery. It's much less invasive than the chemicals. And knowing you, you get combative when you awake from anesthesia!"

"You can say that again!" I said. "But now, I've lost my diary. What am I going to do now?"

"Your new Xychronian jumpsuit as all the amenities that you once had, plus more" she replied.

"Plus more?" I asked. "Like what?"

"First of all, it will protect you from the elements. Remember the jumpsuit they gave you in camp? This one is far more advanced. This one is fire-retardant, heat resistant, and resistant to freezing cold weather."

"Is that all?"

"No." Just merely think about what you want to record in your diary, and it will record your thoughts. So be careful of what you really want to say."

"Anything else?"

"Yes," she added. "You don't have to log on or log off any more.

There's one other feature that I almost forgot to mention. Your new jumpsuit has cloaking capabilities. It will give you invisibility on any planet except for Xychron."

"That's fantastic! But why the exception of Xychron?"

"This is for security and safety reasons. Being invisible on the streets will not protect you from the vehicles on the streets. They cannot see you. So when you are on other planets, be careful." she said, "However, there is one thing that we need to do."

"What's that?" I asked.

"We need to program the days of the week into your new jumpsuit."

"How do we do that?"

"Simply remember the days in Xychronian terms," she said. "We have a similar cycle like that on Earth. There are seven days of the week beginning with what you called as 'Sunday.' Sunday is Sunctus. Monday is Munctus. Tuesday is Septus. Wednesday is Vintus. Thursday is Quatus. Friday is Cinctus. And Saturday is Virtus."

"Let me see if I have this right," as I repeated the days back slowly. "Sunday is Sunctus … Monday is Munctus … Tuesday is Septus … Wednesday is Vintus … Thursday is Quatus … Friday is Cinctus … And, Saturday is Virtus!"

"That's right" she said. "Well done! So what's today?

"I don't know. The last time I saw you it was Vintus before I went to sleep. But since then, I lost track of time."

"Today is Quatus. Now if you ever need help, just think 'help day,' and a hologram will appear before you and will list out the days of the week. Give it a try."

So I merely thought about it and said to myself "help day" and sure enough, a holographic image appeared before my eyes listing the days of the week.

"Now, for the months of the year," she continued. "Again, we our calendar is very similar to Earth's. We have a twelve month calendar and the names of the month are a very similar also. So what you would call January is Janre. February is Febre. March is Mare. April is Abre. May is Mai. June is Junre. July is Julre. August is Augre. September is Sepre. October is Octre. November is Novre. And, December is Decre.

Do you think you have it? Your jumpsuit has been recording that. Just say 'help months.'"

"Help months," I said. "January is Janre. February is Febre. March is Mare. April is Abre. May is Mai. June is Junre. July is Julre. August is Augre. September is Sepre. October is Octre. November is Novre. And, December is Decre!"

"Perfect!" she said. "Now the time is ten-hundred hours. We operate on the twenty-four hour clock here."

"It is now," I said. "Ten o'clock."

"Now," she said, "There's just one final thing to program … the year. On Xychron, the current year is 3309."

"So," I said, "On Xychronian equivalence, the children were born on the eleventh of Abre 3308 is that correct?"

"That's correct. And the birth records will reflect that."

"So I believe we're ready to go home. What do you think?"

"I think so too! Let's get out of here."

CHAPTER 38

Project Noah's Ark

In the evening after supper, we retired into the living room where we took the twins. The kids had grown considerably since we have arrived, but they had still not begun to walk. However, they were little speed demons. I even had a hard time catching up with them and this castle provides them with a lot of room to zip around in.

We've set up toddler gates to entrances just so they wouldn't go past certain areas. Especially to those leading up or down stairways. And, there were several leading to the living room area.

I was talking and doing a little reading to Kathy as Beverly came crawling up to my chair. She climbed up my legs.

"Look honey!" I said to Kathy. "I think Beverly is going to start walking today."

Our eyes were fixed on Beverly as she struggled to gain her balance on two feet. After establishing her first stance, she stood at the base of my feet with a great smile. Then she turned to Kathy.

"Come here, Sweetie!" said Kathy.

Beverly attempted to take one small step forward unassisted. I was almost ready to help.

"No," Kathy said. "Let her do it on her own."

Then she took another step forward, then another. Yet, another. Then, Beverly discovered her newly found way of moving around the castle and walked towards Kathy as we looked in amazement at her accomplishment. When she reached Kathy, she gave her a big hug.

Meanwhile, Byron's day in the sun was about to happen very quickly. As Beverly was struggling to stand up. Byron was rolling on the carpet giggling with Christine and having a grand time.

Then, as Byron crawled to Christine, he attempted to standup with her aid.

After gaining his balance, Christine helped him turn around while standing and pointed him in my direction.

"Come here!" I said to Byron. "Come to daddy!"

Then, Byron began to take his first steps. It was a miracle. Both children walking on the same day. I know our lives would never be the same.

The kids eventually became very tired after all the excitement in the living room, and it was past their bed time. After we put them to bed, we returned to the living room. I was still interested in the story about this space exploration that Kathy always talks about, and I thought now would be a good time to find out more about this adventure.

"Kathy?" I asked. "You mentioned bits and pieces about this space probe that was launched in ancient Napajan. Could you tell me more about that probe?"

"Sure. As you know, the ancient city of Kamanpura on the island of Napajan was an advanced civilization of the world around the days of the Aztecs and the Mayan Indian tribes. It existed around the time of Atlantis."

"I've heard of Atlantis," I said. "But why hasn't Kamanpura nor Napajan ever been written recorded into the history books?"

"That's because the nation was too small. It was often over looked compared to the other great civilizations of the times. But actually, Napajan had a more advanced civilization than any other. It was visited by more outer celestial visitors than any other civilization at the time. The government had a gift for foretelling events well into the future."

"So what happened? How did this exploration come about."

"Project Noah's Ark," she said. "was initiated by the original great Monarch of Napajan who resided in the ancient capital of Kamanpura. He foretold that great catastrophic changes were about to happen on Earth so he created a space probe that included couples of every race in the world and every animal that ever existed onto this starship to find a planet suitable for sustaining life like as it were on Earth. That probe led to here, Xychron three-thousand-three-hundred-nine years ago."

"Was he on that expeditionary team?"

"Yes, he led the team. He was commander of the starship. Napajan was the only country to have such a vehicle in its days."

"Did he have any relatives?"

"Yes. I am one of his descendants. He also left behind brothers and sisters on Earth. Many of the relatives fled to the United States in the 1930s when civil strife broke out in Napajan that ousted the reigning monarch and replaced it with another one.

"So, your people are actually humans transplanted?"

"Exactly. We've just adjusted throughout time to a different environment."

"Then what about the institution of marriage? When we left, interracial marriages were outlawed."

"Interracial marriages are common practice here." She said. "That's why you see a lot of people with mixed blood. There's no one dominant race here on Xychron. That's why we consider ourselves as one — one race, one being."

"Then what about gays and lesbians? Back on Earth, they were treated very harshly and inhumane."

"Why should they be treated any differently than anyone else?" she said. "They contribute just as much to our society as anyone else and should be treated as equals and no differently. They have been accepted into our fabric of society since the inception of our civilization."

"So, if your civilization existed for more than 3000 years, what does that say about the original lunar exploration projects that the United States performed in the 20th Century? They say they put the first man on the moon."

"And that is correct. However, we had no use for the moon. The moon couldn't sustain life there. Human colonies have existed on other planets long before the United States ever put a man on the moon!"

"Then why wasn't this ever made known?" I asked.

"Governments always kept it a secret in fear that there would be a panic among its people. It was a way to control the people of nations. It was a way to hold back progress."

"So this is how Xychron got its start?"

"Yes."

"Then does Xychron conduct any commercial commerce with anybody?"

"We occasionally do some business with some countries on Earth. But most of our commerce comes from other planets. We're very selective of whom we do business with. Some planets tend to be warring planets. Earth is a borderline planet. We are very selective of the nations we do business with there. As for the warring planets, we don't do business with them, nor they with us."

"But, you said that you don't manufacture any weapons here. What do you use for your defenses?"

"Our minds. Our minds are our first line of defense."

"But how can that be? Your minds can't stop a nuclear attack."

"You'll be surprised what the total mind can do. Remember that I taught you how to travel from place to place using your mind?"

"Yes."

"You can use your mind to control the rate of speed, the rate of motion, the time of day, and so forth. If you shot a bullet at me, I can slow the speed of that bullet the time it leaves the gun! It would never touch me!"

"That's impossible!" I said. "No one is that fast."

"That's true. But the speed of a bullet is very slow! Watch. Throw something at me as hard as you can."

So I looked around and found a rock that was used as a paper weight. I threw it at her as hard and as fast as I could. As soon as it left my hand, it was as if it went into instantaneous slow motion. She stepped out if its trajectory. Then the rock went back into real-time, full motion. The rock flew right past her without even coming close to her.

"We have the ability to see what's going to happen even before it happens," She said. "Then we can take corrective measures in defending ourselves without having to resort to a counter weapon."

"Eventually, you will learn how do to do this over time. If there were a nuclear attack, we can immediately evacuate and escape using mental teleportation to a safe planet at a moment's notice. Our children are taught this in pre-school. The twins will be taught this when they go to the Palace School."

CHAPTER 39

First Day at School

When the twins turned three years old we decided to send them to Palace School. We hadn't seen Kathy's parents for a while and they'd been dying to have a big ceremony for us and have been pushing us to at least renew our wedding vows Xychronian style. So, we departed our village in our star cruiser for a flight across the pond and landed at the place where we were greeted by the Emperor and the Empress.

By now, I have mastered the art of mental-teleportation commuting and have found it quite easy. I struggled at first with a few misses during a couple of errands. But I eventually have become a lot better at hitting my destinations. In fact, I've become so good at it that Kathy and I go on excursions together using this mode of transportation. We've been to Earth and back for some short vacations using her old house as our retreat and taking some walks up to Henniger Flats which were reminiscent of the old days. The only thing I can't do anymore is take the shortcut! Just before we departed Earth's orbit, we left the planet intact giving them a second chance hoping that the message will get across and will have an impact on their society. Hopefully this had stemmed the destruction of Earth. Apparently, it had – at least, for now. At least, the times when we returned to the vacation house, it was still there.

We were given a tour of the Palace School as it had been a while since Kathy attended, and it had been renovated and rebuilt since then. It was much larger and looked more like a small campus now, she said. We were taken into some of the classrooms where the children were learning about different things including learning about different evacuation exercises. In fact, when I walked into one room, the kids disappeared on an evacuation exercise — then, reappeared about 30 seconds later.

We left the twins with their first teacher. It was a sad moment. They didn't want to leave our sides, and both kids had terrible separation and emotional experiences. Byron was holding onto my leg tightly and didn't want to let go as he cried for about five minutes. Beverly was having similar experiences with Kathy. Finally, we got them to let go of us and we hugged them both and assured them that everything was going to be fine and gave them our love. Then their teacher escorted them into the classroom where they immediately adapted to the new surroundings as if were night and day.

We walked back to go visit for a while with mom and dad. Kathy and her mother went in one direction, and the Emperor took me in another direction.

"Gordon," the Emperor said, "there's one room here that I have to show you."

We walked together through a long hallway as I stopped to look again at more artwork along the way. Kathy and the Empress joined us at another point along the way as we resumed our walk along this long hallway towards this room that the Emperor wanted to show me. A couple of the staff members standing at the entrance to the room opened the doors to a great hall. At the head of the hall was the throne of the Emperor and Empress.

"Here we are," the Emperor said. "One of these days all of this is going to be all yours, my son and daughter."

The great royal court was adorned with marble floors, tapestry, and royal purple curtains draped from ceiling to the floor, stained glass windows, and high arches. At the head of the hall were the thrones of the Emperor and Empress. As I stood before the throne, I stared stunned and in absolute fascination and amazement at the Seal of the Emperor that was hanging behind the Emperor's seat. My ring was an exact replica of the seal, a golden image of an eagle raised with the head looking to the right and both wings spread over the head. I held my hand up.

"This is amazing!" said Kathy. "Your ring is exactly the same as that seal!"

The Emperor came over to examine the ring.

"Gordon, my son!" said the Emperor. "You are true heir to this throne. You are the ancestor of the original Monarch of Napajan! Welcome to the Palace of Xychron, Prince Sakata!"

"But is this all true? Can I really be a descendant of the original monarchy?"

"There were only two rings made, and from what Katherine has told me, you have both of them. Only the possessor of these rings has the right to the throne."

"That means, the true heir to the throne of Xychron has come home!" said Kathy.

"Precisely! We are going to have to have another big celebration!"

CHAPTER 40

Exchanging Vows

As we promised the Emperor, the day came when we decided to exchange our wedding vows before the Xychronian people. It was Kathy's dream to have a big ceremony, and she didn't let her parents down one bit.

The ceremony was held on a mountain top grotto with a crystal clear lake, a gentle flowing river and a small water fall with a lot of trees. There were guests of thousands gathered along the riverbed, and a cliff served as a natural altar where we stood before the high priest of Xychron.

Xychron didn't have any churches, cathedrals, synagogues, mosques or temples like on Earth. That's because Christ never came to Xychron as he did on Earth. Hence, Christianity was never established on this planet. As Kathy said, there wasn't a need for these institutions or buildings because people talked to God here daily – in the open. This was just a ritual ceremony.

"Prince Gordon Sakata" said the priest. "Will you have this Woman to be your wedded Wife, to live together after God's ordinance in the holy estate of Matrimony? Will you love her, comfort her, honor, and keep her in sickness and in health; and, forsaking all other, keep yourself only unto her, so long as you both shall live?"

"I will," I said.

"Princess Katherine" said the priest. "Will you have this Man to be your wedded Husband, to live together after God's ordinance in the holy estate of Matrimony? Will you love him, comfort him, honor, and keep him in sickness and in health; and, forsaking all other, keep yourself only unto him, so long as you both shall live?"

"I will," said Katherine.

"I, Gordon Sakata," I said as I stared into the eyes of Kathy. "take thee Katherine to be my wedded Wife, to have and to hold from this day forward, for better for worse, for richer for poorer, in sickness and in health, to love and to cherish, till death us do part, according to God's holy ordinance; and thereto I plight thee my troth."

"I Katherine," replied Kathy. "take thee Gordon Sakata to be my wedded Husband, to have and to hold from this day forward, for better for worse, for richer for poorer, in sickness and in health, to love, cherish, and to obey, till death us do part, according to God's holy ordinance; and thereto I give thee my troth."

As the priest continued with the ceremony, I couldn't help but gaze into Kathy's eyes once again as if we were back on the tower of the Megasphere. She was stunning, to say the least. But this time, she wore a wooden tiara adorned with flowers and ribbons which made her look even more beautiful than when we were together during our first wedding ceremony. The only difference was that we had our own two children as our "witnesses" during the exchanging of our vows and it was really a commitment to them as well.

After the ceremony, everyone gathered at the castle for a grand party that lasted through the night. The whole world celebrated as events were televised on holographic screens all over the village.

"Tomorrow my son," said the Emperor, "the celebration continues. Please come to the Royal Concert Hall as my guest to hear the Royal Choral Society."

"I would look forward to that very much, sir." I said.

"I understand they are preparing Beethoven's *Ninth Symphony* for our enjoyment," he said.

"I know that piece quite well." I responded.

"You and Katherine will join us our Royal Box."

The next evening, we joined the Emperor and Empress in the royal concert box at the Royal Concert Hall. On stage was the Royal Symphonic Orchestra with a Chorus of one-thousand.

The concert hall's lights dimmed as the conductor appeared on stage. There was a loud applause, then silence as the conductor raised his arms and the orchestra started with the opening movement of the *Ninth Symphony*. As the orchestra was playing, I could identify parts of Beethoven's previous nine symphonies as the orchestra built to the climax of the fourth movement. Then, the chorus started their contribution of the stirring climax of "Ode to Joy" filling the halls with a thousand voices.

The audience in the concert hall responded with a rousing applause, screams, and shouting. It was amazing that Beethoven himself had the same reaction when he conducted the piece. But, he couldn't hear the audience response until they turned him around because he was deaf at the time he conducted this piece.

"Thank you very much for a wonderful treat" I said to the Emperor."

"This is only the beginning of the festivities. Please join us at the Royal Football Soccer Stadium tomorrow evening."

Now what could have he had in store for us at the Royal Soccer Stadium?

So Kathy and I spend some quiet time in the city.

"These buildings still astonish me!" I said to Kathy. "I still can't believe how big and tall they are!"

"They are quite impressive aren't they?" she said. "The biggest building is the Andromeda Complex. There are over 500,000 people working there."

"What do they do there?" I asked.

"It's the official Xychronian government building. It houses the Parliament, Senate, and the Xychron World Court."

"What's that real tall structure there?" I asked, pointing to another structure that must have stood over 5,000 feet into the sky.

"That's Xychron Tower. Come on. Let's go to the top."

"I thought you were scared of heights?" I reminded Kathy.

"That was back on Earth," she said. "The Megasphere Tower is flimsy compared to this one. Standing on the Megasphere Tower will scare anyone from anywhere!"

"How do we get up there?" I asked.

"Think hard!" she said.

No sooner than I thought about it. We were standing on the top platform of the Xychron Tower overlooking the night lit city.

"What a beautiful sight!" I said to Kathy.

"Do you like it here on Xychron?"

"Very much so. I feel very much at home now."

"That's good. Mother and Father are very pleased to have you as part of the family. He's always wanted a son-in-law. And I really struck it lucky with you! A real prince even!"

"I'm very happy and honored to be part of the family." I said as I turned to her. "I really love you, more than you think."

"I know, my dear. I love you very much also … more that you will ever know."

We embraced each other there at the top of the tower and kissed each other forever. Well, it seemed like it went on forever. Then as we both settled down. Our thoughts brought us back down to ground level.

The next evening, we went to the Royal Soccer Stadium as we were invited by the Emperor and sat in the Royal guest box.

"Gordon," said the Emperor. "It is my pleasure to present to you, by command performance, the Royal Emissaries and the Imperial Marauders Drum and Bugle Corps who will be performing their field shows for you this evening and for your entertainment. I understand you have seen the Royal Emissaries in rehearsal."

"Yes." I said. "Just a few days ago."

"They will perform first," the Emperor said.

The Royal Emissaries marched onto the field with 124 young adults dressed in brightly colored costumes of red, green, white and silver. They were followed by the all-male Imperial Marauders, also 124 strong, were dressed green, black and white uniforms. Both gave very entertaining performances which were like that of half-time shows during football games back on Earth. But I was really astonished to see and hear how professional-like they performed on the field, which was their stage.

"Thank you so very much for another splendid evening," I told the Emperor.

"Don't mention it, my son," the Emperor said. "I hope this will be the start of a magical life for you and Katherine, for the rest of your lives together."

"I am very happy to be your son-in-law, your Highness," I said.

"Just call me dad, Gordon," he said. "That's what Katherine calls me. Let's just keep it in the family."

"Okay, Dad." I replied. "I kind of like that. I haven't been able to call anyone my dad in a long time."

CHAPTER 41

Princely Duties

The next day, I was left to my own devices. Kathy and Christine went on a short trip to tour a medical facility on the other side of the planet with the Empress. Unfortunately, I wasn't invited on the tour, so it was my time to be a bachelor once again.

I decided this would be a good time to go to the vacation home to see how it was standing since we haven't been there for a while and the house probably needed a little picking up. So I informed my staff and left my contact information with my personal assistant and set my mind to go back to Pasadena.

I arrived in the year 2010 to find that the house really needed a dusting job. It looked like nobody lived here for centuries. And, that could have been quite accurate. The royal staff doesn't keep a vacation staff here regularly, so it's pretty much up to Kathy and I to keep the house up each time we come here for a visit.

I forgot that this was the year that the moon had its greatest gravitational effect on the earth's surface. Somehow I felt this was the wrong time to be here. Nevertheless, I started to do some dusting around the house, polished the furniture and turned the television on.

Looking at the news, which was a little crude compared to the 23rd

Century style of broadcasting, I learned that the state's government was closing down a lot of emergency medical centers due to budget shortfalls. The state couldn't afford to keep them open. People had to travel longer distances to get emergency medical assistance. This was not good in these times, because cars didn't move as fast as those in the 23rd Century, and there was much more traffic congestion on overcrowded highways.

Continuing with my reconstruction efforts on the house, I managed to do a little construction work on the framework of the house. There was always talk about the "big one" hitting the area. So, I worked on reinforcing the framework of the house as I made several trips to the hardware supply shops in the area and fixed the plumbing as well. This was probably why it was able to withstand major catastrophes throughout the centuries when I first started dating Kathy (or Wendy) in the 23rd Century.

But after I finished my projects here, I was still surprised to see that even in the world today, how little prepared people were for major catastrophes. People just took things for granted. They often said that it was too costly as if money was more important than saving lives.

I didn't have a car of my own. When I made the trips to the hardware store, I got a ride in the neighbor's pickup truck since he was going to the same place which made it convenient. Besides, I really wasn't well versed on driving those antiques anyway. I knew that there were shelters for the homeless in the city, so I called a local market and placed a large order for food and had them deliver it to the nearest food bank. I thought it would be the least I could do be for I went back home.

After I was satisfied on the work I did on the house, I set my mind to return back home to the year 3309. As soon as I arrived, I was informed by my personal assistant that the big earthquake finally struck the Los Angeles area in February 2015. The damages were tremendous and horrifying. People were displaced from their homes. Many people lost their houses. Insurance companies that were supposed to have assisted, didn't pay one nickel and left the state with a lot of people just holding the bag for themselves. And since emergency medical centers were prematurely closed, a lot of people died because they couldn't get immediate medical attention — all for the lack of money and ill-preparedness on government's part. What a tragedy!

There were cries for help and assistance. Very little came their way. The federal government pledged all the help it could give. But it was too little, too late. The federal government was too busy fighting a war in Iraq and terrorists in Afghanistan. They already failed once in responding to another catastrophe in New Orleans earlier after Hurricane Katrina devastated the city. What a poor example of government emergency response that was. Many people died as a result of that mess.

However, Los Angeles was a different story. It was simply going to cost too much to put Los Angeles back together again. I think that is why the federal government turned its back on California once again like in many other situations in the past.

Going back was too much of a nightmare. It reminded me about the tragedies of the treatment of people in the 23rd Century. Yet, the pattern of not learning by their mistakes seemed to have carried on from generation to generation. I guess that is probably what led to the demise of Earth. Yet, man continually is repeatedly given a "second chance." How long this will continue is anyone's guess. But, I'm quite sure; the clock is ticking for man and Earth. One of these days, there will be no second chance.

CHAPTER 42

Homecoming

I was about in the gardens one morning taking my usual, casual constitution around the castle grounds when I approached the weeping-willow near the lake where Kathy and I like to sit and talk. No sooner than I began to sit down with her on my mind, she then appeared from her trip.

"Good morning dear," she said. "How have you been without me?"

"I've missed you very much. Welcome back home." I said. "How was your trip?"

"It was very interesting. They installed a new imaging system at the university that will scan your entire body in less than 5 seconds. Then it will produce a four-dimensional image for the doctor's review and it will also give him a preliminary diagnosis of the problem or problems if there are more than one. It's really interesting!"

"Did they find anything wrong with you?" I asked.

"Absolutely nothing! I'm perfectly fine, thank you. What have you done while I was gone?"

"I went back to the vacation house in the year 2010. The house was a mess."

"Oh really? What did you do?"

"I fixed up the house here and there. I also shored up the structure of the house before the big one hit L.A."

"Did it withstand the earthquake?" she asked.

"It was still standing in the 23rd Century, wasn't it?"

"Now that I come to think about it. Yes it was."

"Any way, before I left, I sent some food over to the food bank to help the less fortunate."

"That was very generous of you."

"It was the least I could do."

"Thank you for your work."

"Don't mention it" I said. "I did learn some interesting things that happened during that time."

"Like what?"

"Just before the earthquake it, the state shut down a lot of emergency medical centers because they ran out of funding."

"Money again! It's all about money! When will they ever learn that it needs to be about people? They'll never learn!"

"Not to change the subject, but …"

"But what?"

"How did you know I was here in the gardens?"

"That was easy! Your tracking module in your head gives me your precise location anywhere in the universe!"

"Anywhere?" I asked.

"All I have to do is concentrate on your thoughts," she said. "It's that simple! It's even better than the tracking module that you had from your bionic arm! That one was rather crude. Besides, the signals are much stronger."

"My Lord!" I said, "What is this universe coming to?"

"It merely brings us closer and closer together," Then she kissed me lightly on the cheeks. "I missed you very much, my love."

Then we continued kissing as usual, on the lips. And, it was nice. My lips had felt like there had been long neglected for the past three days.

"You know?" I said to Kathy. "I lips and my stomach have this terrible craving for a glazed donut!"

"A what! You'll never find one of those here on Xychron! And, don't you dare bring any back from Earth! Gordon Sakata, if I ever catch you sneaking away to Earth and bringing back junk food, I'm...I'm..."

"I just can't remember when was the last time I ever had one."

"And you're doing well by not having one either! Have you seen any obese people on this planet?"

"No, come to think about it."

"That's because we don't serve junk here on Xychron! Look at all the problems the RNA had. It really had a problem with obesity. Especially with the children!"

"You're right," I said.

"And, the children ..." She added "started to have diseases that were typically found in adults. Isn't that correct?"

"That's correct!" I said.

"Do you want our children growing up like that?"

"Well," I said, "not really."

"Very, well then. That settles it! Now, do you still have a craving for a donut?"

"Well, no," I replied, "A cheeseburger maybe."

"Oh hush!" she said while putting her hands over my mouth.

CHAPTER 43

Dedicating the Twins

Back in the Republic of North America, it is customary to dedicate babies, usually before a minister and a congregation. In some Catholic churches, they baptized the baby with or in holy water depending on who did the ceremony. On Xychron, children are dedicated when they turn four years of age and are taken to the high priest.

We left our castle that morning to fly across the pond to pick up the twins, and the Emperor and the Empress at the Palace, and continue our journey to the grotto on top of the mountain where we exchanged our vows. This time, it was to dedicate the children before God.

The high priest began the ceremony:

"I thank God for parents, who are willing to dedicate their lives and the rearing of their child to God. Today you are joining in covenant with God and these witnesses, that you will raise these children in God's house and in a Godly home, for God's glory. To the Parents: This service is not one for salvation of the children, but the dedicating of yourselves to be Godly parents. If it is your intention to present your children to God, and to pledge yourselves to bring these children up in the nurture and admonition of the God, Please answer, WE DO, to the following promises. Do you dedicate yourselves to God and His universe of worship?"

"We do," all of said.

"Do you dedicate yourselves to raise your children in a Godly home?"

"We do."

"Do you this day recognize these children as gifts of God, and thank Him for this blessing?"

"We do."

"Do you this day dedicate these children to God?

"We do."

"Do you here this day promise to give these children every possible benefit of home, school, and of universe of worship?"

"We do."

"Do you here this day ask God's blessings upon its life, to guide, guard, and direct it through all its years?

"We do."

"Bless and protect the family." said the high priest.

We thanked the priest for his services as we departed the grotto back to the palace.

"That was a lovely service," said the Empress. "How did you like it dear?"

"It was very nice, my dear," said the Emperor. "Gordon, what did you think of it?"

"Well, it was nice and short." I said. "It was certainly not like my dedication ceremony."

"Oh really?" replied the Emperor. "Do you remember anything about your dedication ceremony?"

"I have to admit, Sir, I was really too young to remember."

We all laughed as we proceeded to the small private dining room for lunch.

This time, it was truly a family event. All six of us were gathered around the dining table. The Emperor and the Empress together flanked by myself and Byron on one side, and Kathy and Beverly on the other.

"The twins are doing very well in school!" the Emperor said.

"That's good news!" I said. "What have they been doing?"

"Both of them have mastered the art of mental-teleportation and have learned that skill to evacuate in case of emergencies. The teachers will inform you where the emergency evacuation locations are if you need to find them."

"Beverly," he continued, "is a whiz in mathematics. Byron, on the other hand uses his mathematical skills in conjunction with his artistic and musical talents and continues to amaze everybody."

"Wow!" said Kathy. "That's great!"

"I think both kids have mom's intellectual gifts," I said. "I never was one to be very smart."

"But," Kathy interjected. "I think they also have your artistic talents as well, my love."

"I think," the Emperor said, "that both children have a good balance of both mom and dad within them. I think their future will be very bright."

CHAPTER 44

The Grand Tour

After lunch, we dropped off the twins at the Palace School and said our good-byes to the Emperor and the Empress. Little did I know that Kathy had a special surprise for me today. I was already blissfully happy by the dedication of the twins. But she decided it was time for my grand tour of the planet. I've never visited the other places on the planet before. This was going to be quite an experience, and I was looking forward to it very much. We travelled a lot between the castle and the palace, and Earth and back. But we never had time to tour the rest of the planet. And, there was a lot to see. Unlike Earth where there are many nations, each continent is like a district – or a zone – that specializes in some form of commerce be it in industry, manufacturing, or business. There are districts which have very large universities and are dedicated towards education.

Besides myself and Kathy, there was an entourage of staff, business, and government leaders who boarded the starship. No, we weren't going to another planet. It's just that there were so many of us that the starship was the largest vehicle that could take us around the planet for this tour.

Kathy headed the exploration as we first began touring the capital in flight. We hovered over several key landmarks as she showed me some interesting points of interest. One of the things that impressed me was just how immaculate the cities, towns and villages were kept.

"Kathy?" I asked. "Do you have street sweepers to clean your streets? Everything here is so immaculate. They're so clean you can almost eat off the streets!"

"We do have cleaning vehicles that sweep the streets periodically," she said. "But by and large, there is very little that can be tossed out. Every citizen is responsible for keeping the streets and highways clean. There are disposable receptacles in key areas in the cities and villages that destroy litter automatically. There's no need to pick up these containers and take the refuse to a local landfill where it pollutes the environment."

"I also noticed that you don't have any areas of poverty or any low-income neighborhoods." I observed. "Back on Earth, there were shantytowns all over!"

"People on Xychron are treated equally. There are no classes of rich or ultra affluent people. Yet, we have no poverty as well. Everyone earns the same as you and I, the Emperor and the Empress. Everyone is guaranteed quality housing, and as you have observed, our housing standards are very high. By Earth's standards, these are really mansions. We'll fly to another continent."

We headed eastward over the large ocean that separated the capital and where the castle was located on. On the castle's continent were mainly industrial and manufacturing complexes.

"We're now hovering over our industrial continent." she continued. "Here, you will find a primarily industrial complexes and buildings. But as you can see in the far distance over there, there are villages where workers of these industries live. Again, the workers have the same amount of life credits as the Emperor, and they are not paid for doing their work. In return, they are guaranteed life-long employment even though they are allowed to leave and find other kinds of work whenever they desire."

"When workers leave a company, are they allowed to keep their benefits?"

"Their life's benefits are provided by the government. Not by the company," she said. "On Xychron, everyone has a right to work without the fear of being laid off. In your own words, we do not have the paper people syndrome as you described back on Earth."

"Amazing! Is that why you don't have the problems of homelessness? By the way, how did you know about the paper people syndrome on Earth?"

"We extracted that information from the memory cells of your old bionic brain," she said. "But exactly, Xychronians are not displaced from their work or their homes like the people on Earth. Let's take a peek at the world's university where I was at a few days ago."

We flew to the next continent as we toured the university campus.

"This is the sight of the Xychron University Hospital. This is where a lot of the research and advances are made in medicine." she said.

"Is this were you got the scanning demo?" I asked.

"Yes," She said. "On Xychron, every individual is entitled to medical care. It's not like the health care system in the RNA where people had to pay in order to get prescriptions and medical care. Here, you just walk into the clinic, and they will take care of you – no questions asked. It's all covered by your life's benefits. You found that out by using some of your life's benefits while you were in the hospital."

"Yes." I said. "I fully understand what you are saying."

"As for the climate," I asked. "Is it always this nice around the planet?"

"Yes," she said. "We don't have the pollution problems that Earth had because we make every effort not to contaminate the atmosphere. You know all too well that the atmosphere is very delicate. We had found ways not to pollute the atmosphere by using processes that are environmentally friendly. All manufacturing processes have to be cleared by the Xychron Ministry of Manufacturing and Engineering Standards and Practices. This governing body has restricted the dumping of anything into the waters and oceans. That's why our waters are crystal clear compared to the waters on Earth."

As we cruised around other parts of the planet, I was shown various forms of animal life and ocean life. Life is very similar to Earth but definitely more abundant.

"As for politics …" I asked.

"Our politicians are not paid like they were in the RNA government," said Kathy. "We have no corruption in our government since even if you took a bribe, you have nowhere to hide it. It all goes into your account. And at the end of the year, your account balances out automatically so that it is equal to everyone else's balances – no more, no less. If you have an excess in your account, the excess is placed into a general fund. Besides, if you accepted a bribe, you normally would be removed from office. Political favors are banned and weren't allowed since the beginning of this civilization."

"What about political parties? Do you have political parties on Xychron?"

"We don't have organized political parties like the RNA had on Earth or as other nations had in their countries. Our politicians are, pretty much, independents. There are groups that gather with similar views and ideas. But Xychronian are encouraged to think and express themselves freely and individually without influence by one political ideal or philosophy. Largely, legislation and policies are adapted by consensus. If anyone objects, he or she just stands aside, but they are allowed a dissenting opinion during the debates. One of these days you will visit the houses of the Parliament and the Senate. Discussions there get quite interesting at times."

"And crime?" I said. "Where are criminals sent to?"

"We don't have as much crime here like there was back on Earth. That's because we don't have weapons. We do have detention facilities for misdemeanors. And for the major felonies, the prisoners are sent to a prison facility on the farthest of the three moons, Zandor which really isn't a prison facility so to speak. It's more of a colony for serious offenders in our society. It's our way of separating the undesirables," she said.

"So, paradise, or so to speak. Isn't as it seems after all."

"Correct. And I had said that before. We are not a perfect society. There is just one more spot that I have to show you before our tour ends."

The starship hovered over the farming region of Xychron. We barely cleared the farming fields that we could have practically touched the plants from the window.

"Does this plant look familiar to you?"

"It does, indeed. But is this legal here on Xycrhon. Marijuana was an illegal substance back on Earth."

"We grow hemp here regularly and it's a very important commodity for Xychron. With it, we can manufacture clothing, paper, and use it for medicinal purposes. Unlike on Earth, we don't cut down our trees and use them for paper. That is why you see our forest so dense with green trees."

"Amazing!" I said. "What else do you use this plant for?"

"We use it also for paint and cleaners, food, fuel, cosmetics. But the primary use is for paper, clothing and textiles."

Eventually, the starship returned back to our castle.

"Well, here we are, back at our home. We're not going back to the palace since there's no need to. So, we'll just depart here. How did you like your tour?"

"Very interesting," I said. "Thank you for the excursion. You taught me a lot!"

We departed the starship, and as it flew off across the pond back to the palace.

"There's one more question. You said nothing gets dumped into the ocean."

"That's correct."

"Then what happens to all of the business that gets flushed from the bathrooms?" I asked.

"We try to recycle as much as we can here," she replied. "All of that stuff gets treated at regional treatment centers and recycled into fertilizer. Talk about recycling. You'll also notice that we don't use paper plates here also. Especially the Styrofoam kinds that you used on Earth. That's because they are harmful to the environment, and they can't be recycled. We use stoneware here as you've noticed."

"One final question before we retire." I said. "Why was life so difficult on Earth? Why did people have to struggle to make a living?"

"That's because governments on Earth made life difficult to begin with. They created barriers between themselves which naturally caused distrust. And within their borders, they created social classes that separated people which created even more distrust. And while all this was festering, there was this tumor that grew among them like "cancer" in one's physical body — doubt. People frequently doubted other people's opinions, life styles, disrespect for religion, a disrespect for each other. This cancer that festered among the peoples of the Earth eventually became malignant. It seemed like there was no turning back. Man was destroying his own self. Remember that we respect ourselves as 'one body' here on Xychron. The body has to take care of itself. On earth, man did not treat himself as 'one body' but continually took in upon himself to tear him apart. Essentially, he was tearing 'the body' apart. God has established and created model civilizations all over the universe — Xychron is just one of them. A body can heal itself if it desires and if it takes careful steps to do so."

CHAPTER 45

The Transfer of Power –
A New Era

Several years later as the twins were about ready to enter high school, we were summoned to the palace abruptly. Rather than taking the cruiser, Kathy and I decided that it would be faster to teleport on our own, so we set our minds on the palace and arrived within seconds.

We rushed into the living room to find the Emperor and Empress sitting side by side on the sofa.

"We got here as soon as we could, Father." said Kathy.

"Gordon, Katherine, please have a seat," the Emperor said. "The reason why I summoned you here is that my wife and I have decided to retire immediately and to turn the throne over to you."

"But why, Father?" I asked.

"Doctors have told me that I am in failing health and I don't have very long to live. While I'm still alive, Juliana and I would like to visit some of the wonders of the universe and get around for a while. You know, relax. I think it is now a good time to turn over the reins to you."

"But, Father," I said, "I am really unprepared to become Emperor so suddenly."

"You will be a natural, my Son." He replied. "It's in your blood. You and I have come a long way."

"I will never forget you, Father." I said. "Write us a postcard once in a while during your journeys."

"That we will do," he said. "I have instructed staff and the leaders of government to prepare transfer of power ceremonies two days from now in the Royal Court. At that time, you will take your oath of office and be declared Emperor of Xychron, and you, Katherine, shall become Empress of Xychron."

"We are speechless, Father." I said. "This has really taken us by surprise."

"I am sure you will do well as our new leader, my Son. Let your faith and soul guide and keep you."

"Thank you, Father."

We retired to our residential quarters in the palace.

"I really wasn't expecting this so soon," I said to Kathy.

"Well, you really knew it was going to happen eventually," she said. "It just so happens to fall sooner than you really expected, my dear."

"I am humbled and honored by the experience and opportunity." I said. "But I'm also really scared. I never led a country before, let alone an entire planet! I even had a hard time keeping my own apartment in one piece even!"

"You always wore that ring! You had to have known that there were mystical and magical powers of that ring."

"I always thought that it was only folklore." I said. I really didn't think it was going to lead to this! Not even beyond my wildest imagination had I ever thought it would come to this!"

"Let's back up for a moment," she said. "In your wildest imagination, did you ever think that you were ever going to marry a princess?"

"Absolutely not!" I said. "In fact, I didn't even think I was going to live this long. I thought for sure I was going to die and be buried alongside of Gordon I on that mountain before you rescued me. Then, I thought I was lucky just to have married someone like you on the platform of the Megasphere Tower, princess or not."

"Did you ever see me coming?" she asked.

"No. I can't say I have." I said.

"Do you recall a letter that was addressed from me to you in your dreams?" she said.

"It's one of those dreams I clearly remembered. It had your name on it – Princess Katherine Kusumatsu. But I can't recall opening the letter. I think the dream fizzled out, as I don't remember the details after that."

"That was me trying to communicate with you," she said. "That was my form of 'text messaging.'"

"This is really unreal!"

"You know now that you can do anything if you put your mind to it."

"You're absolutely right."

"Let's summon the kids here."

"That's a good idea."

As soon as I said that, the twins appeared in our quarters.

"Hi Mom, Dad. Did you call for us?" asked Byron.

"Yes, Son," said Kathy. "Your father will become Emperor in two days. Grandfather Gabriel said that he is going to retire."

"Really?" said the twins. "That's great news!"

"Thank you, Byron and Beverly." I said to the twins. "When I become Emperor, I hope you two will be at my side to support me. I'm going to be a nervous wreck!"

"Oh dad," Beverly said. "You'll do just fine. We'll be there at your side."

"Thank you, my princess," I said as I embraced and hugged her tightly.

The following morning, we gathered in the Royal Palace Plaza as thousands of people gathered to hear the announcement by the Emperor.

"Fellow Citizens of Xychron! It is with great joy that I announce to you my official retirement from the throne as your Emperor. Tomorrow, you shall have a new Monarch!"

There was a loud noise of surprise from the crowd.

"Do not be dismayed." He continued. "My wife Empress Juliana and I are happy to relinquish the throne to Crown Prince Gordon Sakata and Princess Katherine. They will become your new leaders as of 1000 hours tomorrow morning! During our retirement, we plan to go on a major voyage visiting the great wonders of the universe!"

"For the past forty-five years," he said, "it has been my greatest honor serving you, the citizens of Xychron. Now, it is time for me to pass the sovereignty to a new generation. I wish you well and God speed to all of you!"

The cheers of the crowd rose to a deafening level as chants began to stir among the crowd. "Long live the Emperor!" they chanted.

We escorted the Emperor and the Empress to the Royal Starship as they departed on their voyage into the universe. It was definitely a heartbreaking moment. It would be a while until we would see each other next. And I hoped the occasion would be soon. But I knew that the Emperor loved to travel, both forward and backward into time. I was rather anxious to see what he discovered in the future.

We walked back into the palace where I was asked to assume a few royal duties, review the guest list for tomorrow's indoctrination ceremony.

"Sweetheart," I asked Kathy. "Do you want to see this list with me?"

"Sure!" she said as we sat down together on the Emperor's sofa in his office.

"This is quite a list," she said. "It has all the dignitaries and celebrities on the planet. Also, there are a few guests here that are from other planets as well."

"Mr. Maxwell," I said to my personal assistant. "Is this going to be a closed or open ceremony?"

"It's a closed ceremony, Sir." He replied. "There simply wouldn't be enough room for everybody in the Royal Court. That's where the indoctrination ceremony has always been traditionally been held."

"What are the possibilities of moving it to a larger venue?" I asked.

"But it has been always held in the court, sir. Do you have somewhere else in mind?"

"As a matter of fact, I do," I said. "I want the whole city invited!"

"The whole city, Sir? There's nowhere in the city that will be able to accommodate such a size of audience, sir."

"I believe there is," I said. "The Royal Football Stadium!"

"Well," he said, "the venue does seat over 500,000 people. That could be a possibility."

"Make it happen!" I commanded.

"Very well Sir." He replied. "I'll take care of the details right away."

"The Football Stadium?" asked Kathy. "It's never been held there before."

"I want this ceremony to be the people's ceremony — an open ceremony." I said. "This is their monarchy, and we are their servants."

"I agree with you 100-percent!" she said. "What about the post ceremony celebration and reception?"

"We'll have it outdoors in the stadium for everyone to enjoy!" I said. "Why should only a select few enjoy the occasion? Besides, with a venue that size we can have a mass combined choir singing great choral works as a build up to the induction ceremony itself."

"Wow! You have quite an imagination for your indoctrination."

"You can only live this moment once in your life." I said. "We should make the most of it."

"This is going to be fun and exciting!" she said.

"Yeah. I don't think I'll be so nervous if I'm not in such a formal setting as the Royal Court."

After working on several other items of business, we retired to the dining room for supper.

"You know," I said to Kathy. "Christine is here. It would sure be nice to have Ed here with us."

"We can have him here by tonight!" she said. "I'll send Chris on a mission to Earth on our starship."

"Wait a minute," I said. "What do you intend to do?"

"Haven't you heard of alien kidnappings? It's done all the time!"

"But what if he doesn't want to come?" I wondered.

"Don't worry, we have our ways! Besides, he'll recognize 'Bonnie.'"

"Christine!" said Kathy. "Please come here."

Christine entered the living room.

"Yes, Ma'am!"

"I have a little job for you. Please go to Earth and bring Ed back here right away."

"Yes, Ma'am. I'll be back in two hours."

She leaves the room for the starship.

"Two hours?" I asked. "Is that all it takes?"

"That's about all it takes for an abduction." Kathy said.

Two hours passed. Then there were footsteps heard leading into the living room.

"We're back!" said Christine.

"Hello, Ed. Welcome to Xychron." I said.

"Gordon?" he asked. "Is that really you?"

"Yes," I said. "It's really me in the flesh"

"I thought you died during the war." he said. "They said you were missing in action."

He paused and looked towards Kathy.

"And may I ask who you are?"

"This is my wife Princess Katherine. But you knew her as Wendy."

"Wendy? Is that really you? You have really changed!"

"Yes," said Kathy. "I really don't look like my old self. I've changed somewhat — I even surprised Gordon."

"But where am I?" he asked. "The last thing I knew, I was following Bonnie into this store. And, the next thing I know, I'm here. Is this a dream?"

"It's no dream," I said. "You are on the planet Xychron."

"Where is Xychron?"

"You're on a planet just on the other side of the Sun."

"Is there really such a place?"

"You're standing right on it!" Kathy said.

"But why did you bring me here?" he asked.

"We wanted you to celebrate in our new life as Emperor and Empress of Xychron tomorrow!" I said.

"Emperor and Empress of Xychron?" he asked. "What's this all about? I didn't know you had royal blood in you, Gordon."

"I didn't really find that out until I got here also, Ed. Do you remember that ring I always wore?"

"The one with the eagle?" he asked.

"Yes, that one," I said. "It matched the Royal Seal of the Emperor. I found out I was heir of the throne. I am a descendant of the original Monarch of Napajan."

"Get out of here!"

"No." I said. "It's really true!"

So we took him down to the Royal Court and showed him the seal hanging over the throne and the ring. He was convinced.

"Your Highness ... Your Prince ... your Majesty ... Gordon, I really don't know what to call you," he said.

"Just call me Gordon. Come on. It's been a long day, and you've been traveled a long way, Ed. Let's get some shut eye. Tomorrow's going to be an even bigger day."

The night passed swiftly. We were awoken by the palace staff at 0600 hours, and I was quickly prepared for the day. We had breakfast in the small dining room, and the twins were dressed in their formal dresses. Byron had on his tuxedo, which was really dapper. Beverly wore a long gown, and I waited anxiously for Kathy to make her appearance.

"Good morning," said Kathy as she walked regally into the dining room. "How is everybody today?"

"Just fine and nervous," I said. "You, however, look absolutely stunning and extremely regal. Are you really my wife? Am I really your husband?"

"Gordon?" she asked.

Kathy wore a long, fancy, egg-shell white formal dress with a purple sash. Purple and white were my family colors. After breakfast, we were asked by the staff to take some formal pictures. We took a few as a family, then as individuals.

Then, it was time to depart for the stadium. We got in the transport vehicles, which was actually a long motorcade as we ever so slowly made our way through the winding streets of the capital leading to the soccer stadium.

Citizens lined the streets waving flags and cheering and wishing us well as we returned the gesture through the shaded windows. The crowd cheered and cheered even louder each inch of the way. It seemed like it took an eternity for us to even reach the stadium grounds entrance.

When we finally arrived at the gates of the stadium, it became increasingly difficult to drive through the multitudes of people, crowding around the transport vehicles to take a peek inside. In the background, I could hear music of the combined choirs as they entertained the audience inside the stadium. They were joyously singing their hearts out. And as we inched our way through the stadium tunnels, I couldn't help but think of the fable of the pauper that turned king only that, this time, this wasn't a fairy tale. This was real!

The transport vehicle exited the tunnel and entered into the stadium as a deafening roar could be heard for miles around. A new leader was about to be inducted as Emperor, and the crowd rose to its feet with anticipation of the event. Event security was attempting with all its might to clear a passage for the vehicle. It wasn't like a regular football stadium on Earth where there might have been a track surrounding the field itself. That would have been too easy. This field was designed for soccer — it had no accommodations for track and field events.

We crawled ever so slowly, closer and closer to the induction platform. There, the great seal of the Emperor hung high with the flags of the Emperor and Xychron flying and the thrones of the Emperor and Empress waiting for our arrival and appearance on the grand stage.

We finally got out of the transport vehicles and were escorted to the platform. Awaiting at the top of the platform were dignitaries and invited guests. At the podium was the Chief Justice and the High Priest.

"Prince Gordon Sakata?" asked the Chief Justice. "Are you now prepared to take your oath of office?"

"I am." I said as my voice echoed through the huge stadium filled to capacity. Then there was silence.

"I, A. Gordon Sakata the II, vow to change nothing of the received Tradition, and nothing thereof I have found before me guarded by my God-pleasing predecessors, to encroach upon, to alter, or to permit any innovation therein; to the contrary: with glowing affection as her truly faithful student and successor, to safeguard reverently the passed-on good, with my whole strength and utmost effort; to cleanse all that is in contradiction to the Royal order, should such appear; to guard the Laws and Ordinances of Xychron as if they were the divine ordinance of Heaven, because I am conscious of Thee, whose place I take through the Grace of God, whose Monarchy I possess with Thy support, being subject to severest accounting before Thy Worldly Court over all that I shall confess; I affirm to God Almighty that I will keep whatever has been revealed and whatever the first councils and my predecessors have defined and declared. I will keep without sacrifice to itself the discipline and the rite of the universe of worship. I will put outside the universe of worship whoever dares to go against this oath, may it be somebody else or I. If I should undertake to act in anything of contrary sense, or should permit that it will be executed, Thou willst not be merciful to me on the dreadful Day of Divine Justice. Accordingly, without exclusion, We subject to severest excommunication anyone — be it Ourselves or be it another — who would dare to undertake anything new in contradiction to this constituted Constitution and the purity of the faith, or would seek to change anything by his opposing efforts, or would agree with those who undertake such a blasphemous venture. Thank you in advance for your help!"

"By the powers vested in me," said the Chief Justice, "I declare you, A. Gordon Sakata II, Emperor of Xychron! May God be with you always! Congratulations!"

The crowd immediately rose to its feet and let loose a thundering ovation.

The crowd settled down as I stood at the podium alone. There was complete silence. It was so quiet that a pin drop could be heard in the stadium.

"Citizens of Xychron, Citizens of the Universe!" I said in my opening remarks. "Empress Sakata, Princess Beverly Sakata, Prince Byron Sakata, Members of the Parliament, Members of the Senate, Members of the Judiciary, Honored Guests: I come before you as a humble servant, honored to have been called to the duty as your Emperor of Xychron. As I take this task with a sense of great humility and responsibility, I seek your prayers, blessings and support, and also the blessings of God, that I may be blessed with the wisdom and courage to lead such a great society well during the next era to come."

"We on Xychron live in a blessed world where all citizens are guaranteed employment, living income, medical care, and guaranteed quality housing for life. Unfortunately, we cannot speak for many civilizations on other planets in this universe! On other worlds, people are displaced from their homes and jobs and are denied medical care and the basic rights to live in dignity. We cannot and should not tolerate these acts to continue against the humanity of the universe while a tyrannical minority continue to cloak their veil of darkness among these nations in the universe."

"Let us serve as a beacon of light — a ray of hope to those who have been discouraged and dismayed by the destructive evil forces in their lives. Let us show them that there is a better way."

"In this universe, nations war against nations; worlds war against worlds. We also cannot stand aside and permit this to continue. We must continue to promote peace and tranquility in the universe so that war and fighting are made obsolete. Let it be that nations shall not lift up swords against nations; and worlds shall not lift up swords against worlds, forevermore."

"We also dwell in a society where we live and treat each other as equals with dignity and respect as citizens of this universe as well as citizens of Xychron. That is not so on other worlds. Let us be an example that people can co-exist in equal harmony through the acceptance of each other regardless of race, color, creed, religion, and sexual influences. If we can accept each other for what they are — citizens of the universe — then, people of other worlds can do the same. We must help them raise their levels of thinking in order that they can remove their barriers and walls that separate them causing social injustices, racial and sexual prejudices. Let us help them realize that each individual is not just a person of a city, state, country, or planet, but a citizen of the universe with inalienable rights guaranteed by their Creator."

"Thank you once again. God bless Xychron and His Universe!"

Kathy came by my side and stood as we greeted the crowd by

waiving back. Byron and Beverly joined me at my other side as we, as a family stood for the first time as a Royal Family.

I turned towards Katherine and tried to talk to her over the deafening roar.

"I know you're having a hard time hearing me, Dear!" I said, "But, I just wanted to say I love you my Empress Katherine Sakata!"

"I love you too!" she shouted back, "My Emperor Gordon Sakata!"

We embraced each other once again. And in front of the masses, we gave each other a huge kiss. I was elated and overjoyed. That was the happiest day of my life. I was greeted and embraced by other guests and dignitaries on the stage. Ed and Christine came up and hugged me and offered their words of congratulations and well wishes among others.

Then, the grand celebration began. The formal music changed to that of joy and celebration. There was dancing in the stadium and the partying was non-stop until early the next morning.

CHAPTER 46

Chromlys and Mychrox

I was totally exhausted the next morning and decided to just during my first official day as Emperor. I slept in most of the morning and woke up late in the Xycrhonian afternoon which would have been around lunchtime. Byron and Beverly had already departed for school. By the time I woke up, Kathy was already tending to business as Empress.

After having a light lunch, I took a casual walk out into the palace gardens and gazed at the three moons which made themselves so ever present in the orange daylight sky. As I was looking up at Chromlys, Mychrox and little Zandor in the back, Kathy met me in the gardens.

"It really continues to amaze me how big Chromlys and Mychrox are compared to Zandor." I said to Kathy.

"Well," she replied, "now that you are Emperor, you are now entitled to top secret information."

"Top secret information?"

"Yes. Chromlys and Mychrox are Xychronian-made."

"What?" I asked. "They're not naturally made?"

"No." she said. "Chromlys is the Emperor's flagship. It's the royal starship. Mychrox is the backup ship, just a little smaller, but capable of doing the same things.

"I thought you said Xychron didn't manufacture weapons."

"They're not weapons. Those are our emergency vessels of evacuation. That is where the children were taught to evacuate in case of a planetary emergency."

"Oh! Now I get the picture."

"The two ships can accommodate an entire planet's civilization for an entire generation and travel at ultra-light speed across the universe."

"What's on them? Or, what's in them?"

"First of all, your emergency intergalactic quarters are on Chromlys. Inside both are many compartments and quarters that can accommodate Xychronians as well as people of other planets. They both carry many satellite vehicles that can be used to evacuate inhabitants off of other planets. I believe on Earth, they were called 'life boats.'"

"But what else have you used them for?"

"We have occasionally used them to rescue inhabitants from other planets and take them to other places in the universe."

"But how do you find other habitable planets in the universe?"

"Both starships are equipped with planet finders and navigational systems to find inhabitable planets in the universe. The system also catalogs which ones are friendly and which ones are not."

"Have they ever been attacked by hostile forces?"

"Many times." she replied. "But the advanced onboard defense systems have made them virtually indestructible."

"But why were they made in the first place?"

"First of all, the original ship that our ancestors used to migrate here from Earth was way too small for our modern day use now. We needed a bigger ark. As times progressed, so did the population of the Xychron. Therefore, a second one was built."

"So, with the two ships used together, we can evacuate an entire planet the size of, say, Earth?"

"Exactly!"

"I think there's some unfinished business that needs to be taken care of."

"Have something in mind, do you?"

"How about a little trip back to Earth? Like… a state visit?"

"And exactly what do you have up your sleeve?"

"I'll need to gather my advisors and defense council right away."

We walked back into the palace. We parted in the hall as Kathy went into the living room to greet some guests. I continued to my office and summoned Mr. Maxwell.

"Maxwell, please assemble all the advisors and defense council to the conference room at 1900 hours."

"Yes, your Highness!"

"And don't call me 'Your Highness!' I replied. "I prefer doing away with the all the formalities. Just call me Gordon, please."

"Yes, Gordon."

Later in the evening, my advisors and the defense council met in the conference room with the Galactic Federation Ambassador Romula.

"Ambassador Romula, ladies and gentlemen, members of the defense council, I've called you together to announce that I plan to evacuate the inhabitants of Earth."

There was a little rumble in the room. Then there was silence as the Ambassador spoke.

"But Emperor Sakata," said Ambassador Romula, "we have received no distress call from Earth. On what do you base this evacuation necessity?"

"When I left Earth, the planet was being overtaken by machines – droids and robots. Humans were being displaced from of their habitations and forced into un-natural living conditions, into poverty and starvation."

"Emperor!" replied the Ambassador, "You can't just go in and evacuate inhabitants without a reason. Besides, that is an internal matter. Not an intergalactic concern."

"I disagree Ambassador. It's an obvious humanitarian necessity. Inhabitant's lives are being destroyed due to the greed of a few of their people. Ms. Pebblestone, what is the current status of Earth?"

"Emperor," said Ms. Pebblestone, "Earth now has an unemployment rate of 95%! Over 90% of their people are homeless."

"Is this cause for action or not, Mr. Ambassador?" I asked.

"Well," said the Ambassdor, "I have to admit, our data is a little out of date. Very well. I support your concern. Exactly what do you plan to do?"

"I think a royal visit to Earth is in order. Generals, summon everyone to their stations. We'll depart at daybreak."

CHAPTER 47

Voyage Home

Morning call came all but too soon. It was 0400 hours and the sky outside was still dark. Kathy woke me up from a deep sleep as she informed me that daybreak would soon be upon us. So we quickly prepared to depart for the Starship Chromlys. We teleported ourselves aboard the Chromlys and were greeted by Admiral Park.

"Good morning, Emperor and Empress Sakata." said Admiral Park.

"Good morning!" I replied.

"The Chromlys and Mycrhrox are ready, sir!"

"Very well, Admiral. Set course for planet Earth."

"Yes, Emperor. We'll be there in a few hours."

"Oh, and Admiral…"

"Yes, sir?"

"Please summon the Generals to my quarters."

"Right away."

We went into my quarters where I had a map of the RNA drawn. The generals were gathered around the conference table with Kathy sitting among the advisors.

"When we arrive at Earth, I want to begin immediate construction on our conference headquarters at this location in New Mexico. As far as

I know, there is absolutely nothing there. The exact location is latitude 30°24'14.42"N, longitude 106°41'48.57"W. I think we should build an airstrip to accommodate their airships and a first class conference facility. How fast can we build this site?"

"We'll have it built it in one day." said General Peak. "It will be up so fast, they won't even know what happened."

"Very well." I said. "General Alinson, please start broadcasting announcements to the world leaders to plan on making a summit trip to this location in five days."

"Yes, sir!"

Messages from the Chromlys began transmitting to Earth for all the world leaders to converge at the designated location in New Mexico. Many were skeptical of the messages and considered them a prank.

On Earth, astronomers were astonished to see to anomalies on their instruments heading towards the planet at such high speeds. Warnings were being sent the world leaders but were often being ignored.

In the White House in Washington D.C., President Henderson was at his desk in the Oval Office having a meeting with his General Staff. He was suddenly interrupted by his Chief Science Advisor Williams.

"Mr. President!" said Williams.

"What's the matter?" asked President Henderson. "Is this really urgent?"

"Yes, sir. There are two large size objects rapidly approaching Earth. Both of them are larger than our own moon."

"That's impossible!" said General Gomez. "Nothing can be that large and fly that fast."

"What can they be?" asked the President. "UFO's?"

"There's no such thing as extra-terrestrials!" said Admiral Carpenter.

"Then, what the hell could be flying that fast through space?" the President asked.

"They could be two huge asteroids." said the advisor.

"Can we shoot these out of the sky General Brooke?" inquired the President.

"You bet. When they get into range. We can demolish both of them!"

"Then make it so."

"Yes, sir!"

Back on the Chromlys, Admiral Park announces of the intercom, "Emperor, we are now entering into Earth's orbit."

"Very well." I said.

On Earth, people who had homes immediately went out into the streets to look up into the skies. The streets were crowded with people. Vehicles stopped on streets and highways as people got out of their cars and office buildings to see two huge moon-like objects orbiting the planet.

"President Henderson." said advisor Williams. "Two spheres have just entered earth's orbit. They are definitely extra terrestrial."

"Where could they have come from?" the President asked as he gazed out the windows of the Oval Office.

"Sir. There have been messages sent from space inviting all world leaders to meet for a summit at latitude 30°24'14.42"N, longitude 106°41'48.57"W. We didn't pass this along, sir, because we thought it was a hoax."

"Exactly where is this place?"

"Somewhere in New Mexico, sir"

"New Mexico?"

"Yes, sir. But according to our records, there's absolutely nothing at this location. It's just a dry river bed."

"And who did you say this message went out to?"

"We assume it went to all the world leaders."

"Well, for now, we'll just ignore the invitation for now. I don't think it's very important. If it's that important, we'll send Secretary of State Johnson out there. Or, maybe Vice President Buckley."

On the Chromlys, orders were given to start construction of the conference site. Crews from both the Cromlys and Mychrox teleported down to the exact location to begin construction. On Earth, it would normally take a construction crew several years to complete a world class facility. Xychronians are capable of finishing a major project in a day.

First the airstrip was laid with Xycrhonian synthetic landing materials able to accommodate the large airships. Then the bulk of the construction proceeded quickly with the conference facility itself which included an auditorium, conference hall, dining facilities, and hotel accommodations, using all Xycrhonian materials and equipment.

The next day, General Alinson reported back that the conference facility was ready for summit and all personnel were in place to receive the guests.

"And what if they don't come?" asked Kathy as we looked at 3D hologram of the conference facility.

"I think they will be convinced after we dispatch our calling cards all over the planet."

Chromlys and Mychrox are both equipped with fifty emergency transport vehicles (ETVs) each as large as cities to evacuate inhabitants of a planet in case of an emergency. Each pod can teleport a city's population in one transmission.

"General Alinson, are the ETVs ready to be deployed?"

"Yes, sir!"

"Very well, then. Deploy the ETV's to strategic cities of the Earth as planned."

"Yes, sir."

When General Alinson issued the command, the pods were deployed from both spheres. The massive armada made its way towards Earth and hovered over their respective assigned cities.

Back in the White House, President Henderson gazed out the windows of the Oval Office as one of the evacuation pods hovered over Washington DC. Vice President Buckley entered into the Oval Office.

"Buckley, what do they want?"

"I don't know Mr. President."

The Chief Science Advisor enters the Oval Office.

Mr. President!" said Advisor Williams.

"What is it, Williams?"

"We received word that there are vehicles like these hovering over one-hundred cities around the world. Most of them are hovering of the RNA, sir."

"What are they after? Has anyone tried to communicate with them?" asked President Henderson.

"They are asking all world leaders to meet for a summit in three days at the location in New Mexico, sir."

"But there's nothing there in New Mexico!" said the President.

"Well sir," said Williams, "That's not totally correct."

"What? You said before there was nothing but a dry riverbed out there."

"Our latest satellite pictures have indicated that there have been some activity in that area. Pictures have revealed a landing strip and major building construction out there."

"What kind of construction?" asked Vice President Buckley.

"Well," said Williams, "it appears to be a major conference facility."

"But how can anything go up that fast?" asked the President. "That's impossible!"

"Well sir, you're not going to believe this, but you can see this for yourself. Here are the satellite pictures from yesterday."

Williams showed the satellite pictures from the previous day.

"As you can see, there was nothing there yesterday. But if you take a look at the photos taken today, there is definitely something."

"Buckley, whoever we're dealing with is not of this world!" said the President. We need to find out who they are, where they're from, and what they want. In the meantime, I think I need to address the citizens. Arrange for television air time right away."

"Right away" said Vice President Buckley.

Several hours later, President Henderson addressed the citizens of the RNA on television.

"Good afternoon," said President Henderson as he sat behind his desk in the Oval Office addressing his speech to a television camera. "Citizens of the RNA, please do not be alarmed at the recent series of events that have occurred in various parts of our nation. We are being visited by travelers from far beyond this planetary system. Their purpose of their visit is still unknown. We believe their visit to be peaceful and so far, they have not made any offensive attack on our nation, or any other nation in the world."

"As far as we know, there are one-hundred of these space vehicles hovering over cities all over the world. But just in case, I have placed our defenses on high alert and we stand ready to defend ourselves in case they decide to attack. In two days, leaders of the world will meet for a summit at an undisclosed area in New Mexico with their leaders. We assure you, there is no reason for panic and continue with your lives as usual. We will keep you informed of any events through your emergency broadcasting stations. For now, do not travel very far from your dwellings should there be a necessity to evacuate your neighborhood. Thank you and may God bless and protect the RNA."

Around the world, leaders of their countries were pleading with their citizens for peace and calm. Most of the pleas were being ignored. Many people were in a state of hysteria as people began to pack their precious belongings, got in their cars, and headed out of the cities. The poor and the homeless, however, were stranded in the cities and had no choice but to stay put in their shantytowns, tin shacks, and cardboard dwellings. On the highways, however, there were massive traffic jams, road rage, and vehicles breaking down on the highways.

On Chromlys, I consulted with the evacuation task force to determine how were we going to get the people off of Earth in an expedient, but peaceful manner. Amanda Lester, the evacuation coordinator, and Keiko Sakai, the human psychohistorian, were present in my conference room.

"Okay, so the evacuation pods have been deployed to 100 cities on Earth. What would be the best way to evacuate the people we've come to save off the surface of this planet?"

"Emperor Sakata," said Ms. Sakai, "I recommend doing it in two phases. The first phase would be sending a subliminal signal notifying all those affected to prepare for departure and to gather at certain designated points."

"But how will they know to come to the rendezvous points?"

"They have been pre-programmed at birth to recognize a simple musical message. Only those who know of this piece will know to come to the designated areas." she said.

"Wait a minute!" I said. "Are you saying that we play the role of the fabled *"Pied Piper of Hamlin?"*

"The capability always existed in them." said Sakai. "The second phase is to play a secondary subliminal song which they also know which will tell them exactly the time of departure. At that time, they will be teleported onto the emergency evacuation pods and brought here to Chromlys and Mychrox."

"Good. Then once we have them on board, where are we going to take them?"

"There's a planet very similar to Earth." said Ms. Lester. "It exist in the Mondradian Planetary System in the Cyclovian Galaxy. The plant is called "Egressos." It's an uninhabited planet, but the territory is part of the Galactic Federation of Light. I have contacted Federation leaders to send forces to join us there and help these Earthlings build a new civilization there for them.

"How long will it take us to get there from here?"

"We have calculated that the distance from Earth to Egressos is about 6 light years. Or, about one week – seven days on Earth's time in our cruisers."

"Very well. Chart a course for Egressos. Once we have the people on board, we will set journey for there right away."

"Ms. Sakai, when will you start to transmit the subliminal message?"

"As soon as you begin your summit with the world's leaders, we will start the transmission, sir."

"Thank you very much for all of your work."

As the two departed from the room, I stood and looked out the window down at Earth. I couldn't help remembering my life on earth. The days of being out of work; living in a closet, living in a homeless center; caring for elephants. Then, thinking about the inhumanity of man towards fellow men. The cruelty of how some people can be towards others – the misery that they bestowed upon other peoples' lives just so a relatively few people on the surface of the Earth could live in a life of luxury while the rest of the world suffered in starvation, lived without a home, and struggled to make even the basic of life's necessities. I was near tears as Kathy entered the room.

"Honey? Are you okay?" she asked as she embraced me with a tight hug.

"Yes, dear. I'll be fine."

"If there's any solace in this matter, we have received word that leaders of the world are starting to converge in New Mexico for your summit."

"That's great!"

"So far, the President of the RNA is refusing to come. He has sent the Secretary of State to the summit instead."

"Is that right? I've come all this way and I don't even get the courtesy of meeting him face to face for something as important as this?"

"He sends his regrets. According to his staff, he has other priorities."

"Let's see if he changes his mind if we use a different approach."

"What are you going to do?"

"Simple!" I said. "Change our orbit."

I contacted Admiral Park on the bridge and requested him to change the orbits of Chromlys and Mychrox.

"Admiral Park." I said over the ship's communicator. Change the orbits of Chromlys and Mychrox in mirroring orbits around Earth so that we're blocking the sun's exposure to the full surface of the Earth 24 hours of the day. Make it so not one beam of sunshine reaches the surface of the planet for the next 7 days."

"Yes Emperor Sakata."

Both cruisers were moved so that there was a continuous eclipse of the sun over all the earth. The earth was in total darkness for seven continuous days. During these days, many parts of the Earth fell below freezing all day, all night. Floods occurred in the cities near the beaches since tides were affected because of the new orbits of Chromlys and Mychrox. People who were already in a state of distress began to panic.

"Emperor Sakata," said Admiral Park "You're being hailed by President Henderson on the bridge."

"Very well, I'll be right over."

As I arrived on the bridge, President Henderson was on the bridge monitor.

"President Henderson, I am Gordon Sakata, Emperor of the Planet Xychron. How may I assist you.?"

"Your Highness, it's a pleasure to meet you. But speaking for the world, what can I do to get you to call off the eclipse that you have created on this earth?"

"Accept our invitation to the summit in New Mexico."

"But we have sent Secretary of State Johnson to the summit. Is that not good enough?"

"No sir." I said. "Are you not the leader of your nation?"

"I am."

"And do you not speak for your nation?"

"Well, yes. But in consultation with our Congress. What do you seek?"

"To rescue your oppressed people" I said.

"I don't know what you are talking about. We don't have any oppressed people here."

"I beg to differ with you sir."

"Our people live in freedom and are guaranteed liberty."

"Mr. President, is it not true that 95% of your population is homeless, starving, and living in poverty?"

"Well, yes, that is true. But that is their choice."

"I disagree with you Mr. President. Your people have been displaced by your corporations who have opted to replace your citizens with robots and droids. Many people are living in shantytowns, tin shacks, and cardboard dwellings, are they not?"

"Where did you get your information from?"

"I'm a human sir! A native of Los Angeles, once put out on the streets by your corporate infrastructure, interned in your concentration camp in Manzanar, then sent to the mountains during the War of Napajan to die. This was not my choice!"

"What kind of joke is this?" asked the President. It's physically impossible for some ordinary person to go from this planet and become 'emperor' of another planet."

"You are looking at a living example, sir."

"This all must be some kind of hoax."

"Stay right there" I said.

I teleported myself into the Oval Office as the President was speaking into the communicator.

"Are you still there?"

"I'm right here!" as I stood right before him.

He appeared startled and called for security.

"How did you get in here?" he asked.

"It was simple!"

"This is a heavily guarded office. No one passes without going through security."

Suddenly, Secret Service agents stormed the Oval Office.

"Freeze!" said a Secret Service agent. "Do not move!"

I quietly activated my cloaking mechanism and made myself invisible.

"Your security is totally ineffective, Mr. President."

"Where are you? We hear you, but we cannot see you."

"That's because I can make myself invisible."

"Officer, shoot towards the voice."

"Yes, Mr. President."

"Oh, come now." I said, as the agent fired off a shot.

"If you want something to shoot at, here I am." I disabled my clocking device and reappeared standing next to the President.

The Secret Service agent fired off another shot. But as soon as the shot left the barrel of the gun, the bullet went into slow motion. I pushed the President to one side as I stepped to the opposite side. The bullet went flying by in between us.

"Let's stop playing shoot the Emperor games. You're only wasting your bullets. Your weapons are totally ineffective against me anyway. Besides, I come without a weapon. Search me if you'd like."

The agent frisked me and said, "He's clean, Mr. President."

"Very well, clear the room."

They left the room and just the two of us sat, I in one chair, the President in a chair near by.

"Your Highness, please forgive me for all the confusion and hysteria."

"That's quite all right, Mr. President."

"Previously you said you came here to 'rescue' my people. We did not send a distress call out to anyone."

"Sir, I already knew when I left this planet that your people were already in distress."

"But who has sanctioned you to get these people?"

"The Galactic Federation of Light."

"This Galactic Federation of Light…is there such a thing?"

"Yes," I replied. "But Earth's leaders would not know anything about this because it has remained isolated for centuries."

"But how does one become a member of such a Federation?"

"Your nations will have to come together as one. Then apply as one world to the Federation."

"But that, of course, would be impossible here on Earth. "We have many nations here."

"If you truly desire to become part of a universal community, you will break down barriers and find ways of uniting together. Many other planets had to do the same thing. Some planets like Xychron were already a one nation, one planet society."

"Exactly where is Xychron? I never heard of such a place?"

"My planet mirrors Earth's orbit."

"But why haven't you shown up on our galactic maps?"

"Our sun serves as a natural barrier – a shield, between us. It would be very difficult to detect our presence with your current technology."

"What kind of people are you?"

"My people have come from Earth during the early ages of civilization. My ancestors included the original Monarch of Napajan who led an intergalactic exploration during the times of ancient Greece and launched an ark into space which included couples of every race and nationality of the earth, every kind of animal and ocean life, and landed on the planet of Xychron – a planet identical to Earth. We are humans like everyone else on this planet except for the fact that we have a completely different democratic system of government than yours."

"Where do you intend to take our people?"

"I will reveal that at the summit. Will you be there tomorrow?"

"Yes I will. He replied"

CHAPTER 48

The Summit

Several days later, the leaders of the world converged in the conference center in New Mexico after a brief delay because of the President of the RNA. This time, he acted as a gracious host welcoming the guests to his own land. While he was speaking to the assembly in the great hall, I instructed Ms. Sakai to begin transmitting the subliminal message to earth via all the emergency transport vehicles. An old African-American spiritual, *Steal Away (To Jesus),* was being transmitted to every being who had this tune pre-programmed into their minds.

As this tune was being transmitted, people in shantytowns, inhabitants of cardboard dwellings, underpasses, tunnels, and homeless centers all began to abandon their dwelling places and started a massive migration towards a central pick-up location under each hovering evacuation vehicle. The people were lead by choirs of singers leading them out of their dwellings as they sang the tune:

> *Steal away, steal away,*
> *Steal away to Jesus!*
> *Steal away, steal away home,*
> *I ain't got long to stay here.*

My Lord, He calls me,
He calls me by the thunder;
The trumpet sounds within my soul,
I ain't got long to stay here.

Steal away, steal away,
Steal away to Jesus!
Steal away, steal away home,
I ain't got long to stay here.

Green trees are bending,
Poor sinners stand a-trembling;
The trumpet sounds within my soul,
I ain't got long to stay here.

Steal away, steal away,
Steal away to Jesus!
Steal away, steal away home,
I ain't got long to stay here.

My Lord, He calls me,
He calls me by the lightning;
The trumpet sounds within my soul,
I ain't got long to stay here.[viii]

Mysteriously to the leaders of the cities, the depressed and oppressed, men, women, children, singles, families, poor people, gays, lesbians, trans-gendered, bisexuals were led out of the cities led in the fashion of the "Pied Piper of Hamlin" leading the children out of the city into the mountains. Perplexing as it was, only these people heard and responded to a message that no one else heard. There was massive traffic congestion on the highways leading out of the cities as the masses trooped out and headed toward the appointed pick-up locations.

In fear, city officials called for law enforcement to keep the peace. But there were no outbreaks of violence much to their surprise.

As people were migrating mesmerized towards their designated rendezvous, it was time for me to address the world leaders in the great hall. President Henderson introduced me to the leaders of the World as I teleported myself onto the stage and stood behind the podium.

"Leaders of the World, President Henderson, thank you for coming to this special summit on such a short notice." I said.

"I, Gordon Sakata, Emperor of Xychron, have come to Earth to take your oppressed people and to deliver them to Egressos, another planet far beyond this galaxy for a new life of hope and prosperity."

"How do we know that this is not a hoax?" asked the Prime Minister of Britain.

"Just look into the sky, Mr. Prime Minister." I replied. "Are the two spheres you see a hovering over your cities a hoax or an illusion?"

"How can you say that our peoples are oppressed here?" asked the Prime Minister of Japan.

"Because I once lived among you, as a citizen of the RNA, homeless, out of a job, and displaced by your droids. I can also say, from my intelligence that over 95% of your people are living homeless in streets, tin shacks and cardboard dwellings."

"How can we be assured that our people will be taken to a better place to live?" asked the Prime Minister of Australia. "How can we be assured of their safety?"

"I would have not come all this way if I were not concerned for the sake and well being of my fellow men. I care for your people as a citizen of this universe."

"How do we know that such a place called Xychron exists?" asked the Prime Minister of India.

"Because we have been trading and doing business with them for centuries!" said the Monarch of Napajan.

"When do you intend to take our people?" asked President Henderson.

"They are being gathered in 100 of your cities even as we speak."

"But how do they know to go to a designated area?" asked President Henderson.

"They have been pre-programmed since birth with a coded message.

Anyone who has this message within them will know where and when to appear. It's their invitation."

On huge monitors in the great hall, images were being displayed from all over the earth of massive migrations of people walking to various rendezvous points.

"But you can't take our people without permission." said President Henderson. "Such an act would require a declaration of Congress."

"Really now?" I asked the President. "Well, the laws of the Universe have just overruled your feeble earthly laws. Beside, who gave you the authority to take away their basic freedoms and liberties of speech, expression, and living in a humane and respectable manner? Your government has taken away the people's power and authority to govern by giving that power to a select few in your country, influenced by special interest groups representing corporations of the RNA. Your laws no longer favor nor serve the people, but are skewed to benefit the rich and corporate executives of your country. You have a two-party political system in which there are no real differences or choices for they both are very much equally the same – the only difference is that the two parties use different political rhetoric. But in behavior and action, they are essentially the same – neither serve your people, ignoring the principle that your constitution proclaims a 'government by the people and for the people.' In find this to be highly ironic sir!"

"Your country," I continued, "has led your world in displacing people by putting them out their homes and into the streets of your cities, forcing them into poverty and starvation, and simply destroying their lives by taking away their jobs and denying them essential health care all for the sake of profit and the status quo. In fact, sir, I have had to send more emergency transport vehicles here to your country alone than to another country in the world. That's how bad off your country is sir."

"I won't let them go." said President Henderson.

"Give them hope, Mr. President."

"I'm going to have you arrested for kidnapping!"

"Let's be serious, Mr. President. Your powers can no longer detain me. I am not an Earthling anymore. I am a Xychronian. I'll simply disappear from your detention facilities. You've had a glimpse of my abilities in your Oval Office."

"Leaders of the World, thank you once again for your attendance today, this meeting is adjourned." I said as I transported myself back to the bridge of Chromlys.

On Chromlys, I had Ms. Sakai transmit the second phase of the subliminal message. *Deep River*, began to play as people were teleported from the rendezvous points onto the emergency transport vehicles. World leaders watched as the people were being teleported into the vehicles from earth. There was a rush to contact their national defense and military leaders and instructions were issued to make attempts to stop the evacuation process using all means necessary.

Military vehicles tried to move in closer to the rendezvous but were unsuccessful. A defensive force-field prevented them from drawing any closer than a mile. The protective force fields disabled their vehicles. Tanks, mortars and missiles were used to no avail. The force-fields created a barrier and blocked any military object from entering near the evacuation grounds.

Military leaders were reporting back that their weapons were totally useless in the fields.

The ETV's began making their ascent back to Chromlys and Mychrox. Earth's defensive forces began firing rockets and long-range missiles at each vehicle without success as each trajectory prematurely exploded before it reached its target.

"Emperor Sakata," said Admiral Park, "All ETVs have returned and are accounted for."

"Thank you. How many people did we bring back?"

"Countless… Millions upon millions, sir!"

"Very well. Set course for Egressos, Admiral."

"Yes, sir!"

Chromlys and Mychrox went into mirroring orbits and began increasing their orbital speed around Earth to break away from the planet's gravity. In the process of doing so, major tidal effects were occurring on the earth's surface. Near coastal shorelines in each country, waves began to grow increasingly larger as the two moons increased their cruising speed. Eventually, there were massive tidal waves that caused major flooding in cities. The friction of the moons' flight causing an abnormal increase in the Earth's rotation also caused massive fires to structures and buildings in cities and small towns. Nuclear weapons were also exploding as well as nuclear electric generating facilities. The departure of Chromlys and Mychrox left a everlasting "calling card" to earth's civilization. It was like having to start all over from scratch.

Meanwhile, on Chromlys and Myhrox, there was joy and elation of the millions of people that were evacuated from earth. There was a sense of hope as these travelers looked forward to a new life in "paradise."

CHAPTER 49

Crossing Over Into Campground

During our course for Egressos, I met with the planning and transition team headed by Kathy in the conference room.

"While you were down on Earth talking to the world leaders, I had a conference with the Galactic Federation of Light." said Kathy. Here is a model of what Egressos will look like by the time we get there.

She displayed a three-dimensional hologram of the main city and the surrounding areas.

"The Federation is hard at work right now putting this together" she said. The city is modeled after Xychron. This should give them a good start."

"This is quite impressive. It sure beats what they were living in before."

"Each person or family will have a mansion for themselves. There are provisions for farming and agriculture in the surrounding areas. In addition to this area, there will be plenty of room on the planet for them to expand and grow."

General Alinson entered the conference room as we were looking at the model of Egressos.

"Pardon me, Emperor Sakata." the General. "My staff reports that the guests are now settled in and have been issued new travel clothing suitable for their voyage to Egressos. We are now gathering them into the main assembly halls on both Chromlys and Mychrox so you can address our guests at the grand feast."

"Very well." I said. "I'm looking forward to joining them soon. What do you think of their new city?"

"It's very impressive sir. I think it will be a great blessing to them compared to the living conditions they had to experience back on Earth."

We all departed from the conference room. The General went back to his quarters as Kathy and I went back to our quarters to prepare for the grand feast. As we walked back to our quarters, I felt a sense of personal satisfaction that I was able to fulfill a goal of serving my fellow man on Earth in some small way – by giving hope to people who lived daily in despair. Dehumanized by their governments and literally tossed into their streets to rot, they are being taken to a place where they can now live in dignity and be given the opportunity to flourish in a community within the universe.

Several hours later, Kathy and I stood before the masses that we evacuated from Earth. Millions of people on Chromlys and millions more on Mycrhox. The atmosphere on both vessels were joyful and festive.

"Fellow travelers," I said, "I, Gordon Sakata, Emperor of Xychron and my wife Empress Katherine, welcome all of you aboard Chromlys and Mycrox. In just a few short days, you will be arriving at your new home on the planet of Egressos."

Three-dimensional models were projected throughout the assembly areas aboard both vessels. All the guests looked with utter joy and amazement.

"There," I continued, "you will begin new life of prosperity, dignity, and respect. Not as citizens of separate countries as you had on Earth, but, united as one nation — one planet."

Deafening cheers roared through the chambers on Chromlys as well as Mychrox.

"Not only will be people of Xychron be there to support you and help you get your new civilization started, but you will have the fullest support of the universal community through the Galactic Federation of Light."

"On your new planet, each one of you will be guaranteed a mansion for your permanent living dwellings. Gone are the days where you will have to survive in a tin or cardboard box or shack."

"So, enjoy this feast, have a comfortable and pleasurable voyage to your new homes, and I'll see you on Egressos."

As Kathy and I were leaving the platform in the assembly area, a tall, slender African-American gentleman approached.

"Your Highness, sir?" he asked. "My name is Akachi Toledano."

"Nice to meet you, Mr. Toledano. Please, just call me Gordon" I replied. "We're not into the formalities on Xychron."

"Yes, sir." he said. "The people have asked me to see if you are the one who was prophesied to return to Earth to save us?"

"You mean, like your 'savior?' No. I am just a humble person who felt that there was a need to do something for the people like yourself and free you from despair and hopelessness. That's all. I too was one of you."

Then, more people drew nearer to our discussion.

"People think you are the Chosen One sent from Heaven to save us." he said.

"No, I came of my own accord. But we all know God does strange and mysterious things."

"So," he said. "You really are the Messiah who has returned to the earth to claim his own."

The crowd started to become ever so silent. I felt like I was some kind of preacher as I was being televised over jumbo monitors aboard the Chromlys and the Mychrox.

"No. Absolutely not! What I am saying is that we each have a measure of God in us. That's why Jesus said, 'the Kingdom of Heaven is at hand.' You always had the power to make changes among yourselves. However, you permitted yourselves to be enslaved by the tyranny of the greedy rich and corruption among your governments. And, unfortunately, the churches of every denomination played right along with the corruption and the secrecy of the minority who always wanted to keep this power so secretive among you."

"They say it takes three points to make a 'level playing field.' This principle also applies to the science of surveying. As with a person, there are three elements that makes up a 'whole person' – the adult self, the parent self, and the child self. Most of us act on two levels – on the adult self and the parent self. The child self is often ignored and is often secluded within us. In a way, we can say that we are all guilty of child abuse.

"On earth, you have let your parent selves set your rules and regulations, set what you should do and what you ought to do while the adult sides of yourselves allowed you to think, make decisions, and solve problems. But since you've kept your child selves bottled up inside each of you, you never fully let yourselves feel and react truly to various conditions and situations. And it is the child within you that will set you free and lead you."

"Your educational systems have not done a good job in developing your inner child. They had taken away arts, music and drama education programs in schools, denied students recess and nutrition. By and large, they denied every opportunity for the inner child to be creative and expressive during the day. The schools did more to suppress rather than encourage child development in favor of "adult" driven activities and subjects that said 'you can to this, but you can't do that.' All under the excuse because 'there was no money.'"

"At the adult level, the inner child's creative time was also suppressed as well. When employers took away jobs and gave them to droids, they literally took away the 'playground' for the adult. To many adults, work was a form of 'playing' outside the house. It was an opportunity for the inner child to come out and be creative. Employers denied that opportunity for the whole person by giving their jobs away to robots all for the sake of maximizing profits."

"So, consequently, what had happened on your planet? There was a serious imbalance of living on earth. Life was spinning only on two axes – the adult and parent axes. There was a genuine disregard for feelings and reaction for the adult selves and parent selves cared less about what the child selves felt. Hence, there were massive layoffs and a destruction of individual and family lives all for the sake of money, corruption, and greed. Of course, that in the long run had its consequences – bankrupt nations, states, municipalities, and companies."

"On the other hand, the world has let the child self in some people run ramped – without discipline. That is, the parent self of society (the government) has essentially failed to discipline the child. It has not taught the child to share. But instead, has manifested greed in the individual. Hence, there was a glutton of corporate greed in the RNA and in the world. In every individual, there has to be balance among the three elements. If individuals do not possess balance, then there is imbalance in the world. One 'self' is going to dominate the other. In this unfortunate case, the child self of a few had dominated the passive adult self and ineffective parent self."

"Your churches have raised you well in becoming good parents and good adults. But they often secluded the inner child within. The church has always taught you how to be passive, and to be submissive to people in positions of authority whether in government, corporation, or the church. You were often conditioned to respond to something when instructed to do so. If you challenged someone in authority, you were chastised for it. In some cases, severely punished for your actions, and rarely were you ever given the freedom to freely express yourself without negative consequences or retribution. Rarely would you receive praise for what you had done. By and large, rewards for your behavior resulted in incarceration in some parts of the world."

"Take, for example, shepherds and their flocks of sheep. In the case of the world, the shepherds were fulfilled by the roles of the church leaders, governments, and corporate leaders. The sheep were essentially 'the people.' The majority of you were always conditioned to fulfill the passive role of the sheep – to serve at the pleasure of the master. Leadership and money was not used to serve the people, it was used to control people's minds. Money was used to influence governments and policy – not to benefit the people, but to benefit corporations. Money, therefore, became the priority over the needs of the people. It gave relatively few people power and authority in governments, corporations, and churches. There was just enough money on Earth for the rich minority to retain control and influence over the majority. Whatever was left, the people had to either fight for, or live without. That's why in churches, you were taught to live passively and give generously to the church. In reality, very little money went to meet the needs of those truly in need. Over sixty-percent of the wealth went into the coffers of the operations and administration of church headquarters. Just look at the massive artwork and material riches that the major churches of the world possess. If they sold their treasures, there really would be no need for the shantytowns in which you once dwelled. The church is not about material things or possessions, nor a building. The church, in reality, is in each one of you. If you want to give to a church, give to yourself first for that is where God is."

"This power was to be freely had by everyone. It was the power to live in prosperity and abundance. Take a look for yourselves. There were only a few hundred people in your governments. There were several thousands in big corporations and businesses. Yet, when you add up the total number of people within these groups, they made up only a fraction of the world's population. Millions of people had the power to make changes to rid themselves of corruption in their governments and had the power to govern big businesses and corporations. Yet, on Earth, it was the exact opposite. The minority ruled and dictated to the world. The kingdom of heaven couldn't be established because it was constantly being locked out by the ruling minority. The submissive majority never took the courage nor the responsibility to assert itself as the 'dominating force' and to declare 'enough is enough.' But the powers have always resided among the people since the creation of man."

"Therefore, I encourage each of you to fully love and embrace the child in you for that child will make you whole. On Earth, there have been many illustrations of angels as being represented through children and infants. The child in you is like your angel. Let the child in you be your guiding spirit. Do not let it die.

"Anyway, sir. On behalf of my people, I want to thank you for saving us."

"Don't mention it. The pleasure is mine."

As I shook his hand, others started to crowd around me to get a glimpse of me and to touch me. Then out of spontaneity, they all began to sing the lyrics to the song, *Deep River:*

> *Deep river — my home is over Jordan,*
> *Deep river, Lord, I want to cross over into campground.*
> *Don't you want to go to that Gospel feast,*
> *That promised land where all is peace.*
> *Deep river, Lord, I want to cross over into campground.*[ix]

As they continued to repeat the song, Chromlys and Mychorx continued to trek across the deep river of the universe – the darkness of space filled by the stars and planets which zoomed quickly by as we were travelling faster than light speed towards Egressos, a land where all is peace – a new campground.

As for the people left on Earth, only time will tell if they have learned a lesson. One thing is for certain, when one civilization comes to an end, another starts anew. Will the "wheel" recreate itself on Earth once again? Will a new generation of people enslave yet another generation of people? Will the people of earth ever learn the lessons of the past? Or will the status quo remain as generation after generation never breakout of their repetitive lifestyles? Will societies on earth ever progress and advance with time? Will nations still continue to use war, destruction, and killing as an answer and solution to their problems? Yes, as for the people on earth, they too will have a "new campground." But they are going to have to rebuild without the people who helped build their world, countries, cities, and municipalities. Yes, only time will tell.

CHAPTER 50

Paradise

About seven earth days later we arrived in Egressos' orbit. A sparkling new city awaited the travelers arrival as the crew began to prepare the transfer of the guest to the surface of the planet. I was walking towards the bridge and was eventually joined by Admiral Park.

"Emperor, we are now transferring the all the guests to the ETVs as they will be transferred to the city soon."

"Good. Is the city ready to receive them?"

"Yes, Emperor. All reports indicate that they are very excited and looking forward to receiving them."

"And is the transition team in place?"

"Yes, sir. General Alinson will remain here during the transition and will help the Egressonians establish their government. Our forces will remain here for a while as planned to assist them establishing trade and commerce with the Galactic Federation of Light and will eventually pull out once the Egressonian government feels it is the appropriate time they can become fully functional and independent."

Soon, the ETV's departed Chromlys and Mychrox for the planet taking millions of travelers to their new homes. The people arrived at an air facility in a very large meadow with tall grass and blooming flowers.

Before the people were dispersed to their new mansions, I was asked to address the guests one last time. Kathy and myself teleported ourselves down to the meadowlands from our quarters. It was a beautiful sight. Certainly a land of paradise compared the living conditions these people had back on earth. The meadow reminded me of the grotto back on Xychron without the running water.

"People of Egressos — former Earthlings — General Alinson. Welcome to your new home!"

A thunderous cheer arose from the crowd.

"Soon, you will be escorted to your new mansions where you will no longer live in pain, suffering, poverty and hunger. We have journeyed across the universe a long way and I hope you will find this place acceptable in your new life. I wish you well in your new lives here on Egressos. May you all prosper."

"Although I must part from you for now, this is not a farewell. Let this be the start of a forever lasting relationship between your planet and mine. I leave you with General Alinson during this transition as he will assist you in creating your independent government. He and his forces will remain here until it is time that your government feels it can operate as a fully functional and independent nation planet of your own and which time at which time General Alinson will withdraw our support forces and return them back to Xychron. At no time do we seek to colonize your planet."

Then, there was a deafening roar from the massive crowd.

"So, at this time, I bid you good bye for now and good luck."

The next several hours were the most exhausting time of my life. Greeting and hugging practically everyone while they waited to be transported to their mansions. General Alinson's staff did a remarkable job assigning each individual and family to their new mansion on Egressos. The transportation vehicles operated like precision clockwork. There were tears of joy in each individual that we hugged. You could tell not only that they were exhausted from travelling, but overjoyed to be moving into a real home – a mansion no less to speak. I was personally and emotionally touched by each individual.

As soon as we said our farewells to the last person to board the transport, we teleported ourselves back up to Chromlys for our voyage back home to Xychron.

"Admiral Park," I said from my quarters, "set course for Xychron."

"Yes, sir!"

Unlike breaking away from Earth's orbit, Chromlys and Mychrox gently broke away from Egressos' orbit as the two vessels gradually gained super-light speed towards Xychron.

About ten days later, we arrived at Xychron's orbit. We teleported ourselves back to the palace as if nothing had ever happened. Well, not really. We got back home in the middle of the night while the city was asleep.

I guess word got around fast on Xychron. I really was exhausted and needed rest. The rest of the city wanted a hero's party. Mr. Maxwell and Christine woke us up at 0600 hours and said that the city had a grand celebration planned for the two of us.

"No, Max!" I exclaimed. "I need my rest!"

"Sir, the people are expecting your presence. You are a hero!"

"I'll be their hero tomorrow. Let me sleep in today."

"Don't you know that Xychronian Emperors never sleep?"

"I'm starting to find that out" I said exhaustedly. "Okay, but just this once."

I got out of bed, showered and prepared myself for the day's events. Kathy was already up, bright-eyed, and energized. "How can you be so energetic?"

"Don't you know?" she said.

"Don't I know what?"

"Xychronian Empresses never sleep."

"Oh, thanks a lot. You're no help at all!"

"Good morning, sweetheart!"

"Good morning, my love!"

After having breakfast, I went into my office to attend to some state business before going out into the public for the grand celebration. From what I heard, there was quite an event planned for the day. I have never been to a hero's welcoming, let alone being treated like a hero myself except for that moment on Chromlys. I just felt like an ordinary person who had to do what was right.

As I prepared to leave the office, the sun's rays beamed through the windows and caught my attention. It was like the sign of a brand new day. It reminded me that it was also the sign of a brand new day for people in another part of the universe. As I looked up towards the sky, Kathy joined me and looked out the window as well.

"Well, do you think they will be happy out there on Egressos?"

"I can only hope I've done the right thing." I said. "But I just could not see how anyone could have lived in such conditions as they did on that other planet."

"Do you think they will be able to survive as a new civilization?"

"It's almost like repeating the voyage of the Monarch of Napajan back in the ancient civilizations of Earth. He foretold a great disaster to mankind and did something to save the species, didn't he? He had the courage to remove some people from Earth to start a new civilization here on Xychron. And the human race benefitted from that experience.

"If you had a wish, what would that one wish be?" she asked.

"I only wish that people will never have to live in such terrible living conditions anywhere else in this universe, on any planet again. And that no species ever be held under the bondage of any form of slavery or oppression, no matter what it be called or labeled, not here, nor there, anywhere – never, forever."

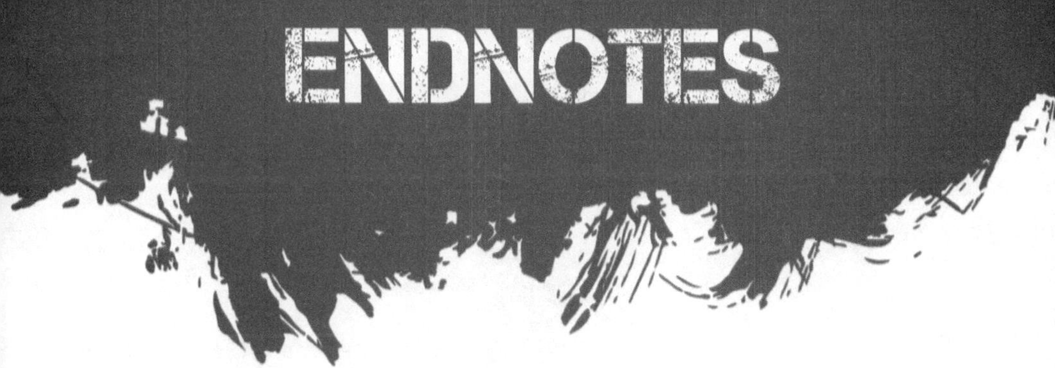

i. Based on President Franklin D. Roosevelt's Speech to Congress for a Declaration of War, December 8, 1941.

ii. Abraham Lincoln's Annual Message to Congress, December 1, 1862

iii. Abraham Lincoln's Annual Message to Congress, December 1, 1862

iv. Abraham Lincoln's Annual Message to Congress, December 1, 1862

v. The Final Lincoln-Douglas Debates, October 15, 1858

vi. Abraham Lincoln Fragment on Democracy, August 1, 1858

vii. From Abraham Lincoln's Gettysburg Address, November 19, 1863

viii. *Steal Away (To Jesus)* – An African-American Spiritual by Wallace Willis, ca. 1862.

ix. *Deep River* – An African-American Spiritual, anonymous.